THE LONGEST ROAD

Recent Titles by Pamela Oldfield from Severn House

The Heron Saga
BETROTHED
THE GILDED LAND
LOWERING SKIES
THE BRIGHT DAWNING

ALL OUR TOMORROWS
EARLY ONE MORNING
RIDING THE STORM

CHANGING FORTUNES
NEW BEGINNINGS
MATTERS OF TRUST

DANGEROUS SECRETS
INTRICATE LIAISONS
TURNING LEAVES

HENRY'S WOMEN
SUMMER LIGHTNING
JACK'S SHADOW
FULL CIRCLE
LOVING AND LOSING
FATEFUL VOYAGE
THE LONGEST ROAD

THE LONGEST ROAD

Pamela Oldfield

This first world edition published 2008
in Great Britain and the USA by
SEVERN HOUSE PUBLISHERS LTD of
9–15 High Street, Sutton, Surrey, England, SM1 1DF.

British Library Cataloguing in Publication Data

Oldfield, Pamela
    The longest road
    1. Bereavement - Fiction 2. Fiction - Authorship - Fiction
    3. Book editors - Fiction
    I. Title
    823.9'14[F]

    ISBN-13: 978-0-7278-6645-5   (cased)
    ISBN-13: 978-1-84751-069-3   (trade paper)

All Severn House titles are printed on acid-free paper.

Typeset by Palimpsest Book Production Ltd.,
Grangemouth, Stirlingshire, Scotland.
Printed and bound in Great Britain by
MPG Books Ltd., Bodmin, Cornwall.

Prologue

Merle Place, near Maidstone, Kent. 1915

As soon as Clare opened her eyes she remembered and the terrible certainty descended once more. Simon was dead; killed in action somewhere in the mud of the Somme. The world would keep turning without him, but she was now alone, and at twenty-three all her hopes for the future had gone with him.

Get up, Clare. You have to get up. You have to get through the day – and tomorrow and the day after and . . .

Someone knocked on the door and she scrambled out of bed. It would be one of the girls trying to get her to work before Matron did her rounds.

'Just coming!' She rushed to open the door and found Greta waiting there, already in her blue dress and white apron – the unofficial uniform of the volunteer ward maids.

'You should room with us,' Greta grumbled. 'You're always blinking late and one of us has to come haring down here.'

'I'm sorry.'

'Why should we have to chase after you?' Greta said crossly, glancing enviously around the room. 'Just because you own the place and you think you're posh!'

Clare's home, Merle Place, was now a hospital where wounded servicemen were sent to recuperate until they could be sent back to fight.

'I've said I'm sorry. You didn't have to come for me.' She splashed cold water on to her face, neck and hands from the bowl on the little table.

'Yes, I did. Caroline sent me. She's always currying up

to you.' She adopted what she hoped was a 'posh' voice. '"Go and fetch Miss Wishart or she'll be in trouble." I think it serves you right if Matron catches you!' While Clare was drying her face with the towel, Greta stomped out, her shoulders stiff with disapproval.

'Wait for me!' cried Clare, but Greta was already halfway down the steps to the tack room below. From the window Clare saw her running back in the direction of the big house. Alone in the large room above the stables, Clare cleaned her teeth and struggled into her clothes, then ran down the stairs and out into the stable yard.

Jimmie, the gardener-cum-groom-cum-handyman, had already cycled in from the village and now glanced up and smiled. He was slipping a bridle on to a horse, preparing the animal for his first work of the day – pulling the big mower over the lawns. Once Merle Place had boasted elegant gardens, but now the trees and shrubs were mostly neglected and only the lawns were kept under control. On fine days the soldiers would enjoy them either sitting in their wheelchairs or stumbling about on crutches.

If only that shell had fallen a few yards further from Simon then he might have ended up here; safe for a few months while his injuries healed. I could have been with him. I could have helped to nurse him back to health.

But then he would have been sent back to play out his part in the war and how could she have let him go? Beneath the patients' smiles they all knew what awaited them when they recovered and were well enough to take up their rifles again and fight on.

Clare rushed towards the house.

Jimmie said, 'Tut, tut! Late again!' He looked embarrassed and Clare understood. He didn't know what to say to her now that her soldier sweetheart was dead. Nobody knew what to say to her. Nobody knew how to help her through the first agonizing days.

'Good morning, Jimmie!'

She ran on. There was no sign of Greta ahead of her.

Keep going, Clare. Just get through today. Keep busy.

You're not the only one who has lost someone you love. Forget your own problems and think about the patients.

Merle Place had been taken over by the government six months earlier and turned from a private house into a hospital. The huge ten-bedroomed house which had been left to her by her grandfather was temporarily no longer her responsibility. She was simply another ward maid – with one difference. She was allowed to live separately in the small flat above the stable block.

The front door was already open and a military truck, with a large red cross on the side, was parked outside. The day's intake of wounded men was being helped down from the rear of the vehicle. New patients. One of them whistled at her as she rushed past. She managed a brief smile and dashed into the hall (which now smelled permanently of antiseptics and Jeyes Fluid) and from there into the large front room – a room which had once been her grandparents' elegant morning room. It was now the staff room.

Clare found a seat next to Caroline, one of the trained nursing staff, who smiled and whispered, 'Just in time!' Seconds later a freshly starched Matron swept in and silence fell.

One of the Sisters read out the rota for the day and Clare was assigned to the meal trolleys.

Down to the kitchens. Push the trolleys round the wards. What will it be today? Breakfast of porridge with bread and jam to follow – or maybe scrambled eggs on toast. A lunch of corned beef hash and peas or perhaps fish cakes. Supper of cheese sandwiches and a slice of currant cake.

Not that Clare had an appetite. It had shrunk to match her failing zest for life, but Caroline, acting like a mother hen, did her best to see that she didn't lose too much weight.

Keep thinking, Clare. Keep your mind on anything and everything. Anything to keep the grief at bay.

She would smile and joke with the patients. 'Good morning, Sergeant Willow. Feeling more awake today? You were snoring fit to burst yesterday.'

'Better for a sight of you, miss, that's for sure, but don't tell my missus I said so!'

'How are you, Corporal Tanner? Got a tip for the two thirty?'

'Come a bit closer, darling, and I'll whisper it in your pretty little ear!'

Sometimes what they whispered was quite shocking to ladylike ears, but Clare understood and forgave them. The men hid their fears anyway they could, while the lonely women hid their heartache.

One

At exactly five to nine Clare set down the jug of hot water and tapped on her cousin's bedroom door. Was he awake? Probably not, she thought with a resigned sigh. He would think nine a.m. ridiculously early to drag himself from his bed. Nervously, her hand went up to her hair which she had swept up into the usual untidy mass, but which she had secured with more hairpins than she would normally use. She had also dressed with care in a grey skirt and jacket over a white blouse with her mother's pearl brooch at the neckline. This last was to give her confidence, but so far it hadn't worked and her stomach churned with anxiety.

'Come on, Donald!' she muttered and, hearing nothing, knocked again more loudly. 'Are you awake—'

When she received no reply to her third knock, she opened the door and peered in. Donald was sitting on the edge of his bed, ruffling his dark hair and scowling. As usual he reminded her of a bad-tempered pixie. He wore a nightshirt that had once belonged to his father who had been a much larger man altogether.

'I know!' he grumbled, before Clare could say anything. 'The chappie from the estate agents is coming at ten thirty. I'll be—'

'At ten, Donald,' she corrected him. 'Not ten thirty. I need you to greet him with me, otherwise he'll think I'm a woman on my own and he'll try to cheat me.'

'You are a woman on your own.'

She ignored the hurtful words, having heard much worse

from him. 'I know, but it looks better if we are united – at least at the beginning. You don't have to come all the way if you get tired.' She carried the jug across the room and put it on the washstand, next to the bowl.

'I *will* get tired,' Donald told her. 'And I won't come far. Certainly not round the grounds. This was your idea, remember? Your crazy little scheme to sell our home and buy something smaller. Share the proceeds and get rid of me in the process. Oh, don't think I don't know.'

Clare hesitated, wanting to say more, needing to deny the truth of what he said, even though she *did* hope that he might accept some of the money and buy himself a flat. At the moment, however, Clare needed his full co-operation – he had to get washed and dressed and have his breakfast so that Mrs Parks could clear away the meal. The dining room was one of the most impressive rooms with the least faded curtains and the least worn carpet.

'I'll leave you to it, then,' she offered. 'Please open your windows when you come down . . . freshen the room.'

Donald was not a believer in fresh air, convinced that if his heart didn't give out, his lungs would do so. His room always smelled of hair oil, cigarette smoke and the various lozenges and medicines he took. He had developed some early symptoms of heart disease, which had brought about the deaths of various aunts, uncles and grandparents in the past. Being Donald, he had accepted his lot with a resigned attitude, and in 1914 had neatly turned it to his advantage as the army had refused him as below par and had found him clerical work in a factory. Since the war started he seemed to ignore the fact that life was harder. They now made do with a minimum of servants and the pace of life had changed.

As soon as the war ended and Merle Place had been returned to Clare, he had invited himself to stay for a visit but had then apparently decided to stay on indefinitely. With ten bedrooms, she had been unable to claim lack of room, and also, if pressed, would admit that she found his presence vaguely reassuring. The large decaying house, set in several acres, was pleasant enough in the summer when the sun shone through its huge windows, warming the mostly empty rooms and lighting the long, silent passages. In winter Merle Place was often gloomy and full of shadows. There were times when Clare missed the bustle of the hospital, and the days passed agonizingly slowly.

But now she had something to occupy her mind – she was selling the house and today the estate agent was coming. Downstairs she made straight for the kitchen where Mrs Parks, the housekeeper, and Jimmie Smith were finishing their breakfast of tea and toast.

Jimmie smiled at Clare. 'I've done all the downstairs windows,' he told her. 'Finished them last evening, just before it got dark. Inside and out! Your Mr Yates will be impressed. Specially if the sun comes out. Nothing like sparkling windows to lift a place.'

And it certainly needed lifting, she thought. The thin May sunlight could only do so much. The house had that look of genteel neglect that hinted at a lack of money.

'Thank you, Jimmie. Whatever would I do without you?' Clare returned his smile.

It was true, she honestly did not know what she would do without him. Jimmie Smith was cagey about his age, but she guessed he was around fifty, although he never shirked any work. He told her he was just as happy up a long ladder, clearing out gutters, as he was guiding the big mower behind Jonty, the horse.

Mrs Parks put the lid over a tray of bacon and tomatoes and prepared to carry it through into the dining room. She had been one of the cooks at Merle House during the war and had agreed to stay on afterwards. Now Clare trailed after her, her pleasant face ruined by an anxious frown. As she helped herself to bacon and buttered a slice of bread, she tried to compose herself and think herself into something approaching confidence.

I must appear friendly but businesslike and I must insist that we agree a fair price. I won't lie about the repairs that need to be done . . . and I shall offer a single agency for three months only if he agrees to take a lower percentage.

Donald appeared and she poured the tea.

'You look very nice,' she told him, eyeing the clean shirt beneath the waistcoat she had made him for his last birthday. Donald was four years older than Clare, and they had never enjoyed a close friendship.

He rolled his eyes by way of answer and glared at the bacon and tomatoes. 'No eggs again?'

'Jimmie says they're not laying.'

Collecting the eggs and feeding the half dozen hens was another of Jimmie's jobs.

'Perhaps he should feed them more corn.'

'We don't have much corn. They have to forage for themselves most of the time.'

There was an undeclared feud between Donald and Jimmie, she knew, mainly caused by Jimmie's unspoken criticism of what he termed 'laziness' on her cousin's part. There were plenty of jobs that Donald could attempt which would ease Jimmie's burden, but which her cousin claimed were beyond him.

Clare sympathized with Jimmie but tried to ignore the muted hostility between the two men. Donald was lazy, she knew, but she felt unable to accuse him in case his heart trouble really was as serious as he claimed. She toyed with the idea of asking the doctor, but that would be a rather extreme measure and she couldn't bring herself to risk the doctor refusing due to patient confidentiality. Whenever she decided to tackle her cousin on the subject, she drew back at the last moment and said nothing. Suppose Donald *were* to do some vigorous weeding or bring in a scuttle-full of coal, and it strained his heart and he collapsed . . . She would never forgive herself.

'I wonder what he'll say,' she remarked. 'Mr Yates, I mean. I wonder what he'll think of the house. We've done all we can to smarten it up. A real spring clean. Jimmie's done the windows, Mrs Parks has wiped down all the paintwork that shows and Molly has beaten the carpets half to death. I've made up two of the empty bedrooms and put flowers on the window sills and polished the furniture to help get rid of the damp smell.'

He gave her a sour glance. 'By that little catalogue I presume you mean that I've done nothing. I tidied up the boot room, as I recall.'

Clare said nothing. Her cousin had *started* to tidy it, but after ten minutes had retired to his room with an alleged pain in his chest which he blamed on his exertions, leaving the rest of the work for their young housemaid Molly.

Clare left the room before he could start an argument and went into the kitchen. Mrs Parks was standing there looking lost.

'If I'm not to do anything that will steam up the windows before this man has seen the kitchen, what *am* I to do?' she asked. 'And what is Molly to do when she arrives? You don't want the place smelling of ironing . . .'

'I've told her not to come in today. She's coming tomorrow instead.' She prayed that the housekeeper would accept this but doubted it. Mrs Parks was a very opinionated woman and occasionally tried to bully her mistress in subtle ways.

'I suppose I could tuck myself away in the sewing room and check the laundry,' Mrs Parks offered. 'Sort out what wants mending or turning sides-to-middle.'

Clare seized the idea gratefully. 'Then when he's gone you could do the lunch and leave a little early.'

It was agreed. Mrs Parks cleared away the dishes and Donald settled himself in the morning room with a copy of *Field and Horse* while Clare wandered nervously from room to room, hoping the estate agent would give them a reasonable valuation. Finally, when the time came and went she fled into her study and closed the door. More than anything she wanted to sit down at her desk and write the next instalment of her serial for *The Ladies Own Journal*. Only when she was writing could she escape totally from her narrow existence and from the constant worries of everyday life. The money she earned, little though it was, helped to defray various expenses and gave her a false feeling of independence. Unfortunately the money her grandfather had left her was almost all gone, hence her decision to sell Merle Place which Clare reluctantly accepted had become a very large white elephant.

Before she could sit down the bell rang and she heard Mrs Parks hurry to the front door. Clare took a small mirror from one of the desk drawers and checked her appearance before making her way downstairs. Mrs Parks passed her on the stairs, on her way to the airing cupboard where the linen was kept. Mr Yates was waiting for her in the morning room, his bowler hat on the table beside him.

'Mrs Wishart! A pleasure to meet you.'

He held out a plump hand, which Clare shook, encouraged by his smile. 'It's *Miss* Wishart,' she told him.

'Now, you do surprise me.' He was short with bold dark eyes and a confident expression. 'What a pleasant day for such a pleasant enterprise! I've been looking forward to seeing more of Merle Place.' His smile broadened. 'As a child I came here on several occasions to play in the gardens while my father talked business with your father and grandfather. Estate business, that is. There was more land then.' Seeing that she look confused, he added, 'My father is Edward Yates, bank manager, now retired.'

'Ah, I see.'

'You haven't always lived here, Miss Wishart.'

'No, my mother was very delicate and died young and my father thought I would be lonely so I was brought up by my aunt. She had a son called Donald, who is staying here so you'll meet him. After she died I moved back here to join my father and help nurse Grandfather who was a widower – and then my father died in a tragic accident.'

'So your grandfather left Merle Place to you – the sole beneficiary?'

'Yes. Unfortunately he and Donald's father had had a serious quarrel many years ago and the two men were never reconciled. None of them came to his funeral. It was all rather sad but I have offered some of the proceeds of the sale to Donald.'

'Which he no doubt accepted?'

'Of course.'

After a little more polite chat, Clare suggested that they

make a start. Mr Yates produced a notebook and pencil and prepared to make notes.

'This is the kitchen,' Clare explained, 'and there is, of course, a walk-in larder and a small ice house in the garden. We have running cold water from an excellent well which has never run dry, as well as hot water heated by the stove. The copper is situated outside in the outhouse, which also provides space for drying clothes in wet weather.' Clare realized suddenly that Mr Yates was staring at her with exaggerated amazement.

'My dear Miss Wishart, you are a natural! If you were a man I would suggest that you became an estate agent.'

Clare felt herself blush at the unexpected praise. 'I've been practising,' she admitted. 'I want you to see the best of the house and not only the faults – of which there are a few.'

He laughed. 'Show me the house that has no faults,' he said. 'I can assure you there is no such place. But we should press on, I don't want to take up your morning, Miss Wishart . . . or should I call you Clarinda Hart?' He gave her a sly look.

Clare found herself stammering with embarrassment. She had believed the secret of her writing was safe. 'Oh . . . Oh, that.' She laughed. 'You know!'

'We all know,' he told her. 'Everyone knows that in print you are Clarinda Hart. An author, no less.'

'Hardly an author,' she protested. 'Just little stories. I-I find it amusing. It keeps me out of mischief!'

'Now, that's a shame. We should all get into a little mischief now and again. Even lady writers.' He gave her a bold wink, but hurried on immediately. 'Forgive me, Miss Wishart, my mother always claims my tongue runs away with me. But on we go.' He studied his notes. 'Lead on, Macbeth.'

They were in the dining room when Donald finally appeared. Clare made the introductions, referring to him as 'my cousin Donald Wishart'.

Donald nodded cheerfully. 'Sad about the poor old place – it's falling down around our ears! You'll be hard-pressed to find a buyer. You'll need someone with more money than

sense or one of those blighters who made a fortune from
the war!'

He was trying to make a joke about the property's short-
comings, but Clare was horrified. 'Donald, what a thing to
say! It's a lovely old house. It just needs money spent on
it.' She glanced at Mr Yates, but he just winked at her again.

'I'm finding much to admire,' he said firmly. 'Houses
like this are very much in demand from people with deep
pockets who want a small country estate. You are well placed
for the train service to London and are not too far from
Folkestone for the ferry service to Boulogne.'

Donald shrugged his thin shoulders. 'Well, now that I'm
here,' he said, 'I might as well take over from my cousin.'

Mr Yates, however, was having none of it. 'Oh, but I
insist that your cousin stays with us. I'm finding her an
excellent guide. She does live here, after all, whereas you,
Mr Wishart, are a guest.'

There was an awkward silence.

Donald said, 'The property was left to Clare on the understanding that she would sell it eventually and give me a
small share of the proceeds. There are no other claimants.
Not that I'm pressing for my share. I'd prefer to stay here.'
He gave a short laugh. 'But by all means carry on without
me. The prospect of trailing round is hardly exciting and
my health is precarious.' He gave a short bow and walked
stiffly away.

Dismayed, Clare said, 'Oh, dear! Now he's offended.'

Mr Yates whispered, 'We can manage very well without
him, Miss Wishart. So, shall we continue?'

Upstairs, they duly inspected the bedrooms, which Mr
Yates assessed as generously sized.

'I understand this house was requisitioned as a hospital
during the war,' he said.

'It was. These bedrooms each had six beds in them.
Occasionally some of the ex-patients call in to take "a peace-
time look" at it. One day a mother turned up whose son
had died here. She wanted to see the room where his bed
had been and she asked a lot of questions.' Clare frowned
at the memory. 'It was rather upsetting actually because she

obviously thought I'd remember all the details about all the young men who passed through here, but I don't. There were so many. But she wanted to learn something to comfort her so . . . so I made a lot up about how he was a bit of a favourite and we were all shocked when he relapsed. It was quite uncommon. I felt uncomfortable to be telling lies, but I didn't know what else I could do for her.'

She thought of the relief she had seen on the faces of so many young and wounded men and what a haven of peace Merle Place must have seemed. 'Sadly, many who were cured were promptly returned to active duty in France and went away with false cheerfulness – back to the muddy hell of the trenches.' Clare sighed.

Mr Yates asked, 'Where were you during that period?'

'I stayed on, sleeping in the large rooms at the end of the stable block, where Jimmie now lives. I was given a very basic training and worked as a ward maid – not giving injections or anything like that, but doing the unskilled jobs so that the trained nurses could concentrate on their work. We changed the beds, helped with minor things like serving the meals, checking the stores, pushing the wheelchairs. We did learn to read thermometers and occasionally change dressings, but . . .'

He was looking at her curiously. 'That must have come as a shock for a young woman like you.'

She smiled. 'It did, rather. We were looked down on by the qualified staff, and rightly so, but I like to think we contributed to the war effort in a small way.'

'You also relinquished your home!'

'It was requisitioned, yes. It was a strange time.'

'It's less than two years since it ended,' he said, 'but sometimes it seems another life. Most of us began to think it never would end. Did you lose anyone?'

'My favourite cousin and his best friend Simon were killed on the same day – at the Somme.' Her voice shook. 'They were conscientious objectors, but they had volunteered to be stretcher bearers. A single shell killed them both.' She didn't add that she had been engaged to her cousin's best friend. 'When the war started there was a rush to volunteer and the two of them took the King's shilling, expecting a great adventure.'

To Clare's dismay, they had both disappeared into an army training camp with hundreds of other starry-eyed men and were soon sent to France. There were three letters from Simon, neatly bundled and tied with ribbon, in the bottom left-hand drawer of her desk – a drawer she rarely allowed herself to open. The hurried letters in his familiar pencilled scrawl never failed to make her cry and undermined her fragile attempts at creating a new life without him.

'How terrible!' Mr Yates exclaimed.

He was genuinely shocked, Clare thought, and she quickly changed the subject before he should enquire further.

She showed him the attics, which had once housed her grandfather's servants and then led the way downstairs again and out into the grounds.

'Most of the land was sold off,' she explained, 'but several acres were kept back. Sadly, it's more than our gardener can manage without help so, as you can see, much of it is over-grown. It could be wonderful again – look there! That's the old rose garden. In my grandfather's day there were thirty different varieties.' She led him further out among the weeds and pointed again. 'That was the herb garden which was part of the kitchen garden. You can see what's left of the big greenhouse – some of the glass in the roof is cracked. We used to have peaches and we still do have a few grapes.' She sighed. 'I don't think those times will ever come again. It feels sometimes that although we won the war we lost something vital from the country. Something indefinable. So much change – and so fast. The twenties seem light years away from the days before the war.'

'But it was a war to end all wars,' he said. 'Or we hope it was.'

With effort, Clare pushed the sad thoughts from her mind and stared round. 'What haven't you seen . . . Ah, yes! The water. It's really a large pond although it has been described as a small lake. It's beyond the brambles to our right so watch your step. You don't want to snag your trousers.'

For a few minutes they stood beside the large expanse

of water edged with rushes which had been overtaken by weeds. A simple landing stage had partly rotted away, but a half-sunken rowing boat was still moored to it. 'I can remember seeing my grandparents in the boat,' Clare told her companion. 'It was years ago. I must have been about five or six, and Grandmother was holding a parasol and although I didn't know the word "elegant" then, I recognized the scene as precisely that!' She laughed softly, moved by the glimpse into a happier past.

Glancing up at him, she was surprised to see something in his eyes that had nothing to do with his work, but more to do with admiration . . . or was it pity?

When he had gone, Clare returned to the house and found Donald in the sitting room with his feet on a footstool.

He glanced up irritably. 'He took his time. An hour and a half! What's the verdict, then? How much is the old pile worth?'

'He couldn't say immediately. He's going to write to us when he's discussed it with his partner. He says he rarely sees such a large property and if it were in good order, it would . . .'

'But it isn't, is it? That's the whole point. It's creaking at the seams, cold and draughty, and probably full of dry rot. It's a shadow of what it ought to be, and I bet you will never sell it!'

Clare bit back resentment at his words. 'That's what makes it difficult to value, of course. He also thinks we might need a foreign buyer or someone with what he calls "new money", and we should be prepared for a long wait.'

He grinned suddenly. 'That suits me. I'm in no hurry. I'm quite happy here.'

As Clare glared at him, a sudden spurt of anger surprised her. 'That's because it's so easy for you,' she snapped. 'You make no plans to leave, you contribute nothing and expect to be waited on hand and foot!' Breathless, she gulped air. 'The house is mine because for whatever reason it was left to me. I shall sell it when I choose, and if you find it so unworthy why not move out?'

Donald raised his eyebrows. 'Hoity-toity! That's not like you.'

'You don't know what I'm like. You hardly know me and for some reason you have never liked me. You rarely speak to me most days and you never spend any time with me.' Her heart was thumping. Confrontation always upset her. She wondered why, on this day of all days, she had chosen to defy him.

'That's because you were a spoilt brat! Little Miss Perfect.'

'I'd lost my mother! You have no idea what that was like for a child.'

'You were always telling tales – getting me into trouble!'

'Only because you were always tormenting me with your sly little pinches. Hiding my dolls . . . and scribbling in my story books!'

He did not deny it, but grinned instead. 'I know you'd miss me if I went elsewhere.'

'That's where you're wrong.' Clare was beginning to panic. She had gone too far and now there was no turning back. She drew a quick breath and said, 'On the contrary, I'd be perfectly happy if you left me on my own. Just go home, Donald!'

Donald stood up, thrust his hands into his pockets, sauntered over to the French windows and stared out. 'Too bad, cousin of mine. The room I had which I called home, was relet eighteen months ago, soon after I came here. I have nowhere to go.'

That was news to her. Depressing news. Clare put a hand to her head where a small pain was developing behind her eyes. Her eyes were playing tricks on her and she groaned inwardly, recognizing the start of a sick headache.

Turning from the window, he saw her expression and his eyes narrowed. 'Don't tell me! You're about to resort to tears!' he said.

Clare could think of nothing crushing to say, so she threw him a withering look, spun on her heel and left the room. His laughter followed her up the stairs so she slammed the bedroom door behind her and then sat on the edge of the bed, trembling with a deep misery laced with anger. 'You're going,' she said furiously. 'I'm going to sell this house and never see you again.'

She lay down on the bed without bothering to remove her shoes, reached for her ancient teddy bear and clutched him to her chest, then took deep breaths until her heartbeat slowed to normal and she felt marginally better. Surprised, she reviewed the last few hours. She had managed to survive the estate agent's visit without making a fool of herself and had finally told Donald that she wanted him to leave. All in all it had been extremely stressful, but she felt she had achieved something. So it wasn't all bad, she consoled herself. In fact, if she were going to get one of her sick headaches and it seemed likely, at least it had been worthwhile.

Two

Jimmie's expression was thoughtful as he noticed Mr Yates being shown round the property. He had harnessed Jonty to the big roller and was preparing to subdue a few mole-hills and flatten the wide expanse of lawn in front of Merle Place. He had been introduced to Mr Yates an hour or so earlier and was now forced to face up to an unpleasant truth. Mr Yates was an estate agent. Clare Wishart was going to sell the old house.

'So where does that leave me?' he demanded. Obviously, he would be out of a job and would lose his home as well.

At the sound of Jimmie's voice, the horse flicked his ears to and fro; Jimmie took this as a sign that Jonty was listening.

Kneeling, he slipped on the first leather shoe to cover the front hoof, then shifted position to do the same with the second shoe. The soft leather prevented the hooves from making indentations in the well-manicured lawn. A bit ridiculous, in Jimmie's eyes, to strive so hard for a perfect stretch of grass when the surrounding garden had run amok, so to speak. Weeds, brambles, and dead shrubs abounded.

With Jonty pulling the roller and Jimmie steering it, they made majestic progress to and fro while Jimmie tried to concentrate on his personal problems.

'Miss Wishart won't see the need,' he said, with a shake of his head. 'All she thinks about is her stories, but she's letting life pass her by.'

Jimmie's idea of a woman's life was to have a husband and children. It had been good enough for his mother and thousands like her, so why wasn't it good enough for Clare Wishart? Ever since he had first set eyes on Clare he had loved her and wanted to marry her. But Clare, he was sure, had no desire to marry him – or any other man. Her beloved had died in the war before they were even properly betrothed. They said she considered herself a widow and would remain so. If that were true what chance did any man have of winning her over?

Jonty stumbled suddenly, breaking Jimmie's train of thought. 'Hey up! What's up with you?'

He had probably caught sight of a cat or a rabbit, thought Jimmie. Poor old Jonty had always been a nervous animal and as he grew older, he grew worse and tended to shy at the least little thing.

'What have I got to offer someone like her?' he said aloud. 'Quite a lot!' he replied firmly, but he wondered would she ever see things that way. He guessed her age to be about thirty so there was still time to marry and have a family, but only if he could persuade her. Somehow he had to jolt her to her senses, but he had no idea how this was to be achieved and there was no one to whom he could turn for advice. His parents were long gone and his only sister, Dorothy, lived in Hornsey in north London. Not that she'd be much help, he mused, since her own marriage to Eric had been a wretched failure. Eric had abandoned her and their son for another woman and Dorothy had become very bitter. She was hardly likely to encourage him to court a woman who was a good bit wealthier. Or *would* be wealthier if she sold Merle Place. It wouldn't seem right.

But poor Miss Wishart must be lonely, he reminded himself, as he reached the shrubs that edged the lawn and steered the pony round and began to roll the next strip of billiard-smooth grass.

Jimmie felt sure that Clare must feel lost in the mainly empty rooms of Merle Place. How much more comfortable they could be together in a smaller house. He had a little money tucked away. Unless . . . did she have a reason to dislike children? Surely not. Most women were at home with children. Maybe she would also like a dog. He could train a dog and the children would love to have a pet.

Jonty came to a sudden halt and shook his head as if the

flies were bothering him. Jimmie cried, 'Giddy-up, you daft creature!' and they moved slowly on again.

Normally Jimmie would be hustling the animal, eager to finish what he considered a boring job, but today he wanted time to think about Clare. All he really needed, he decided, was to get up enough courage to ask her if she had any plans to marry and settle down. If she really wanted to go on with her stories, he wouldn't object, but surely she wouldn't want to because she'd have better things to do with her time. Jimmie's mother had despised women's magazines, refusing to have any in the house. Time-wasters, she had called them. He had said so once to Mrs Parks, who had raised her eyebrows and said, 'Best not tell the mistress that!'

The only possible stumbling block that he could imagine was another man, but he had watched the situation carefully and there seemed to be nobody who might already have designs on her. And any man who might fancy her would have to consider her blasted cousin, who seemed to have put down roots. Donald's presence in the house was probably enough to deter most men. They wouldn't know what to make of him, loafing about as if he owned the place.

'How she tolerates that wretched man, I do not know,' he grumbled.

Slowly but surely Jimmie was talking himself into a plan of action and by the time he and Jonty had finished rolling the lawn, he had made up his mind about Clare Wishart. At the first sensible opportunity, he must find some courage and sound her out.

Donald was waiting outside the old greenhouse, when Jimmie turned up soon after midday. Donald called a greeting, then pulled out his watch and glanced at it before returning it to his waistcoat pocket.

He had been telling Clare for months now that Jimmie was a time-waster and should be sent packing and replaced with a younger, more energetic man.

'Overslept, did you?' he cried with false jollity. He himself had only just finished his breakfast, but Jimmie wasn't to know that. 'Doesn't take you all this time to roll the lawns, does it?'

Jimmie gave him a thin smile. 'I've also been sawing a rotten branch off the big chestnut tree,' he said. 'Not easy with only one pair of hands. I could have done with some help.'

'You should have asked me. I'd have done it for you.' With one hand tied behind my back, he thought.

Jimmie unlocked the greenhouse door. 'I did ask for you, but the mistress said you were still asleep. Didn't want to spoil your beauty sleep, I daresay.'

Donald shrugged angrily. 'Nothing to get up for in this place.'

You'd be surprised, Jimmie thought. All the rest of us find plenty to do. He disappeared inside and Donald followed him reluctantly, pushing his way cautiously past an unwieldy bundle of canes tied together with string and brushing his hand against a massive stinging nettle that had established itself below the bench.

The old greenhouse had settled into a permanent decline since the days when a team of gardeners produced most of the household's vegetables and fruit, although the original vines still trailed half-heartedly across the glass roof, which now had several missing panes. Others were cracked and all were greened with neglect. The floor was littered with earth, flowerpots rested in heaps in the corners and a motley collection of old watering cans, rakes and forks huddled at the far end. A faint smell hung in the air – a mixture of dried earth, mildewed wood and damp vegetable matter, which had been brought in from the compost heap in two buckets.

'What a horrible smell,' Donald said bad-temperedly. 'I'd pull this place down if it were mine.'

Ignoring the remark, Jimmie made his way between the benches to inspect his seedlings – tomatoes, marrows and cucumbers, green and healthy, between five and seven inches high. He examined them closely and, with careful fingers, picked out a few small weeds.

'You haven't planted them out yet, then,' said Donald accusingly.

'Too early. Might still get a frost. May can be a tricky month weather-wise. Excuse me.'

Donald had stepped up close and Jimmie pushed past him with a little more force than was necessary. Donald recognized the rebuff and his mouth tightened, but he told himself he was too smart to show his resentment. Instead, he said, 'Miss Wishart's retired to her room. She has one of her sick headaches. Prone to them, I'm afraid. Takes after her mother in that respect. Probably the result of her time with the estate agent yesterday. I suppose she told you she's selling up. Where will you go then?'

'We shall both be looking for a new home.' Jimmie looked at Donald. At least I'm not an unwelcome guest, he thought. 'I'll manage. I value my independence.'

Donald filed away in his mind the fact that the handyman had made no protest. Was that simply loyalty to an employer or something more? His eyes narrowed. Surely Jimmie had no illusions about 'the mistress'. Whatever Clare's faults, she was way above Jimmie on the social ladder, and if she ever married – which Donald doubted – it would be to someone with much better credentials and a far better position in life. Crossing one leg over the other, he adopted a nonchalant pose. Leaning against the bench with his arms folded, he watched Jimmie as he worked.

'I daresay my cousin will give you a reasonable reference when you go. Someone will take you on.'

'I'll worry about that when the time comes.' Jimmie walked away, pretending to study the vine that trailed above them.

Donald knew that he was longing to be left alone so decided to remain. 'So, you cut down the branch of the old chestnut tree. That was Clare's favourite. She used to have a swing suspended from that branch.'

'Miss Wishart asked me to cut it off. She thought it was rotten and might fall and hurt someone. I should have noticed it myself.' Jimmie, his hands on his hips, stared upwards at the knotty vine that was just coming into leaf above them. 'Nasty bit of blight, that!' he muttered. Reaching for a bucket, he filled it from the rainwater butt and added a handful of something from a bag which he pulled from beneath the bench. He stirred it without comment then reached for a slim copper pump and filled it with the mixture. Before Donald realized what the handyman was doing he began to spray the overhead vine and Donald, standing directly beneath it, was thoroughly wetted.

'Hey! Watch what you're doing, you idiot!' he shrieked, abandoning his indolent pose and leaping sideways to escape the liquid which still pattered down on to his head and shoulders.

Jimmie paused and turned innocently and began to apologize. 'There isn't really room for two in here,' he explained.

'Not if one is a complete idiot.' Furious, Donald brushed himself down, using his handkerchief to wipe away the worst of his shower. He then retreated with as much dignity as he could manage.

Outside, he somehow resisted the urge to find a brick and throw it through the glass roof, and wandered back to the house with the conviction that the accidental watering had been nothing of the kind and with a sense that he had certainly lost that little encounter. Jimmie Smith was brighter than he looked, he thought, with a frisson of reluctant admiration. 'But you won't beat me next time!' he told the absent gardener grimly. 'Two can play at that game.'

It was just after four the same day and Clare had escaped into the study, where she'd pulled the heavy curtains together to restrict the sun's glare and then had sunk gratefully into the big, high-backed leather chair which had once been her grandfather's. She had taken aspirin and her headache was slightly diminished, and she now wanted to put Mr Yates' visit out of her mind.

She was trying to complete part seven of a serial she was writing for *The Ladies Own Journal* and was preparing to submerge herself in the fiction; to worry only about her heroine and less about her own problems. Glenda was locked in a loveless marriage, but had met a man she secretly loved . . . It was so much more relaxing than wondering if she should sell Merle Place and how to get rid of cousin Donald.

While she pondered the next paragraph, she carefully sharpened a second pencil and then arranged paper, pencils and eraser in front of her. On her left she had a mug of tea which she had brought up with her and which she began to sip thoughtfully. The study was a large, shabby room lined with beautiful leather-bound books which her grandfather had cherished. Sometimes she imagined that she could still smell her grandfather's favourite pipe tobacco or hear faint echoes of his soft, gravelly laugh. In his study she felt like a writer.

Only the scope of her writing disappointed her because a few pages in a magazine did not satisfy her. She had an idea for a novel, but had no idea how to go about such a daunting task without advice from someone knowledgeable. The only person she knew in the publishing world was Edina Masters, her editor, and Edina did not offer help in any form. All she wanted from Clare was the five pages required each month for the next edition and had no further interest in her career.

With a sigh, Clare told herself to make a start, but instead she took a small tin from the bottom left-hand drawer of the desk, opened it and surveyed the almond biscuits which Mrs Parks had made two days earlier. Carefully choosing the two biscuits which contained the most almonds, she closed the drawer and heard footsteps approaching along the passage. Donald burst into the room.

'That damned Jimmie!' He threw himself into an armchair and glared at her.

Clare glared back. 'Can't you see I'm busy? I've come up here to work.'

Ignoring her, he picked up her second biscuit and popped it into his mouth whole, crunched it and swallowed it. 'Any more of those?'

'No!' She pushed the drawer shut with her foot. 'And your manners are appalling!'

'Yes, Mama!' he mocked, rolling his eyes. 'One of these

days he'll go too far. Jimmie, I mean. I'm warning you, cousin of mine. Who does he think he is, for heaven's sake? He's a sight too big for his boots, that man, and I came near to boxing his ears.' He recounted his grievance in graphic terms. 'Lord knows what was in the liquid. It might have been acid.'

'Acid would kill the vine. It wouldn't be acid. It was probably just a weak Bordeaux mixture. Don't worry, you'll survive.' She wasn't quite sure what she was talking about, but she hoped Donald would be impressed.

He was not. 'It could have been poisonous,' he persisted. 'Or I might have been blinded if it had gone in my eyes. The man's a menace. If you don't get rid of him, I will.'

Clare wanted to shake him. He was going to ruin what was left of her day with his tantrums. 'You'll do nothing of the sort. He's employed by me, not you, and I've warned you not to get in his way,' she said firmly. 'He's got work to do and he doesn't enjoy your interference. Stay away from Jimmie and you'll be quite safe.' She kept her face straight but she wished she could have witnessed the incident. Poor Donald was no match for Jimmie.

Donald shook his head. 'You are so gullible, Clare. You can't see the man is lazy and is taking advantage of you. If I had a decent ticker I could do his job in half the time.' From habit he laid his right hand over his heart and contorted his face as if in sudden pain. 'I'd have given anything to have fought in the war, but they wouldn't have me. I'd have made a good officer, given half a chance.' He sighed heavily.

Before Clare could be forced to listen to the familiar complaints, she said, 'You'll have to excuse me, Donald, I have to work.'

He grinned. 'Scribble, scribble! I could write a book if I wanted to. I've got plenty of experiences to draw on. That's what you need to be an author. Experience of the world.'

Clare bit back her impatience. She had heard it all before. 'You've got plenty of time, Donald,' she said sweetly. 'Why don't you make a start on your book? I promise to buy the first copy!'

Ignoring her, he went on. 'You can't write a decent love story if you've never been in love and you can't . . .'

'But I have been in love! I was going to be married. Have you forgotten already?'

For a moment he regarded her blankly and then he nodded. 'Oh, yes! Simon, wasn't it? Alistair's friend. I'm sorry, Clare.' He had the grace to look contrite. 'Yes, that was terrible. The two of them dying together. I'm sorry.'

She forgave him instantly, but picked up her pencil and waited, pointedly, for him to leave.

He heaved himself from the chair with a great show of reluctance. 'I mean it about Jimmie. You're going to have to sack him anyway when you sell the house. He might as well go sooner than later.'

'That's for me to decide, Donald.'

He shrugged. 'I thought that since I'm here, I might as well give you the benefit of my advice. It's a big responsibility for a woman.'

Clare closed her eyes. If she replied the conversation would never end because Donald liked to have the last word.

Seeing that her head was now bent over her writing pad, he finally wandered out, closing the door behind him with exaggerated care. Clare was left to try and recover her enthusiasm. To help her settle back into the right creative mood, she helped herself to another biscuit, closed her eyes and munched thoughtfully.

Later that evening Clare went in search of Jimmie and discovered him on his knees, bedding out antirrhinums on the far side of the lawn. Seeing her approach he scrambled to his feet, brushing grass cuttings from his trousers. His face lit up as she drew near.

'I've set three colours for this bed,' he told her. 'Pink, white and red. I thought they'd go well together. Nice hardy little things.'

Clare nodded appreciatively.

'Yellow and orange for the other side. They should do well there.'

He took a rag from his pocket and rubbed at his earthy hands.

She said, 'I want to talk to you about when the house is sold – if I ever find a buyer. Maybe you could pop in when you've finished here and . . .'

'I've been hoping to talk to you, Miss Wishart.'

'Have you?' She looked at him in surprise. 'Is something troubling you? I shall give you a most wonderful reference, Jimmie, so I'm sure you won't have a problem finding alternative work.'

'It's about that . . . Or rather, it's about what comes next.' He frowned. 'Because I've been thinking. You'd be alone, you see, with no one to turn to.'

He took a deep breath and stared down at the newly planted antirrhinums.

Puzzled, Clare tried to decide what he actually meant but failed. She said, 'I'm afraid I can't keep Merle Place on, Jimmie. It's desperately in need of repair and there is no money available. I know it will be a disruption for you, but I've told you I shall give you a good reference and that's what I want to talk to you about. I know several people who would value your services and . . .'

'But I'm more or less committed to you, Miss Wishart!' He threw her a despairing glance. 'That is, I'd rather be with you. There now, I've said it.'

'Oh, Jimmie, I know you're very loyal, but I probably shan't need a gardener or a handyman if I buy myself a little cottage somewhere. I haven't quite decided what to do after Merle Place is sold. It's strange to think of living somewhere else, but Merle Place should be put to a better use. When I recall it during the war . . . It was important to so many people. I sometimes thought of it as a beehive with bees buzzing in and out and everyone so purposeful. Now I just seem to drift. I really shouldn't be rattling around in it alone.'

Jimmie was staring at her so intently that she began to feel uneasy.

He said, 'My point exactly! But suppose you weren't rattling around on your own. You don't know what the future might bring. I mean you might . . . you might marry. Had you thought of that, Miss Wishart?'

Taken aback, she stammered, 'Marry? Whatever put that idea in your head, Jimmie? Good heavens! I hope you don't think I might marry Donald!'

'Lord, no! No, I was thinking . . .'

'He is my cousin so that rules him out as a suitor.' Jimmie opened his mouth again, but Clare held up her hand and he faltered to a stop. 'Let's talk again some other time, Jimmie. I appreciate your concern but I have no intention of marrying anyone.'

He looked startled. 'Not ever?'

'I'm not exactly young and there are thousands of women like me, Jimmie, who have lost the men they love to the war . . .' She swallowed hard. 'But life goes on for us. We have to plan for a different kind of future.'

'But you shouldn't think that way,' he told her earnestly. 'You could meet someone else . . . someone who would love you dearly.'

'I'm touched by the compliment but I think the sale of Merle Place is enough for me to worry about for the moment – and I suspect I am seen as a spinster.' She smiled faintly. 'But I must let you get on, Jimmie. Come and talk to me some other time about the reference.'

She walked back across the grass, confused by his attitude but vaguely amused by the notion that he might have imagined her marrying Donald. Did Jimmie wonder about her relationship with Donald? Did anyone else in the village have suspicions about them – and if they did, what could she do about it? She could hardly go round telling everyone that Donald was not only her cousin, but a cuckoo in the nest that she would be glad to see take flight! It was an awkward situation and she was frowning by the time she reached the house.

Three

When Molly walked into the kitchen the next morning it was immediately obvious that something had upset her. Her small mouth was set in a tight line and her brown eyes flashed. She snatched her apron from behind the door, pulled it down roughly over her dark hair and tied the strings behind her, without so much as a 'Good morning'. Mrs Parks took one look at her and poured her a cup of tea.

'Sit down and tell me what's wrong,' she said, with exaggerated resignation, 'and take that look off your face or the mistress will give you a right talking to and might send you home!'

Instead of doing what she was told, Molly burst into loud hiccuping sobs. Mrs Parks stood with her hands on her hips and waited until the worst was over. 'Come on, girl. Spit it out.'

'It's all over the village.' Molly sniffed as she rubbed at her eyes with the end of her sleeve. 'This place is going to be sold and we'll all get the sack.'

Mrs Parks frowned. 'And how did you come by that piece of news?'

'My friend Vi works behind the bar and Master Donald told her. Said it was a secret and she mustn't tell anyone, but Vi told me and she told her husband and he told his mother and . . . Is it true?' Her lips trembled.

'We don't know for sure yet, Molly. That's why you haven't been told anything.' Mrs Parks hesitated over how much she should tell her. 'The man from the estate agent had a look round and is going to write to the mistress and tell her what he thinks. The trouble is that it's not in very good shape – so much needs doing to it. It may be that no one wants to buy it because it would need a lot of money spent on it.'

'But what if somebody *does* buy it?'

'We'll each be given a very good reference so we can easily get other work, so there's no need for all this fuss.' She spoke firmly, but she understood Molly's fears. Clare had taken the girl on when she left school aged twelve and Molly had never worked for anyone else. To her, the prospect of change was bound to be alarming. 'So, wash your face – and say nothing at all to Miss Wishart about all the gossip. She won't be very pleased, that's for sure!'

She began to cook breakfast – boiled eggs and toast – and thought about her own prospects if Merle Place were to be sold. Sometimes new owners would take on the original staff. That might be interesting – as long as they were reasonable and fair-minded and didn't try to pay lower wages for the same hours. Merle Place was within walking distance of the village where she lived, which was handy in bad weather, and the mistress was always willing to let her go home early if her mother took a turn for the worse and had once sent a jar of calves foot jelly to help her recover from one of her turns. Miss Wishart was good like that. A new employer might not be so kind – but on the other hand, with a good reference, she might be able to ask for higher wages. No good asking Miss Wishart for more money because things were very tight; the household could no longer afford the best cuts of meat from the farm and often bought cracked eggs. Mrs Parks sighed.

Molly, somewhat chastened, appeared beside her and said, 'Where shall I start?' Her eyes were red and Mrs Parks tutted. 'You'd best keep out of the way for a while,' she said. 'Take the tea leaves and do the carpet on the upstairs landing, then wipe over all the door handles and finger-plates. By the time you've finished they'll have eaten their breakfast and you can wash up.'

Molly pulled a face. 'I hate that job. The tea leaves make my hands all messy.'

'I've told you before to use the old cotton gloves, but

you never do. Just get on with it. I'm in no mood for any nonsense.'

Meanwhile, in the big room above the stables, Jimmie sat over his writing, oblivious of the time. In front of him was a sheet of paper, which he had folded in half to form a greeting card. On the front he had drawn a very respectable primrose with a suitable leaf, gently shaded in, and had written HAPPY BIRTHDAY across the top. That part had been easy enough – the difficult part was what to say inside the card. He didn't want to make a mistake and have to rub it out, but more importantly he didn't want to say anything that would offend or startle Miss Wishart. Maybe 'Best wishes from Jimmie' would be enough but he wanted something a little more personal that would give her a hint about his feelings for her. So would 'Love and best wishes' do the trick? What he longed to write was 'All my love and best wishes from your devoted friend Jimmie', but common sense warned him against taking such a liberty.

Too far, too fast, he thought. He had decided to lead up to his proposal of marriage gradually so that when he finally managed it, she was ready for it and prepared to say yes. He'd never handle a refusal. He'd be crushed.

He sat back, the old cane chair creaked under his weight, and he stared up into the rafters waiting for inspiration which didn't come. Then he let his gaze move slowly around the room. The bed was narrow and barely comfortable but he had refused the offer of a better one because this was the bed Miss Wishart had slept in during the war and he liked to think that, in a sense, they had shared the bed.

His tabby cat slept on the lid of a small rattan chest which had also belonged to Clare, but which now held a few of his clothes and an extra blanket for the bed in winter. As though aware of his gaze, the cat opened his eyes, blinked and stretched. He had no name because he was never called, but made his way in and out at will by way of the wooden steps which led down from the trap door to the tack room, and from there to the stables. The cat was useful when Jimmie needed someone to talk to, and he kept the mice at bay.

Jimmie glanced at his alarm clock and jumped to his feet. He was going to be late. The card would have to be finished in his midday break and handed to Miss Wishart during the afternoon.

It was blustery but not cold that afternoon when Clare walked into the village to send off her latest instalment to Edina. Now that it was finished and sealed ready for posting, Clare had the usual doubts about it. It was rare for her editor to ask her to make any changes – or to offer comments of any kind – but the nagging doubts remained. Had she made the conversations credible, had she hinted too strongly at the disaster that was imminent, or made the heroine just a little too trusting?

Sarah Tennant was coming out of the post office as Clare waited to go in. They exchanged the usual pleasantries. Clare asked after Sarah's mother, who had just come out of hospital, and Sarah asked Clare how her work was going. As usual it was a brief exchange. Sarah had been to Merle Place on a few occasions for afternoon tea. Clare had joined Sarah twice when she walked her elderly dog, but she was aware that the village considered her continued existence at Merle Place slightly eccentric and was rarely at ease with any of them.

The postmistress glanced up and smiled politely as Clare entered the post office. The shop was empty apart from a small girl choosing sweets from the jars behind the counter.

'A red lollipop, please Mrs Brett . . . No, a liquorice lace.'

'You don't like liquorice, Mary.'

'Oh!' The child pressed two fingers against her mouth. 'Then I'll have . . . a sugar mouse!'

'Pink or yellow?'

'No, I'll have one of those.'

'A barley sugar stick? Right!' Mrs Brett rolled her eyes as she reached for the jar.

Clare's answering smile was touched with sadness. If Simon had survived the war they might well have had children – it had been part of Clare's dream for their future.

When the girl had gone, Clare handed over the package, and it was weighed and priced.

Mrs Brett glanced at the address and said, 'Another instalment? I don't know where you get the ideas from.'

Clare paid her and was about to leave when another customer arrived.

'Ah! Miss Wishart,' she began. 'Is it true you're selling Merle Place? I said never! It's been in the Wishart family for as long as I can remember.' Mrs Murdock, small and round, carried a basket over one arm and clutched her purse in both hands. 'I only ask because there was a young man here yesterday asking about the place. Said he'd been nursed there during the war and wanted to see it again. Nasty scar on his face to prove it. Must have been handsome at one time, though, poor fellow.'

Clare shook her head. 'I didn't see him, but then I went out for a long walk yesterday and must have missed him. The men do sometimes come back. Occasionally they go into the church to give thanks and make a donation.'

'You might recognize him. You worked there, as I remember.'

'There were so many that I doubt I'd remember him.'

She left the two women and started back up the hill, her thoughts reverting to the manuscript that would hopefully find its way to Edina's desk tomorrow. When she reached home she met Mrs Parks who was just leaving and asked her if anyone had called the previous day while she was out walking.

'Yes, there was someone. I should have told you. I'm sorry, Miss Wishart, but it quite slipped my mind. A quiet gentleman, very polite and sort of shy. Wanted to see over the place, but I wouldn't let him without you here. Jimmie showed him round the grounds – not letting him out of his sight, of course. You never know with people, do you? Any old burglar could *say* he'd been here during the war – just to get the lie of the land for thieving.' She buttoned her coat up to the neck and pulled on her gloves. 'Poor chap. What do they call it now . . . Oh, yes! Disfigured. That's what he was. His cheek, right down to his jaw. Sort of . . . crumpled. He had a big scar. Nice eyes, though. Blue and very bright. Reminded me of my uncle. Even when he was an old man he still had these bright twinkly blue eyes.' She smiled. 'He was a one for the women, my uncle!' She turned up her collar. 'He might come again – the man, I mean. He said he's come a long way and is staying in the village for a few days. He told me his name but I've forgotten it. Might have been Lampeter ... No, it wasn't ... Lorrimer?' She shook her head again, gave up, and they parted company.

Clare went inside and closed the door, intrigued by the visitor but not at all sure that he would return. Probably he had seen enough. He would remember the garden because the walking wounded spent a lot of time outside and those in wheelchairs were frequently pushed out if the weather was nice enough. Some of them had carved their initials on various tree trunks even though it was frowned upon. They had scribbled on the walls inside the house, too, but most of it had been washed off since or painted over.

Before she'd had time to take off her coat, she heard the letter box rattle and saw a folded sheet of paper slip on to the mat. Curiously she stared at the hand-drawn primrose with its heading. Was it her birthday? It was, she realized with a start, but who had remembered it?

'Jimmie?' she whispered. It certainly wasn't Mrs Parks or Donald because they had had plenty of time to wish her a happy day but had failed to do so. Not that she cared. Birthdays seemed to have very little meaning nowadays. Inside there were two words in capital letters – FROM JIMMIE.

Smiling with pleasure at the kind thought, Clare pulled her coat on again and went in search of him. He was in the greenhouse, pretending to tend the tomato plants and when he turned, she saw that he was nervous.

'Thank you so much for the birthday card,' she said. 'Nobody else remembered – not even me.'

For a moment he didn't answer, and she saw that he was breathing very fast. Perhaps he had run all the way back to the greenhouse.

'I thought ... that is, I remembered from last year when your cousin, when he called you a middle-aged ...' He stopped, confused.

Clare suddenly knew what he was referring to and felt herself blushing. She had jokingly reminded Donald that it was her birthday and he had said, 'I didn't know that middle-aged spinsters wanted to remember their birthdays.'

'Oh, that! It didn't matter,' she protested. 'He was only joking.'

'He was insulting you.'

'Oh, Jimmie! Please don't even think about it. He didn't mean it.' She knew, of course, that he had meant it to hurt her and she had been hurt, but she could never admit it. To do so would make her appear vain and silly.

'I know it's none of my business but . . .'

Clare could see that this conversation was taking a dangerous direction and searched for a way to prevent it happening. Glancing at the birthday card, she said lightly, 'Let's just forget Donald. This is my birthday and I don't want it spoiled.'

'Happy birthday!' he said hoarsely, and he snatched up the nearest tomato plant and gave it his full attention.

Clare said shakily, 'I'll put your card up on the mantel-piece,' and stumbled from the greenhouse. As she made her way back to the house she cursed herself soundly for her stupidity. 'Fool!' she muttered to herself. 'You embarrassed the poor chap.'

As she hung up her coat, she considered the reason she had spoken so rashly. It was the revelation that Jimmie hated Donald. Really hated him. How long would it be before Donald made one provocative comment too many? She groaned.

Entering the drawing room, she propped Jimmie's card on the mantelpiece because she had said she would, but knew it would only serve to remind her that there was trouble brewing . . .

She poured herself a small glass of sherry and sat down to mull over what had happened and to ponder her options. Suppose Jimmie cared for her in his own way . . . she must not encourage him further. That would be grossly unfair. But she didn't want to lose Jimmie. Clare told herself that she should ask Donald to go, but she knew what his answer would be. He would claim that he had nowhere else to go, no money for rent and no way of earning a living.

'If only I could find a buyer for Merle Place. That would solve that particular problem because Donald would have to go. I'll give him some of the money just to get rid of him and he can make his own way after that.'

The telephone rang the next morning, soon after ten. It had been installed for the benefit of the hospital and Clare had decided to keep it. She knew very few people had private telephones, but she found it useful for her work with the magazine, and one or two other business contacts and tried not to think of it as a luxury.

Mrs Parks was terrified of it and now called to Clare with the usual note of panic in her voice. Clare, who was composing a possible advertisement to put in a property magazine, hurried downstairs to her rescue.

'Clare Wishart. Grayling seven three,' she said.

'It's Edina here,' her editor said warmly. 'Your manuscript arrived this morning for which many thanks. How are you, Clare? It seems ages since we last spoke.'

'Is it all right? The instalment?' Clare knew she shouldn't cast doubts on it, but she was always uneasy until Edina had actually approved it.

'I haven't had time to read it all yet, but I'm sure it will be fine. The plot is holding up well so far, with no lack of pace. I'm very pleased with it as I always am with your work.'

Taken aback by the unexpected enthusiasm, Clare said, 'That's nice to hear. Thank you.' She frowned uneasily and wondered what was coming.

'I had a Steven Flint in the office yesterday,' Edina went on. 'An editor. He's worked briefly for other firms to gain wide experience but has now joined his family's firm which is Bell and May. He's a fiction editor and it seems he is starting up a new imprint for them. He rather likes your work and wonders if you'd meet with him.'

'Meet with him? But why? Bell and May don't do magazines, do they?'

'No, that's the whole point. He thinks you might like to try your hand at something longer than your serials.'

Clare sat down on the small chair beside the telephone, her heart thudding with anxiety. Did she want to hear any more? 'You mean a novel?'

'What else?' Edina's enthusiasm seemed to be on the wane. 'I've been asked to pass on your telephone number to him so that he can talk to you, but I told him I must have your permission first. You must realize what this means, Clare. If you are writing a novel for Bell and May, you won't have time to write for us. You will have to decide between us.'

Clare now detected a certain coldness in Edina's voice. Panic fluttered at the edges of her mind and all the negatives of the situation presented themselves to her. Suppose the novel was no good. Could she survive the failure? Suppose Edina had replaced her and no other magazines wanted her serials. Who was this editor and what would he be like to work for?

With effort, she said calmly, 'I think I'll have to worry about that once I've talked to Mr Flint. If I don't go ahead with a novel there will be no choice to make.'

There was a short pause. 'Naturally we hope you will stay with *The Ladies Own Journal*,' Edina told her. 'Clarinda Hart is very popular. Our readers very much enjoy your work and there is the chance that we may be able to improve on your payment rate. After all, you have been with us for some time and are very loyal.'

Clare blinked with surprise. Surely this meant that she was valued. They didn't want to lose her. She was surprised by a small spurt of confidence and she thought seriously about a meeting with Steven Flint. Yes, she would meet him.

'Please do pass on my telephone number, Edina. At least I can hear what he has to say.' As long as he didn't expect her to travel up to London, she thought. Perhaps he could be persuaded to come to Merle Place. She would serve a nice lunch; Mrs Parks could make the game pie of which she was rightly proud.

Edina said, 'I'll pass it on. But a word of warning, if I may, Clare. A novel is a much more complicated beast and you should give this some serious thought.'

With her head buzzing with excitement after the call ended, Clare sat down, happy with her thoughts until she could wait no longer to pass on the good news. Deciding against Donald, who would pour scorn on the news, she decided to share it with Mrs Parks, who would surely be impressed. However she was brought down to earth again when she entered the kitchen by the sight of Mrs Parks preparing ham sandwiches for Clare's tea and looking distinctly ruffled.

'Your cousin says to tell you that he's taken Jonty and is riding down to the river to do some fishing. He won't be back till late.'

She laid down the knife, put her hands on her hips and glared at Clare. 'He also says that some of your silver spoons have gone missing from that display case under the window and not to blame him. What he means is that it's me or Molly or Jimmie that's taken them and that's a downright lie!'

Clare saw how pale she was. 'I'm sure he didn't mean that.'

'Oh, yes, he did, Miss Wishart. He put it in such a way, you know. I can't recall the exact words but that was his meaning. As if any of us would do such a thing.'

Her voice shook with indignation and Clare did her best to reassure her that even if her cousin *had* meant that, she knew it was nonsense. 'I trust you all utterly,' she said firmly. 'And I'll tell him so and I shall ask him to apologize for his stupidity.' Even as she said it, she began to doubt whether or not she could make him do so. Apologies from Donald were few and far between, but she could try her best.

'Him apologize? Pigs will fly!' said Mrs Parks. She retrieved the knife, cut through the sandwiches and covered them with a clean cloth. 'Molly didn't seem too upset. Said it was probably one of his silly jokes – but Jimmie was furious when I told him.'

'Oh, no!' Aware of Jimmie's opinion of Donald, Clare could see storm clouds gathering on the horizon.

Mrs Parks said, 'Was it important – the telephone call? Not bad news, I hope?'

Mrs Parks saw the telephone much in the way that she saw telegrams – as the bringer of seriously bad news. She disliked having to answer it and dreaded having to take a message. Any that she did take were mostly unreadable and, if readable, often so brief that they were unintelligible, but she was not, however, averse to sharing dreadful news.

Clare, her mind now focussed on the missing spoons (allegedly stolen) and the likely repercussions, sighed and shook her head. 'It was nothing important,' she said.

The telephone call was, of course, very important and that night Clare lay wide awake long after the church clock had struck midnight, trying to come to terms with the fact that she was 'in demand' – or rather her writing was. The idea that her serial instalments had caught the eye of an editor was wonderful, but the prospect of having to deal with the length and substance of a novel had now thrown her into a panic. Although she had an idea for a full-length book, she now felt a growing doubt that she could actually write it.

Other questions crowded in. Would they pay her anything in advance, and if so, what would happen if they didn't like the completed story? Presumably she would have to repay the money. In which case, she would be unable to spend it and without the payments from the magazine, she would have to dip deeper into the small amount of money that still remained from her grandfather's legacy.

Large areas of roof tiles had had to be replaced and the damp ceilings restored. One of the chimneys, in imminent danger of falling in the next high wind, had been repointed, and the old salt-glazed drains, cracked and leaking, had been renewed. A modern stove had been bought for the kitchen, electricity had been installed in part of the house, and the main staircase had had to be treated for dry rot. Jimmie had been engaged to do battle with the overgrown garden and Mrs Parks, who had worked in the Merle Place kitchens while it was a hospital, had been persuaded to return. Clare, after starting the restoration project with stars in her eyes, now realized that it would prove impossible to finish the job without the injection of much more money than she could ever commit – hence her decision to find a new, much wealthier, owner for the property.

Still wide awake when one o'clock struck, she went down to the kitchen and made herself a mug of Ovaltine and, huddled in her dressing gown, sat by the dying embers of the old range and thought about her upcoming meeting with Steven Flint. Was he old or young, she wondered, dour or jolly, helpful or inclined to be critical? Edina had told her very little about the man himself so presumably she had never met him. Would he appreciate the fact that she, Clare, was new to the task and terrified by the prospect?

From thinking about Steven Flint, her thoughts drifted to Jimmie. She focussed her thoughts. In her heart she had guessed some time ago that he found her attractive, but she had found that comforting and had seen no reason to make an issue of it. It was a nice compliment to be admired and she had accepted the fact.

Now, however, she allowed her imagination to take flight. Suppose he was seriously attracted to her – did she feel anything for him? He was older than her; she had almost looked on him as a friendly uncle and had been glad of his reassuring presence in the small household. Had he ever thought of her as someone he might marry. Could she ever return his feelings? She wondered whether he had ever been married and decided to ask Mrs Parks in a roundabout way if she knew anything about his background. It was no use thinking about it. She would never be able to love another man the way she had loved Simon. Anyway perhaps, like Donald, he also saw her as a 'middle-aged spinster'.

'No, he doesn't,' she whispered. If asked to describe him she would say 'mild-mannered, reliable, trustworthy and hard-working'. That's what she would write in his reference when the time came for him to find further employment.

As Clare sipped her drink, the large kitchen grew cooler as the little remaining heat from the range seeped out of the two large uncurtained windows. At night the kitchen was a gloomy place, lit only by a single central light bulb, and when the last of the Ovaltine had gone she went back upstairs and climbed back into the bed. Warmed by the drink and exhausted by her worries, she was soon asleep.

The next day Donald had made an effort and was up in time to eat his breakfast at the same time as Clare – a rare occurrence and one which made her look at him warily as he stared at his plate, obviously deep in thought.

'A penny for them,' she offered.

'What's that?'

'A penny for your thoughts.'

'Funny you should mention money. I suppose you couldn't lend me a few bob, just until I get myself straight. There's a game planned for midday at the Jolly Waggoner and I'm feeling lucky. On a winning streak, actually.'

'Then why do you need to borrow from me?' Clare had heard about the public house in the next village which allowed gambling on games of dice. Donald spent more and more time there – and lost more and more money. Somehow the dice never did roll in his favour so the so-called winning streak was almost certainly a figment of Donald's imagination. 'You still owe me two pounds . . .' She took a deep breath. 'And on another matter, I think you should apologize to Mrs Parks for your comments about the missing silver spoons. The staff are very upset that you seem to think one of them guilty of stealing.'

He cleared his plate, put his knife and fork together, and pushed the plate away. 'My dear Clare, I shall do no such thing. It must be one of them since I don't see why you should steal your own spoons and I certainly have no need of such things.'

Clare swallowed hard. She had no idea how she could force him to apologize and on similar occasions she had given way rather than suffer the bad feeling that always followed an argument. This morning, however, she felt a little more in control and realized that the proposed meeting between herself and Steven Flint was responsible. Perhaps her cousin underestimated her.

She said, 'They may not be stolen but simply mislaid. Even if they have been stolen I am quite certain that they were not taken by Mrs Parks, Jimmie or Molly and . . . and I insist that you apologize to Mrs Parks.'

She held her breath, waiting for the storm to break, but in a flash the answer came to her and she bided her time.

Donald emptied his teacup and pushed back his chair. 'If you think I'm going to crawl to that waspish old woman, you can forget it!' He stood up, the usual smug smile playing around his lips.

'You must please yourself,' Clare told him. 'Likewise, if you think I shall lend you any more money, you can forget that!' She busied herself with spreading marmalade on her toast.

He said, 'Why, you sly . . .' Words failed him.

At that moment the housekeeper came in to the dining room and asked if Clare wanted another pot of tea.

'No, thank you, Mrs Parks, but I think Donald has something to say to you.' She looked sternly at him.

There was a long silence. Clare crossed her fingers. Donald glanced from one woman to the other.

At last he said, 'It seems I upset you, Mrs Parks. I apologize.' Then he walked out of the room, muttering under his breath. 'Lot of fuss about nothing!'

Mrs Parks watched him go. 'What on earth was that about, ma'am?' she asked.

'It's about the missing spoons. We had words about it. I told him to apologize.'

Her face lit up. 'And he did! Glory Moses!'

Clare smiled with her. 'I'm sure they will turn up. We'll forget all about them.'

Ten minutes later she went in search of her cousin and found him sitting in the boot room, arms folded, his legs stretched out in front of him. He glared at her. 'Satisfied?'

She nodded and held out five florins. 'I'll lend you ten shillings,' she told him, 'but don't bother to ask for any more until you have paid back the two pounds, ten shillings you now owe me.'

She turned quickly away and was halfway out of the door when he said, 'Thank you kindly, ma'am,' in a voice dripping with sarcasm.

He'd be mocking her now, she thought, as she banged the door shut behind her. Very likely tugging a humble forelock and insulting her under his breath.

She could hardly wait for the day when Merle Place moved into new ownership. Donald would be on his own then, and he would find life very different.

Four

Jimmie reached up to prune the vine; a job he loved. He was careful to deal only with the straggly lateral growths, some of which had found their way out into the air by way of broken panes. Drawing them carefully inside, he found the first bunch of grapes and studied them with delight. They reminded him of a cluster of match-heads, he thought, as he severed the fragile stem two leaves further on. Tomorrow he would tie the strands to the rusting wires so that the weight of the fruit when it matured could not do any damage. They were dessert grapes by the name of Black Hamburg and Clare always insisted that Jimmie should have the first ripe bunch by way of a thank you for his superior knowledge.

He whistled cheerfully under his breath as he worked, mostly the songs they had sung during the war, even though he had not taken part in the fighting. He'd been a merchant-navy man for a few years when he was young (with a tattoo to prove it) and was no stranger to danger, but he had not passed the physical examination when he tried to enlist to fight in the war. All he wanted now was a peaceful life – preferably with Clare Wishart.

A shadow fell across the window and he looked up hopefully.

Disappointed, he saw Donald watching him, his arms folded, the usual sardonic smile on his face.

'Keep going!' Donald urged. 'Don't let me stop you. I like to see a man at his labours.'

Jimmie's good mood vanished. 'I've nothing to say to

you that you'd like to hear,' he warned. 'If you know what's good for you, you'll leave me alone.'

Donald's smile broadened. 'Oh, dear! Upset you, have I? Oh, I am pleased!'

Jimmie stopped what he was doing, his hands closing into fists, one hand still clasped around the secateurs.

'Don't worry,' said Donald hastily. 'I shan't waste much more time on you. Just wanted to let you know that I saw you last evening, sneaking round the house. Staring up at my cousin's bedroom. Thought I ought to let her know. Nobody likes a peeping Tom, do they, old chap?'

Jimmie let out a gasp. 'I was nowhere near the big house! Wouldn't dream of it – and you know it. If someone was there, it wasn't me.'

'I *saw* you!'

'That's a damned lie!' He tried unsuccessfully to hold back his anger. 'You're a nasty piece of work, Donald Wishart, and if necessary I shall tell her *that*! So, don't get too clever because you haven't got the brains for it. If push comes to shove I'll get the better of you.' He had taken three steps forward and was very close to his tormentor.

Instinctively, Donald stepped back. 'You threatening me?'

'If you don't stop your stupid games, I'll do more than threaten.'

He saw Donald's expression change and knew that at last the man was nervous. He turned back to his work, gritting his teeth with the effort to stay calm. In his youth, he had crippled a man in a fight that his assailant had started, and the dark memory remained with him. Jimmie knew the strength and power of his anger and he had vowed never to let himself be driven into a mindless rage again. Donald, however, couldn't know how dangerous his taunts might prove.

Mercifully, however, Donald now retreated. With a shrug of his elegant shoulders, he turned away and strolled back towards the house. As Jimmie watched him go, adrenaline rushed through him and his hands shook. He tossed the secateurs on to the bench and walked over to the garden shed. Once inside he slumped on to an old chair and closed his eyes. Should he say anything to Miss Wishart, he wondered, about Donald's accusation. He would have to because how else could he deny it? But if Donald hadn't really said such a thing, he, Jimmie, would look a bit of a fool. Perhaps he could sound Mrs Parks out and see if she had heard anything about a prowler.

'No!' He opened his eyes. 'I'll go straight to Miss Wishart.' It might be a good idea, he thought, to let her see, once and for all what a snake she was harbouring at Merle Place.

Minutes later Mrs Parks welcomed him into the kitchen and insisted on giving him a mug of tea and a rock cake straight from the oven.

'Just mind it's not too hot,' she warned. 'It's not so much the cake as the currants. They get very hot.' She watched him eat, enjoying the approving nod of his head and the roll of his eyes which replaced speech while his mouth was full.

When he'd finished he asked to speak to the mistress and was told she was upstairs writing.

'And that dreadful cousin is in the drawing room,' she went on, 'snoring his head off with a book in his lap. Said he was going to do a bit of research. "Into what?" I asked, quick as a flash, but he fobbed me off with a string of big words.' She shook her head in disgust. 'I can't understand the mistress, letting him stay idle, the way she does. I'd get him out and earning his keep, but I sometimes think she's scared of him.'

Jimmie scowled at the idea. 'If I thought for a minute that she was or that he'd ever upset her, I'd give him a damn good hiding, but she always sticks up for him.' He hesitated, wanting to confide in her, but wary of spreading Donald's lies. 'So, could you tell the mistress I've something to tell her?'

'Important, is it?'

'I think so.'

Mrs Parks was sharper than he expected. 'About His Nibs?'

He nodded. 'Up to his tricks.'

'I'll go up and tell her.'

Jimmie waited. A few moments later Mrs Parks returned alone. 'She'll see you in the morning room.'

Jimmie moved outside and gave his boots another go on the boot scraper, then, satisfied with his efforts, made his way to the room where Miss Wishart waited for him. He knocked and entered, and saw his mistress standing inside the window, looking out over the garden.

'I just wanted you to know that it's all lies,' he began. 'I was never outside your windows. I was never spying on you.' He could see by her expression that she didn't understand and went on. 'He's trying to blacken my name . . . sully my reputation and all that, because he doesn't like me. Not that I like him . . .'

'What are you talking about?' Miss Wishart looked bewildered. 'Who is trying to blacken your name? Mrs Parks said you had something to tell me. She didn't say any more than that.'

'Him. Your cousin. He hates me because I see through him.' Jimmie's words came more forcefully. 'Because he knows that I'm on to him!'

Miss Wishart said, 'I think we must sit down calmly, Jimmie, and then we can start again at the beginning.'

She pulled out a dining chair, sat down and rested her arms on the table. After a moment's hesitation, Jimmie followed suit, seating himself opposite her, but keeping his hands and his cap in his lap.

She smiled. 'Now do go ahead and explain what is bothering you. I take it Donald – Mr Wishart – is involved?'

Jimmie nodded and explained what had been said in the greenhouse and how incensed he had been. 'I wouldn't want you to believe such slanderous lies, Miss Wishart. I was at the pub until nine thirty, then I came straight back and went up to my quarters. If there *was* someone in the grounds spying on you, it certainly wasn't me and I saw no one.'

'I would never believe such wicked stories, Jimmie,' said Clare, 'but I can assure you that my cousin said no such thing to me and if he had, I would have sent him out of the room with a very large flea in his ear!' She smiled gently. 'I'm afraid he was trying to upset you and he's succeeded. I shall speak to him next time I see him. Donald has never grown up, unfortunately. I've known him for most of his life and he has never seemed to mature.'

'A rather dangerous child!'

'Indeed. I shall forbid him to bother you when you are working.' She reached out a hand and rested it on the table between them. 'And I shall assure him that I have every confidence in you – which is true. If it makes you feel any better, I find him just as annoying as you do. I hope he will move on before too long.'

'Do him good to find himself a job and do an honest day's work!' Jimmie's nervousness was wearing off. 'My ma used to call people like him spongers!'

Clare withdrew her hand and too late Jimmie realized he had gone too far.

She said coolly, 'Name calling doesn't really help us any further forward.' She stood up. 'I'll do my best to see that he doesn't trouble you again. And now I must let you get back to your garden. Thank you for bringing the matter to my attention.'

Jimmie lumbered down the stairs and let himself out of the front door. Scowling, his mind whirled as he trudged across the lawn towards his shed. Donald had made no accusations about him but he, Jimmie, had been taken in by the pretence.

You've made a fool of yourself, Jimmie lad, that's for sure. Rushing off like that to deny a lot of make-believe . . . but if she's going to keep him off my back that's something. Mind you, I shouldn't have called him a sponger although we all know he is one. Although he knew it was justified he also knew that he had overstepped the mark. Donald-who-had-never-grown-up was still part of the Wishart family. *Of course you had to stick up for him because he's your cousin, and I don't blame you for getting a bit sniffy with me.* But at least she knew now, if she didn't know before, just how devious Donald could be, and for that he had no regrets at all.

Clare worked all morning and after lunch took herself off for a walk that would take her through the village past Sarah Tennant's house. She was hoping that her friend would be in her front garden and might offer a cup of tea and a chat. Clare also wanted to tell someone about Edina's exciting phone call about Bell & May's interest in her writing. She knew plenty of villagers by sight and could name some of them, but apart from Sarah there was no one she considered a close friend and even Sarah existed on the fringes of Clare's life.

Unfortunately there was no sign of her. By the time Clare returned home it was nearly four o'clock and Donald was strolling in the garden with a man she didn't recognize – a tall, round-shouldered man wearing a panama hat and a tweed suit that looked too big for him. As she drew nearer she saw that he carried a walking stick although he wasn't limping. He was probably in his fifties and his bespectacled face wore a nervous expression.

'Ah, there you are!' Donald cried cheerfully. 'Mr Appleton has come about the house but is on the point of leaving. I've given him a whirlwind tour but you can take over now you're back.' He smiled at his companion. 'I'll leave you in safe hands,' he declared and they shook hands.

As Clare regarded her prospective buyer, her heart sank. What had Donald said to him? Nothing good, she thought anxiously. She held out her hand and smiled. 'I'm so glad I didn't miss you,' she said. 'I thought Mr Yates was going to arrange viewings.'

'Oh, but he did,' the man assured her. 'He telephoned and Mr Wishart said I could come over and he would show me round.'

Clare maintained her bright smile despite her growing doubts. She watched Donald stroll back across the grass, his hands in his pockets, a certain triumph in every line of his body. No doubt he had sowed seeds of dissatisfaction, she thought unhappily.

'I hope Mr Wishart explained that I am the vendor. Mr Wishart is my cousin and not connected in any way with the sale of the house.'

'Oh?' He looked surprised. 'I assumed he was your husband.'

'No. He's a member of the Wishart family. We are not related by marriage.' She hoped her irritation at Donald's behaviour was not too obvious. 'I am single . . . Now what can I tell you about Merle Place? I've only lived here on my own, so to speak, since the war, although the house was left to me by my grandfather just before war broke out. I spent a lot of time here with my grandparents when I was a child. I suggest we have a look round and then I could offer you tea and cakes. How does that sound, Mr Appleton?'

Stop this, Clare, she told herself, you're babbling. She looked at him hopefully. Had she charmed him at all? Had she undone any of the harm of Donald's misinformation?

He hesitated and her hopes receded a little further. 'I have a feeling it needs more attention than I expected,' he mumbled rather apologetically.

'It does need some refurbishment,' she admitted, leading the way back towards the house. 'But I can assure you it will repay any investment. I recall Merle Place in its heyday. It was well built and, until the war, was reasonably well maintained. Of course, I expect my cousin explained that it was used as a military hospital for the troops. I worked here myself as an auxiliary nurse.'

'Oh, you're a nurse.'

'Not exactly. More a very lowly ward maid.'

Walking beside her, Mr Appleton reminded her of a heron. He said, 'Mr Wishart explained about the drains. He seems to feel that—'

'The drains? What did he say?' She clasped her hands nervously. 'I don't think there is anything wrong with—'

'And the concealed cracks? He thinks they account for the leaks.'

'Concealed cracks?' Her momentary panic was turning to anger. 'I don't know what he's talking about!'

'The smells in hot weather?' He cast an anxious sideways glance at her. 'He thinks that perhaps you are not aware of many of the defects . . .' He paused. 'That you truly believe . . . I'm sure he meant well.'

Clare fumed silently. Donald had done his work well, she thought bitterly. As they went up the front steps she said, 'My cousin is only a visitor, Mr Appleton, and knows very little about the house or its structure whereas I have been through it with a surveyor and am better informed.'

She led the way into the drawing room. Remembering that

Mrs Parks had gone home earlier than usual she rang the bell for Molly, but it was the housekeeper who answered the summons. Seeing Clare's surprise, Mrs Parks said, 'I sent her home and stayed on myself, not liking to leave you in the lurch. She's been sickly all day – and all yesterday, to tell you the truth. If you ask me—'

'Tell me later, please, Mrs Parks,' Clare said quickly. 'We'd like a tray of tea and cakes, please, and then by all means get off home. I can manage.' Turning back to her potential buyer, she said, 'Do you have any questions for me, Mr Appleton. I'd be glad to deal with any worries you might have.'

He pursed his lips thoughtfully. 'The fact is my sister and I want to start a school for boys – a preparatory school. So many parents seem to work in India or Africa and other far-flung corners of the Empire and they can't find proper education for their children over there. A well-run private boarding school is the ideal solution. You see all those bedrooms would be ideal for dormitories, but with all that damp it might be . . .'

'Damp? That's news to me, Mr Appleton. Do you think we should have another look round since my cousin has obviously confused the issue? To my knowledge the bedrooms have no damp. There may be a slight chill, but you always get that with rooms that are not lived in. There is nothing wrong with the bedrooms.' She thought angrily of the hours they had spent cleaning and polishing, and now Donald had undone it all by talking about damp. 'I suggest that if you are interested . . .'

'Of course the grounds are ideal and the old tennis court could be repaired. The boys will do boxing and cricket, but the staff would enjoy a game of tennis.'

The tea tray arrived and Clare did the honours. Mr Appleton ate three lemon cakes in quick succession. Good. He needed fattening up, she thought. They talked for s ome time about the Appletons' plans for the school, but when the grandfather clock struck five Mr Appleton said, 'Goodness! Is that the time? I shall have to be on my way. I have to catch a train at five twenty-seven and it will take me ten minutes to walk back to the station.'

'I could take you in the pony trap,' Clare suggested, but he shook his head.

'A short walk will do me good – and I saw your horse pulling the roller earlier. He's probably tired.'

'Don't be fooled, Mr Appleton. The vet says Jonty is very fit for his age, though he's a lazy old devil – but we love him. His biggest problem is boredom. He likes getting out on to the roads and especially likes passing other horses.'

Clare walked with him to the wrought iron gates, racking her brains for a way to avoid the refusal which appeared imminent. 'So, if you want to come for a second look, please do – with your sister, perhaps?'

'Oh, yes . . . That's most kind. If she does wish to see Merle Place for herself – and she might – I shall most certainly telephone you or your cousin.'

'Ask for me, Mr Appleton. I do prefer that my cousin leaves the business to me. He means well but . . .'

She left the sentence unfinished. *No he doesn't. He means to scupper my plans to sell Merle Place and on this occasion he has done so. I must speak to Mr Yates and see that he never sends potential buyers unless I say so in person.* She sighed, weighed down with disappointment. Merle Place would make a perfect school. She could almost see the boys playing cricket on the lawn, scampering to and fro between the wickets, or dressed in their pyjamas, scrambling into their beds in the dormitories. She had a sudden vision of herself as a child with Donald and her other cousin Alistair and his friend Simon, chasing each other across the grass on imaginary horses, letting out blood-curdling shrieks as they hurtled in pursuit of imaginary foes. That had been one of the best memories. Donald had always been the difficult one, quick to take offence, sulking and telling tales or refusing to join in. Small wonder he had become a difficult adult with a grudge against the world.

Snapping out of the reverie, Clare shook hands with her visitor and watched him go. He glanced back once and waved his stick by way of farewell and she knew without a doubt that she would never set eyes on him again.

* * *

After supper Clare sat alone in the drawing room, trying to finish a piece of tapestry that was destined to become the padded cover of a footstool. She wasn't particularly interested in the work but felt that it was less tiring for her eyes than hours of reading which would have been her preferred choice. Apart from that, she had been brought up by women who sewed and it seemed to be what was expected. Her mother had decorated all her household bedlinen with exquisite flowers in white and silver silk thread and her grandmother had excelled at crochet. Clare still occasionally wore the delicate cuffs and collars that had belonged to the old lady.

When the phone rang, she threw down the tapestry and rushed into the hall, hoping to prevent Donald from intercepting a call that might be intended for her. To her relief he was nowhere in sight when she lifted the receiver from its hook and gave the number.

The operator said, 'You're through, caller.'

'Is that Miss Wishart?' The masculine voice was cheerful and immediately reminded her of her father. 'This is Steven Flint from Bell and May.'

'Yes, it is.' Clare sat down on the chair. She was breathless with excitement and realized that it must show in her voice. To cover this fact she said, 'I'm sorry. I've just hurried in from the kitchen.'

'I understand from Edina that you are prepared to discuss writing a novel for us. I'm hoping you will come up to London if I can lure you away from your present work.'

'Come to London? Oh, no!' Clare's joy was replaced by deep apprehension. 'I hate trains, Mr Flint. That is, I never come to London. I don't care to travel.' Closing her eyes, she struggled with the panic that was setting in at the mention of travelling to London.

'Oh, dear! I am disappointed. I wanted to take you to the Savoy for lunch. I had intended to woo you with fresh salmon and new potatoes followed by—'

'I'm sorry, Mr Flint,' she said in a hurry. 'I know it's very cowardly and old-fashioned but . . .' She swallowed. 'My father died in a train crash.'

The train had been derailed by a landslip after heavy rain

and her father had been in the first carriage; the only one to fall down the embankment with the loss of five lives.

'Good Lord! That must have been ghastly for you,' Steven Flint said. 'It is me who should be apologizing for bringing back such sad memories. Do forgive me.'

'Of course I do.' Clare banished the dark memories with an effort. 'You couldn't have known.' She shrugged. 'I suppose one day I'll be forced to go by train, but not yet. I see myself as very weak and foolish but it would spoil the day for me.'

'Not at all! It's very understandable. So how do you get about?'

'By pony and trap – I enjoy driving. Or Shanks's pony!'

'It all sounds very countrified!'

They both laughed. Clare said, 'So, is it possible for us to discuss the book by letter or on the telephone? I do want to consider the idea of a novel since you obviously think I am capable of writing one.'

'I have a better idea, Miss Wishart. Suppose I drive down in my spanking new motor car and whisk you off somewhere nice. I take it you are not averse to travelling by motor car.'

Clare narrowed her eyes as she imagined herself being driven by Steven Flint through the village. That would set a few tongues wagging, she thought with delight. 'On the contrary, Mr Flint, I think that sounds rather wonderful. Do you have a chauffeur or do you drive it yourself?'

'I did have a chauffeur but he has taught me the rudiments and I have made several journeys, one of thirty-three miles – and all without any mishaps! I assure you we won't go too fast and you will be quite safe.'

'In that case I shall look forward to it, but it's putting you to a lot of trouble. I feel rather guilty about that.' But not guilty enough, she thought, to refuse the offer.

'Perish the thought. A day out of the office. Better still a day out of dreary old London in the wilds of Kent and lunch with a charming author! Couldn't be better.'

'Will I need a special outfit – a hat with a net to keep out the dust?'

'No, no,' he protested with a laugh. 'You really are living in the Dark Ages, Miss Wishart. It's not an open car. In fact it's very smart and I'm very proud of it. It was a present from my mother to mark my fortieth birthday. But come to think of it, a couple of hatpins might be a good idea so that we can drive with the window open if the weather is particularly fine.'

They finally agreed that the following Monday would be the most suitable day for their lunch and before ending the call he asked her to come prepared with a few ideas for them to discuss.

He said, 'I shall make enquiries and find a nice hotel where we can have lunch and mix business with pleasure. Get to know one another. At Bell and May all our authors are very precious to us and, if you agree to join us, you will be no exception, Miss Wishart.'

A few moments later, after he had hung up, Clare went back to the drawing room in a daze. She picked up her tapestry and bundled it unceremoniously into the bag, tossed it into the sideboard, then laughed aloud as she threw herself on to the sofa. After a moment's thought, she decided not to alert Donald to the coming excitement because she knew he would be disparaging about the meeting and would do his best to spoil it for her. For the time being she would tell no one – except perhaps Sarah Tennant if they happened to meet.

Steven Flint had requested a few ideas. Did she have any? Her mind went blank for a moment, but almost immediately she wondered if a story which featured a chauffeur might be acceptable. Or, better still, a lady driver. She would have to do some research, but the readers might like the idea. Or a woman who lived in a large mostly empty house and who was convinced it was haunted by a former tenant. Yes, that could work. Not that she knew much about the paranormal, but she could research the subject. Springing from the sofa, Clare rushed upstairs and into the study where she settled in her grandfather's chair and reached for pen and paper.

Five

Clare was ready to give up and go to bed when, soon after eleven o'clock, Donald arrived home from goodness knows where. She heard him slam the front door and groaned with frustration. She had worked hard on three ideas to suggest to Steven Flint and had been feeling very pleased with herself and excited about the coming meeting with him. Now all the positive feelings vanished. She guessed that Donald had probably drunk too much and would be in a bad mood. If only she had gone to bed earlier she would have avoided him, but now she would have to go down and face him.

'Clare! You still up?'

With a sigh she closed her notebooks and left the study, closing the door quietly behind her.

'Clare! Where are you?'

As she went down the stairs, she saw him leaning back against the front door, almost unable to stand unaided. Even as she watched him, his legs gave way and he slid awkwardly down to sit on the floor, his head against the letterbox.

He stared at her dully. 'Damn women!' he muttered. 'No pleasing them.'

'I hope you're not referring to me,' she said sharply.

He held out a hand so that she could help him up, but she ignored him.

'Not you, no. Her!'

'Who is "her"?'

Perhaps the publican's wife has thrown him out. She would if he was making a nuisance of himself – and good for her. Her husband is a weak man – wouldn't say boo to a goose – but she has enough courage for the two of them!

Clare closed her eyes at the thought of her cousin being evicted from the pub and the amusement it would cause in the village. She was embarrassed by him and aware that his bad behaviour probably reflected badly on her.

'None of your business!' He regarded her blearily. 'Help me up, can't you?'

Clare took a step forward, then paused. Why did she pander to him like this?

'I'm going to lock up the back of the house,' she said, ignoring his request. 'Then I'm going to bed.'

As she walked towards the kitchen she was aware of him struggling to his feet and muttering obscenities. In the kitchen she locked the door to the cellar, checked that the kitchen windows were secure and bolted the door that led out into the garden. Picking up the scuttle, she tipped some coal in to the stove and replaced the iron lid. Hopefully it would burn slowly through the night and still be warm by the time Mrs Parks arrived.

She turned to see Donald lolling against the kitchen door, his face a mask of desperation.

'Silly cow!' he slurred. 'She's lying. I know she is.'

'Who's lying? What are you talking about?'

'Nothing to do with you.'

'Then why tell me?' She sighed. 'Oh, come here, you idiot! You'd better sit down before you fall down.' Reluctantly she caught hold of his arm, guided him to a chair and sat him down. At once he leaned both elbows on the table and supported his head, groaning as if in agony. Clare mixed water and Epsom salts and handed it to him. 'Drink this and then go to bed,' she advised. 'I'll see you in the morning.'

As she went out of the door, he muttered, 'She's a lying cow!'

'Who is?'

'They're all the same. A snare and a delusion.'

'A snare and a delusion? What are you talking about, Donald?'

He shook his head and Clare resisted the urge to shake some sense into the rest of him.

'You'd be surprised . . .' he began.

Clare was losing patience with him and refused to encourage him by asking for more information. 'I'm going to bed,' she said shortly. 'You'll feel better in the morning.' As she made her way upstairs she told herself that he'd be sober by then and might make more sense. Not that Clare really wanted to know – he was old enough to look after himself, and she certainly didn't want to be drawn in to whatever mess he was in.

Once in bed, she tried to put her cousin out of her mind so that she could enjoy the prospect of the opportunity that Bell & May were prepared to give her, but she could not recapture her earlier sense of excitement. Once again Donald was casting a shadow over her life and it seemed there was nothing she could do about it.

Clare awoke early Saturday morning in time to hear the dawn chorus, but she was in no mood to enjoy the birdsong. She lay awake, imagining what damage Donald could do to her career if he behaved badly while Steven Flint was around. It was a nightmare scenario and it loomed large in her imagination; she could think of nothing else. Something had to be done about him, but she shrank away, as always, from a confrontation. This time, however, it appeared to be the only way to convince him that he was not wanted at Merle Place any more, and that he ought to move out and fend for himself.

Although what he could do was another puzzle. He had no talent and had always survived through the kindness of others or a kind twist of fate. He was always optimistic that 'something would come up' and often it did. There had been a time when he had been lucky with his gambling and won more than he lost, but that period of three or four years before the war had come to an end. In his words 'Lady Luck had deserted him'.

His heart defect had meant that he was not called up for military service but had been hustled instead into clerical work in a factory that made khaki uniforms for the army. Donald referred to it as his 'war effort' and constantly complained about the exhaustion he had endured.

Clare sighed and tried to concentrate on the problems

that Monday would bring. Monday was only two days away, and Steven Flint was going to pull up outside to collect her. Should she offer to show him briefly round the house – or the garden? If so, how could she prevent Donald from tagging along with them? Steven Flint might find Donald charming and amusing company – he could be when he wanted to – and he might not understand why she might want to be rid of her cousin.

Another thing that was causing her some concern was what she should wear. She was to be taken out to lunch by what might well be a handsome stranger and the meeting was part business, part pleasure so she must dress in a way that would be suitable for either. Perhaps her skirt and suit jacket in grey wool – though that was rather dull. Could she wear a dress and light coat – her green dress, perhaps, although it might be too summery and the coat was the wrong green. It might not match the dress and would be too heavy if the weather was fine.

She also wondered if the notes she had made on her ideas for the novel were going to be acceptable or whether she would be sent back to the drawing board.

Clare tried to remember Steven Flint's voice as she imagined what he would be like. What exactly had Edina said about him?

Nothing very helpful, she recalled. Was he young or old, fat or thin, smart or shabby? Would he be fun to be with or dull – or worse still, intimidating. Clare crossed fingers on both hands. *Please don't let him be a bullying type of man – or someone remotely like Donald!*

It was halfway through the afternoon and Clare was busy in her bedroom. Clothes were spread over the bed and every chair as she desperately tried to decide what to wear for her meeting with Steven Flint. Pulling on a succession of outfits, she twirled in front of the large swing mirror, holding a smaller mirror in her hand, and turning this way and that to consider the effect. She was disturbed suddenly by footsteps outside her room.

There was a knock on the door and she recognized Mrs Parks's voice.

'Miss Wishart, that man's loitering about outside – the one I told you about that was in hospital here during the war.'

'Oh, no! I'm half dressed! Ask him to wait in the drawing room, please, Mrs Parks, and give him a cup of tea. Say I'll be down in five minutes.'

Abandoning her clothing decisions, she hastily pulled back on the skirt and blouse she had worn earlier, tidied her hair and hurried downstairs.

Hearing her come downstairs, Mrs Parks hurried from the kitchen. In a discreet whisper she said, 'His name's Alan Latimer. He's a bit odd, but I've given him tea and a slice of cherry cake. He looks as though he needs building up!'

'Thank you, Mrs Parks.' With her hand already on the doorknob, Clare asked, 'Where's Molly?'

'I let her go home, ma'am. I thought you wouldn't mind and I didn't want to disturb you. She was in a funny mood today. Kept grizzling and wouldn't say why. I gather she's had words with that father of hers. I don't know what she's been up to, but from all accounts he's a bit strict.'

Clare nodded, took a deep breath and went in to the drawing room with a welcoming smile on her face. 'Mr Latimer, I'm so sorry to have kept you waiting.'

He was sitting at the table and his mouth was full of cherry cake. As soon as he had swallowed, he stood up and stared at her. She held out her hand, but he ignored it. He frowned slightly as he continued to study her face.

'I know you,' he said. 'You were here. Don't you remember me?' He pointed to the long, ragged scar which slanted down the left side of his face. 'You were one of the auxiliaries. I'm sorry to stare but . . . you're like a ghost from the past!'

'Not a very happy past, I suppose,' she said. 'I don't think I remember you, but you were probably wrapped in bandages for most of your stay. I wouldn't have seen much of your face.'

'No, of course not. How stupid of me.' Belatedly he held out his hand. 'And I didn't remember your name although, of course, I now know it because your housekeeper told me what it was. I feel I shouldn't be intruding like this, but I have something to ask you. Something rather personal.'

'Then why don't we walk in the garden, Mr Latimer? We can talk in complete privacy there with no interruptions.' She thought gratefully that Donald was fishing by the weir and would probably be gone for hours.

Alan Latimer drank the last of his tea and they moved out of the house and into the thin sunshine, which filtered through the trees. It was peaceful in the garden and they strolled slowly along the path towards the neglected rose garden. Her companion seemed in no hurry to ask his question, so she waited patiently for it.

He said suddenly, 'There were bees, weren't there? A couple of hives. Over there.' He pointed towards the area to the left of the rose garden and Clare realized that he was smiling.

'Poor old Chota Peg. That's what we called Freddie. He went too near and got stung and what a fuss he made. And he'd lost his leg. We teased him about that. Not his leg, I mean the bee sting. "It's only a bee sting – it's not fatal," we told him but he moaned and grumbled until Nurse Petty kissed it better!' He gave a short laugh. 'He had a way with women, did Freddie. D'you remember him?'

'Chota Peg?' She frowned. 'I'm not sure. Was he the ginger-haired one – from somewhere in Scotland? There were so many of you, coming and going. It's a very hazy memory.'

Now he was smiling broadly. 'That's him! Lucky blighter. They didn't send him back. Couldn't, could they?' His expression changed. 'Of course I was sent back – my gash soon healed. But not my heartache.'

Startled, Clare registered the change in him but said nothing.

He stopped and turned to face her. 'There was a nurse. Her name was Caroline Turner. I was stupid enough to fall in love with her. That's why I'm here – to try and discover what happened to her. At the time I could offer her nothing and she was very much a favourite with the men. Could have had her pick. I knew I'd be going back and might never return. It wouldn't have been fair.'

As he spoke he was staring round, and Clare fancied he was seeing the gardens as they would have been on a fine May afternoon – there would have been men in wheelchairs or with bandages, more men stumbling along with the aid of sticks or crutches, some learning to walk again with a nurse on either side to make sure they didn't fall. There would have been visitors hovering anxiously over a loved one, doctors in consultation, a few visiting children squabbling over the swings . . .

She said slowly, 'Caroline Turner . . . Of course I recall her. She was so inspirational. Everyone admired her. I'm afraid . . . I'm sorry, Mr Latimer, but she married an airman. I think he was a flight sergeant or something like that. It was right at the end of the war. A matter of weeks before the armistice.'

'Ah, so she did marry.' His tone was flat with disappointment. 'I half expected it, you see. But I had to know for sure.' His face was pale with shock.

With the benefit of hindsight Clare was wishing that she had lied to him, that she had pretended to know nothing about Caroline because there was more bad news. She took a deep breath. 'It's worse than that, Mr Latimer. She was one of the thousands who . . . I'm terribly sorry to be the one to tell you, but I heard from a mutual friend that she died during the influenza epidemic, six weeks after the armistice was signed.'

'Oh God!' he said hoarsely and put up his right hand to cover his eyes. 'How bloody unfair!'

'Yes.'

'After all she did for us – the lads here! We called ourselves the lads – most of them were younger than me. Young Skinner and Bullseye Bob . . . they sent him back to his unit on the Somme and he didn't make it back to Blighty. Nor did poor old Simmons. Trench fever finished him off.' He lowered his hand and Clare caught a glimpse of tears. 'Poor Caroline. Of all people. And they say there's a God!'

Clare couldn't argue with him. Instead she turned to look back at the house. There was no way to comfort him, she knew, but suddenly she didn't want him to go away despairing. She couldn't bear the thought of him alone with his grief. Without thinking she said, 'Why don't you stay and have some supper with me, Mr Latimer? We could have a look round the house if you wish and you could walk in the gardens. It might help to . . . to come to terms with the news.'

At first he protested, but she sensed that his heart wasn't in it and eventually he agreed. He took out a handkerchief, brushed aside the tears and blew his nose.

She heard herself say, 'We do have a spare bedroom. You could stay the night, that is, if you should miss the last train.'

He looked at her in astonishment and she saw a little colour seep back into his pale face. 'Stay here overnight? Oh, my dear!'

Clare was already regretting the offer, unsure why she had made it. Was she just sorry for him, for his disappointment over Caroline? Whatever must he think of her? She said quickly, 'But I expect you are wanting to get home. How silly of me! But we could have an early supper so that—'

He interrupted her eagerly. 'There's nothing I'd like better than to spend a few more hours in Merle Place. How very generous of you.' He was brightening. 'Good Lord! I'm going to accept your very kind offer, Miss Wishart, unless . . .' He was frowning, seeing her obvious uncertainty.

'We won't be here alone, Mr Latimer,' she reassured him. 'My cousin Donald also lives here. He's off somewhere fishing at the moment, but you will probably meet him later.' I do hope he doesn't come home drunk again, Clare thought. It might be wise to see that we get to bed before Donald comes home. 'Donald isn't always home at a reasonable time. He has friends . . . but you are certainly welcome to stay.'

His hesitation vanished as he clasped her hand. 'Thank you so much!'

They spent another half hour looking round the house. Her visitor was surprised by how large the rooms looked without all the beds and he stood in the drawing room with a smile on his face as the memories flooded back.

'This was the day room,' he said, almost wistfully. 'The dartboard was over there – I remember I was quite good at it. Never played since, of course, and Benjy always used to sit by the French windows in his wheelchair.' He turned to Clare with a grin. 'One day he astonished everyone by suddenly standing up and he said, "Sod that! I'm going to walk again!" And he did! Against all the odds. In spite of the doctor's efforts to reconcile him to his fate. Benjy Manners. You must remember him. That was his name and his grandmother used to send him a chocolate cake every weekend. Lord knows how she managed it!'

Later she showed him to one of the rooms. The beds had already been made up for potential buyers' visits and the faint smell of lavender polish still lingered.

He said, 'This wasn't my room, but I see you've painted over the initials that were on the walls.'

'And the not so polite messages!' she reminded him. 'I won't repeat any although some stuck in my mind. We learned a lot by playing at nurses! A little too much sometimes.'

They both laughed.

'Do you think I could stay for an hour after breakfast?' he asked. 'I have my sketchbook with me. Then when I get home I can produce a painting and send it to you as a thank you for your hospitality.'

'By all means. I didn't know you were an artist.'

'I didn't know, either, until last winter when I was laid up in bed with pleurisy and a friend brought me some sketching materials to help me pass the time. From that I moved to a few tubes of paint.' He shrugged. 'That's the way it happens, sometimes.'

Alan Latimer and Clare spent a happy evening chatting in the drawing room. To Clare's relief, Donald did not return early enough to meet their guest.

She had often wondered whether somewhere inside the troublesome man a better person was lurking. *Why don't you let yourself be happy, Donald? You're your own worst enemy.* Perhaps down at the pub he was a different, more likeable person.

* * *

Clare would have been less pleased if she had seen Donald ten minutes later throwing small pebbles up at the window above the stables.

When Jimmie opened the window, Donald said, 'Just thought you'd like to know you've got a rival. I've just seen them looking very cosy, chatting together! Looks like he is staying the night.'

He sauntered away, laughing, but suddenly took to his heels as the stable door opened with a crash and Jimmie came out at speed. Donald fled into the shrubbery, but Jimmie found him and grabbed him by the lapels of his jacket. Even in the moonlight, Donald could see the anger on his pursuer's face and, too late, realized that he had gone too far.

Jimmie thrust his face close. 'Don't you dare talk about Miss Wishart like that. Do it again and you'll be sorry!' Then he shook him violently and hurled him on to the ground. When Donald struggled back to his feet, Jimmie slammed his hands against Donald's chest and sent him flying again.

Winded and more frightened than he would admit, Donald stayed where he was, while Jimmie glowered down at him.

'God, man, you're pathetic! Aren't you going to get up again and hit me back?'

'I'm not a thug like you!' Donald scrambled to his knees and, watching Jimmie warily, tried to decide whether to risk another humiliation. To his surprise, after a moment or two, Jimmie's anger seemed to ebb and he leaned down, grabbed Donald's arms and hauled him to his feet. 'Now you can go straight to Miss Wishart and tell her I've assaulted you. Then I'll tell her why.'

Donald made a show of brushing himself down, refusing to meet Jimmie's gaze.

Jimmie said, 'You're a fool to yourself, you know that? I doubt you've got a friend in the whole world. Not one person who'd have a good word to say about you.'

'Well, you'd be wrong then. You'd be very wrong.'

'Easy to say. Name him.'

Donald gave him a strange look, but refused to rise to the bait. Instead he said, 'What do you know about anything,

Smith? Stuck behind a mower all day or fiddling with your stupid plants!'

'At least I'm working. All you do is loaf about trying to stir up trouble. Take a long look in the mirror some time. You'll see an unhappy man.' Turning, he retraced his steps, and slammed the tack-room door behind him.

Donald stared after him while his pulse returned to normal. He felt his chest for broken ribs. Then, reassured that Jimmie had done no real damage, he stumbled back towards the house. 'As if I haven't got enough worries without you trying to kill me,' he said to himself.

Back at the house he went in by the back door, stamped his way up the stairs into his bedroom and slammed the door. He sat on the edge of the bed and immediately forgot about Jimmie.

He had more important things to worry about. 'So bloody unfair!' he snarled, staring at the faded rug beneath his feet. What had he ever done to deserve such rotten luck? He could have had any woman – and had had several and very nice it had been, too – but this one was special and his feelings for her had surprised him. It hadn't occurred to him that he could actually feel like that about a woman, but it had happened. Then he had to fall for the oldest trick in the book. And there was nobody he could talk to. He was on his own. It was so damned unfair.

Slowly he undid his laces and kicked off his shoes. He should have taken them off in the boot room but had forgotten in the heat of the moment. *That damned Jimmie! How dare he lay a finger on me?* There had to be a way he could turn this to his advantage, but at the moment he was too distracted to plan anything. The trouble was that Jimmie could wind his cousin round his little finger. He sometimes wondered why men didn't see through Clare for the timid little mouse she was. She was pretty in an old-fashioned way, but the war had made changes and women were stronger now.

Mrs Parks was a sight too strong, he reflected, but he was working on a plan to get rid of her. The three spoons were safe enough under his mattress but he must hide something else – something more valuable – so that Clare would have to take action. Once he got rid of Mrs Parks he would stand a better chance of influencing Clare.

I deserve a break, he told himself. So far his life had been one minor disaster after another. His father didn't like him much and had sent him away to a small, second-rate boarding school where, friendless, he had just about survived. Then his grandfather had left the family house to Clare and almost immediately after the war had started. He had spent the best years of his life stuck in a stupid office at the factory in East London, shut in with three useless, graceless oiks who had mocked him and generally made his life a misery. God, how he'd hated it! Nobody understood how he'd suffered. Clare had said that he should count his blessings – at least he wasn't stuck in a waterlogged dugout in France, being shelled by an enemy army. But then Clare was so unsympathetic. He remembered as a child he'd fallen off the swing in their garden and had hurt his hands and knees and was crying and screaming, and Clare had said it served him right for teasing her . . .

He'd finally escaped the hell of the factory, but two years later he felt that the strain was showing and now all he wanted was to stay in Merle Place with her until his jangled nerves had steadied and he could think straight. But no!

She wants to sell the place, he thought, groaning. She wants to be rid of me.

He couldn't cope with that, but she couldn't or wouldn't understand that he didn't want to be on his own. He needed someone to help him. He needed peace and quiet. He wanted something elusive . . . but what exactly?

Donald stifled a sigh. If only Clare would give him enough time, he felt sure he would calm down and start to think sensibly about the rest of his life.

Nothing's going right, he thought and wondered miserably if it ever would.

Six

The following morning Clare and Alan Latimer were
having breakfast when Donald came down. He had
come home late the previous evening so Clare had left him
a note on his bedside table alerting him to the presence of
a visitor. He came in with a cheerful smile, hid his surprise
at Alan's vivid scar, and held out his hand.

'I'm Donald. I'm sure Clare's spoken about me – and
probably none of it good!'

Alan stood and shook his hand. 'On the contrary, Mr
Wishart. I appreciate the kindness your cousin has shown
me. She was sure you would have no objection to my stay.'

Both men sat down and Donald helped himself to stewed
apple.

'I've made a few sketches of your charming gardens,'
Alan told him. 'There is something rather sad and myster-
ious about a neglected garden – if you'll forgive me for
calling it neglected.'

Donald nodded. 'We do the best we can with only one
gardener-cum-handyman, but there's a lot for him to
cover.'

'Do you sketch or paint, Mr Wishart?' Alan asked.

Clare noticed her cousin's reaction. He seemed delighted
by the question.

'I do a little sketching,' he replied eagerly, 'and I believe
I do have some talent, but nobody's ever bothered to
encourage me. I'd love to see your sketches. You might
inspire me to make more of an effort.'

It was news to Clare that he had ever sketched or that
he had any undiscovered talent, but she gave him the benefit
of the doubt. 'Perhaps the two of you could spend an hour

or so in the garden sketching,' she suggested. 'Mr Latimer's train doesn't go until ten past twelve.'

Donald agreed with enthusiasm. He finished his apple and went to the sideboard for egg and bacon. 'Why not stay until a later train and have lunch with us,' he said. 'We don't have many visitors and we'd enjoy some company.' He smiled at Clare.

'By all means.' She looked enquiringly at Alan.

'I'm very tempted,' he said uncertainly.

It didn't take much persuasion for him to say yes. The morning seemed to be brightening in more ways than one. Half an hour later Clare found herself alone, while the two men disappeared into the garden in search of a suitable subject for their work. Clare watched them go with mixed feelings. Her cousin had taken over her visitor and she felt she ought to be troubled, but it was a pleasure to see Donald in such a cheerful frame of mind. Strange to see just how pleasant he could be. It was a side of him she rarely saw.

There's hope for him yet, she thought, and went in search of Mrs Parks to ask about lunch.

In the kitchen she discovered that all was not well. Mrs Parks looked flustered and Molly had been crying. As soon as Clare entered the room, Molly jumped to her feet, pushed past her and ran upstairs.

Mrs Parks said, 'She was late coming in again, but she won't say why. Some trouble at home. A big row. Father's threatening to throw her out.'

'Throw her out! But why, for heaven's sake?'

'Don't ask me. She won't say, but I suspect it's a young man.'

'Young man? But she can't be more than seventeen!'

'Usually man trouble at her age.' She folded her arms over her chest. 'I told her not to bring her troubles to work with her. She must sort it out at home. All these tears and tantrums, taking time off and coming in late. "It's not good enough," I said. "I'll be telling the mistress about your behaviour." That set her off again. I was wondering, Miss Wishart, if maybe you could talk some sense into her.'

Clare doubted it. Hastily changing the subject, she

mentioned that Alan Latimer was staying for lunch. 'Is there enough ham?' she asked.

The housekeeper looked doubtful. 'Unless I make it into a pasty with some onion and a bit of potato. I'd add some hard boiled eggs except that we used up the last one for breakfast.'

'Ham pasty would be perfect. Thank you, Mrs Parks.'

'He seems a very nice gentleman. What a shame about his poor face. He must have been a good-looking man before whatever it was that happened.'

Clare nodded then hesitated. 'Do you think I should have a word with her now? Molly, I mean.'

'Can't do any harm, ma'am. She's that bothered already.'

Clare found Molly upstairs, sprinkling tea leaves on the hall carpet to lay the dust and make it easier to brush up.

'Leave that for now, Molly, and come into the study.'

Molly scrambled to her feet and followed her mistress.

'Sit down, please,' Clare said gently, 'and tell me what's wrong. I may be able to help you.'

Molly shook her head. She sat down, folded her arms defensively around her body and lowered her head so that Clare could not see her face.

Clare waited but no explanation was forthcoming. She said, 'I'm not going to be cross, Molly. I just need to know what's troubling you. You don't look at all well.'

After another silence, Molly raised her head. 'It's Pa,' she whispered. 'He's going to turn me out if I don't tell him who it is I'm carrying on with. That's what he calls it. Carrying on. He doesn't believe I'm in love with him. I can't tell him who it is and I won't because I promised and I love him and if Pa finds out he'll kill him!'

'*Kill him?* Of course he won't. That's just angry talk. He'd be arrested and hanged if he killed somebody. Do be sensible, Molly.'

'You don't know my pa!' She looked up, white-faced with apprehension.

Clare realized that she *didn't* know anything about Molly's father, except he was called Tom Jenner. She had met Molly's mother only once when she had brought the girl for an interview. She had seemed to be a reasonable, respectable woman. The husband had remained an unknown quantity. All Clare knew from odd scraps of information was that he had a small farm, with a dozen or so pigs, a horse, half a dozen goats and a pond full of ducks. Clare bought duck eggs from him from time to time and pork chops when they were available. Molly's mother kept bees and the family always sent Clare a jar of honey at Christmas.

Molly wiped her eyes again and sniffed. Then she sighed. 'I *love* him so much! All I want is to marry him and make him happy. I'm not too young, but *he* says I am.'

'Your father, you mean?'

'No . . . him! My young man. He says I'm too young to get married and so is he. I can't say his name because I don't want him killed.' She looked at Clare desperately.

Clare considered the girl thoughtfully. This seemed to be highly exaggerated but slightly worse than she had expected and she doubted whether she could really help her. Suppose she meddled and made things worse. It really was up to the parents to guide Molly, but the father sounded rather a bully and maybe the mother was under his thumb.

Cautiously she asked, 'Can you tell me this man's name? If I promise not to tell anyone, that is.'

But Molly was already shaking her head. 'He made me promise. He said if I tell anyone then that's the end of us. Either he'll be killed by my father or he'll go away so my father won't find him. I think he's more scared of Pa than I am!'

'Why don't you decide to be patient, Molly? If you agreed to wait a year until you're older – how old is your young man?'

'He's not young, he's about your age. A bit older maybe. He won't say *how* old. He makes a joke of it.' A brief but thin smile lit her eyes. 'He makes me laugh.'

'I thought he said he was too young to marry.'

'He says he's too young at heart! He says it's a big responsibility having chil—? Oh!' With a gasp, she clamped a hand over her mouth.

In the shocked look which passed between them, Clare

knew all. The young man had taken advantage of Molly's
youth and she was expecting a child. Her parents must know
– or suspect. Understanding this left her dismayed. 'You're
going to have a child?'

'No, I mean . . . yes!'

Unable to bear the poor girl's panic-stricken face, Clare
moved away to the window and stared out, hoping for inspiration. She saw Alan Latimer and Donald sitting close
together, busy with their sketchbooks. They seemed to be
getting on well together and Clare hoped that Jimmie would
have the sense to keep away from them. When she had
dealt with Molly's problem, she would go and find him.

'So, Molly, they know – your parents?'

'Yes. Ma guessed.'

Clare turned to look at her. 'Do you think your young
man would talk to me? Would it help at all? He won't be
afraid of me . . . but the thing is, if he could be persuaded
to marry you, would your parents agree? You are very
young.'

'Pa would agree like a shot but Ma . . . I don't know. If
she took against him she might not. She says I might have
to go and live with my aunt for a while and . . . and give
the baby away. She says there's plenty of time later to start
a family when I meet a decent man.'

'But you think your man *is* decent?'

There was a long silence and then Molly said, 'I suppose
you could talk to him, but I'm not really sure. He might
not want to.'

'Perhaps I should talk to your parents first. Maybe they
won't want me to interfere.' She moved back to Molly and
held out her hands to help her up. 'You get on with your
work. Take your mind off it. I'll go and see your parents
and offer whatever help I can – if they want it. Where
exactly is your farm?'

Brightening slightly, Molly gave directions and within
ten minutes Clare was on her way to Frenchies Farm which
belonged to the Jenners.

It was larger than she had expected and was kept in good
repair – no tiles missing off the roof of the small barn and

very little dirty straw in the stable yard. A young lad was leading a horse round while he leaned down to peer at one of its legs. He glanced up when he saw Clare and said, 'Gone lame!'

'Oh, dear. Is it serious?'

He shrugged by way of an answer.

Clare wondered if the lad was also a Jenner – Molly's younger brother perhaps. If she had any brothers. It dawned on Clare that she knew very little about the Jenner family. A thought struck her. Was this young man a suitor? The cause of Molly's problems? But no. He was surely much too young to fit Molly's description.

At that moment a woman appeared in the doorway of the farmhouse, wiping her hands on her apron. Annie Jenner was a large shapeless woman with a good-natured expression on her weather-beaten face. 'Miss Wishart?' she said nervously.

Clare nodded. Moving closer so as to be out of earshot of the lad, she said, 'I'd like to talk to you about Molly if you've a moment.'

'You'd best come in.'

They sat in the kitchen which was large and cool. In a corner of the room, a white duck regarded them with interest from its seat in a cardboard box. Mrs Jenner said, 'Fox got in last evening. We spotted it just in time. It was dragging her away by her feet and one's torn, but it might heal. About our Molly – I'm sorry she's been such a nuisance. Being late and suchlike.'

'It's not that, Mrs Jenner, it's the . . .' Her courage failed her.

'The kid? Yes, bit of a blow, that. My husband's half mad with rage at her and she won't say a thing.'

'I wondered if I could do or say anything to help but – ' she made a helpless gesture with her hands – 'being unmarried myself . . .'

'Well, of course. What would you know?' She frowned. 'We thought it might be Frank's boy, Don, down at the smithy, but he swears it isn't and he never touched her. I believe him though I almost wished it *was* him. Nice chap.

Very well mannered.' She shook her head. 'I'm hoping I find out who it is before my husband does. I don't trust him, the mood he's in. We had a bit of a set to last night and he went out carrying his shotgun. I can tell you I went down on my knees and prayed he wouldn't hurt anyone. Not that Tom's a violent man – don't get me wrong – but his pride's hurt.'

'I can imagine. The trouble is, I think Molly's afraid to say who the man is in case your husband hurts him. If she was reassured that nothing bad would happen to him, she might tell you.'

The duck scrabbled out of the box and limped across the floor and they watched its progress in silence.

Annie Jenner said, 'Well, that's a good sign.' But she picked the duck up and put it back in the box.

Clare said, 'If it was a decent man would you agree to let them marry – if he was willing?'

'God only knows! It'd be up to my husband and at the moment he wants her out of his sight. He's that cut up about it. His precious daughter! He adores that kid.' She sighed. 'Folks will be talking before long – you know how it is.'

'So, you don't have a clue to his identity – you don't know anything about him.'

'I know the first letter of his name – D. I found a note from him tucked inside her pillowslip. I was searching her room – I had to. You may think that's very sneaky, Miss Wishart, but we need to know what's going on. Nice hand-writing, it was. It said "A little present from D". Just that.'

'What was it, the present?'

'A little gold cross on a chain. She's afraid to wear it, of course. I didn't say that I've seen it.' She shrugged.

They talked for another ten minutes or so, but then Annie glanced at the clock and stood up. 'You'll have to excuse me. I've a bit of dinner to cook and my husband will be back soon. What is it about men? They do like their meals on time!' She led the way to the door and Clare had no option but to follow her.

Annie Jenner asked if she wanted a few eggs and Clare

remembered that they did. A few minutes later she made her way home with seven newly laid eggs in a small basket. Otherwise the trip had been a wasted journey, but at least she had tried to be of use. Her conscience was clear, she thought, as she joined her cousin and Alan Latimer in the dining room for lunch.

The table was already laid and Mrs Parks had put a small vase of roses in the middle of the table. The ham pasty looked delicious, the onion had been fried up with the potato and a few herbs, and there was butter and crusty bread. Clare discovered that she was hungry and decided to put the problem of Molly to one side and enjoy the meal.

When Alan Latimer left that afternoon Clare was surprised to feel a sense of loss. She put this down to the fact that his presence had cheered up both her and Donald and the atmosphere in the house, apart from Molly's gloom, was more bearable. That evening, to Clare's surprise, Donald stayed in and after supper they chatted quite amicably in the drawing room while Clare worked on her tapestry.

Donald was waxing lyrical about their visitor. 'A likeable chap,' he told Clare. 'We got along famously. He was surprised how good my sketches were, considering I've had virtually no training. He gave me a few useful pointers about perspective. I won't go into too many details because it's quite a complicated subject, but basically think about it this way – if you stand at the end of a long straight road, it seems to be narrowing so that the far end looks less wide than where you're standing. That's perspective and that's where a lot of artists fail. They get the perspective wrong.'

Clare hid a smile and said nothing. Years ago her art teacher had explained perspective to the class and Clare had found it relatively straightforward. However she didn't want to burst the bubble of enthusiasm Donald was showing. It was so long since he had been positive about anything she was determined to make the most of it.

He went on. 'In fact he felt I showed a lot of promise and suggested that I carry on sketching. This place is wonderful for artwork, apparently – the house as well as

the grounds. Plenty of nooks and crannies and that's important for the shadows.' He narrowed his eyes thoughtfully.
'Shadows, you see, can make or break a picture. Take a
tree, for instance. Look at the trunk. One side is catching
the light and one side isn't . . . When I can afford it I may
well take some lessons.'

'Interesting.' Clare finished with the blue thread, chose
a soft green silk and carried on with her work.

After a moment Donald said, 'All I need is a decent job
– one I could enjoy. I could buy myself some art materials
and take some lessons. It all comes down to money.'

Clare could not let this pass. 'What sort of work would
you enjoy?'

'That's the trouble, I don't know. I haven't tried much, but
I do know I hate clerical work. Being cooped up in a factory
office is deadly. You wouldn't know. Never had to work.'

Clare bridled at once. 'I worked long hours during the
war, Donald, doing very menial, often unpleasant, work.
You try emptying bedpans and see how you like it!'

'But that was in a good cause. That was different.
Everyone admired the plucky little women soiling their delicate hands on behalf of the wounded. Angels of mercy
ministering to our brave boys.'

Offended, Clare hit back. 'You really are despicable sometimes, Donald. You have a very mean, very unattractive
streak in you. May the Lord help any woman foolish enough
to marry you. You'd break her heart in no time.'

The barb flew home and Clare saw fleetingly, by his
expression, that her unkind comment had struck a raw nerve.
She almost fancied she heard him wince.

There was a shocked silence and a chill descended
between them, but after a moment or two her cousin thrust
his hands into his pockets and abruptly changed the subject.

'Alan found it very relaxing here,' he said. 'Soothing.
That's how he described it. He's been suffering from some
kind of disappointment – he didn't say what it was and I
didn't press him – but he is beginning to recover.' He nodded.
'A very nice chap. I told him he'd always be welcome.' He
gave her a sideways glance to see her reaction.

'I'm glad you did,' she said, grateful that the angry exchange had not gone any further. 'I said the same to him. He's good company.'

When the subject of Alan Latimer had been exhausted they fell silent for a while and then Clare said, 'Have you noticed poor Molly? I'm worried about her. She's very unhappy at the moment.'

His attitude changed at once. 'Is she? I don't really bother myself with the servants.' He got up abruptly to pour himself a whisky and brought Clare a small sherry without asking her whether or not she wanted it. He sat down and sipped his drink for a moment, then asked, 'What's she unhappy about?'

'She's in love with someone and her parents disapprove. They think she's too young to be thinking of marriage.'

'Perhaps she is.'

Clare shrugged. 'She's breaking her heart, poor girl.'

'She'll get over it.' He held up the glass and stared at the whisky.

'I'm afraid it's not that simple. She's expecting a baby.'

'These things happen.'

Clare laughed. 'You're not very sympathetic! Haven't you ever been in love?'

He hesitated. 'I've got more sense!' He swallowed the rest of the whisky in two gulps. 'I've certainly never fancied marriage. I saw what it can be like first hand and it wasn't pretty.'

'Your own parents, you mean?' Clare was intrigued. She had always imagined her aunt and uncle to be tolerably happy. Maybe not madly, gloriously in love, though. She had lived with them for some years but had never noticed the tensions Donald referred to.

Donald hesitated. 'They weren't suited. They only married because I was on the way. He did the decent thing and it turned out badly for all of us. I sometimes imagined that they hated each other. Sometimes they didn't speak to each other for days on end. There was always an atmosphere.'

'How awful for you – and for them!'

Donald was looking at her with a strange expression on

his face. He asked, 'Were you really in love with Simon or were you in love with the idea of marriage? Being settled with your own home. Having children. That sort of thing. That's really what women want, isn't it? That's why they want a husband. That's probably all Molly wants.'

'You're wrong, Donald. Molly wants to spend her life with this man. She told me she adores him and will never love any one else. You asked if I was in love with Simon. Yes, I was.' She eyed him curiously. 'I suppose if you've never experienced love it must all be a bit of a mystery – the way the other person takes over your thoughts. Nobody else matters for those first few wild months. When it first strikes you, nobody else seems to exist! You ask about me and Simon – I was deeply in love with Simon and he was in love with me, which means we wanted to be together as much as possible – and that means being married. You won't understand until it happens to you – and I pity you if it never does happen.'

'I doubt if Molly's in love with . . . this chap, whoever he is.'

Clare shook her head. 'I'm sure she is. She is suffering her father's anger rather than reveal his name because if he knows who the man is, he wants to kill him.'

Donald stretched out his legs and regarded his shoes with great intensity. 'Kill him,' he echoed. 'A bit extreme, isn't it?'

'Not at all. Most fathers want to see their daughters happily married and they certainly don't want the shame of an illegitimate baby. They can't bear the stigma. And it's almost the end of the world for the baby's mother who usually has to give her child away knowing that she may never marry and have another child because of the disgrace.' She sighed. 'And the poor baby grows up and never knows his real father and mother. It's really sad.'

'Stop!' Donald stood up abruptly. 'You're breaking my heart,' he mocked. 'Trust you to turn it into a sob story. That sort of thing happens all the time.'

'Not to Molly. And not to the child's father. They'll go through life wondering about the son or daughter they never knew. It's a tragedy, Donald, whatever you choose to think.'

Annoyed by his callous comments, she glared at him. He was standing with one hand on the mantelpiece, his back to her, his face hidden.

He said, 'So, she adores this fellow.'

Clare didn't answer. She was not prepared to listen to any more of his unsympathetic remarks. Now she wondered why she had ever raised the subject with him – she ought to have known how he would react.

He said suddenly, 'Maybe the fellow's got no way of supporting a wife and child. People like you always assume the worst of others.'

Stung into a reply, she said, 'That's hardly going to be a problem. I suspect whoever marries Molly will end up running the farm. They don't have a son. Mr Jenner needs someone to help run Frenchies Farm so a son-in-law would be ideal. Molly's husband would presumably have paid employment on the farm plus good prospects – as well as an adoring wife.' Forgetting her irritation, Clare put down her stitching. 'It's rather a nice farm, actually. I saw some of it when I went over there. Nice family, too. Not that I saw Mr Jenner, but his wife is very pleasant.'

Donald turned, laughing. 'It all sounds very cosy, Clare, very *lyrical,* but you've forgotten one important point – Mr Jenner's planning to kill this future son-in-law! He sounds a mite dangerous to me. Somewhat of a fly-in-the-ointment, wouldn't you say, to a happy-ever-after story?'

'Only if he doesn't make an honest woman of his daughter,' she protested, but her words fell on deaf ears because Donald had walked out of the room, which was his favourite way of ending a conversation that no longer interested him.

Seven

Later that evening Jimmie waylaid Clare as she walked in the garden.

'If I could have a word, Miss Wishart,' he said, snatching his cap from his head and clasping it fiercely with both hands. 'It's about Jonty. The truth is he's not looking so perky lately, and yesterday I had to stop in the middle of the lawn because he was snuffling so and shaking his head like something was bothering him. And he seems a bit slower these last few days. I thought he was just feeling lazy, but now I'm not so sure.'

'Oh, Jimmie!' Clare was at once concerned. 'How is he today? Better or worse? Do you think we should call in the vet?'

Jimmie frowned. 'I don't rightly know, but maybe if we give him a day or two's complete rest. Turn him out into the paddock say . . . It might do the trick. The vet's not cheap and . . .' He left the sentence unfinished. He had gleaned something of the financial position from chatting with Mrs Parks and he was reluctant to worry the mistress for no good reason. 'He's still eating if that's anything to go by. Hopefully it's a good sign.'

Clare brightened. 'I would think so, wouldn't you? Let's do that. We'll forget about the lawn and give him three full days' rest and if he still looks poorly we'll call in Mr Gratton.'

She looked relieved, Jimmie thought. Perhaps now was as good a time as any. He thought carefully about how to introduce the subject. 'It's a big worry for you, this place,' he said, 'that is, you being on your own. Must be a burden for you.'

'It is, I admit, but I feel very hopeful that everything will be for the best.' She glanced round. 'Have you seen my cousin anywhere? He seems to have slipped out without me noticing. Not that I need to know what he's up to, but he usually mentions it if he's going to be out for the day.'

Distracted, Jimmie said, 'I haven't seen him, no.'

And don't want to either. Won't bother me if I never set eyes on him again. Still, best not be rude about him to Miss Wishart. He's her family, if that counts for anything. If Clare was to agree to marry him, Jimmie would arrange to see as little of Donald Wishart as possible.

With an effort, he reverted to his previous line of thinking. 'I know as how you lost your young man in the war, Miss Wishart.' This was so difficult. 'I was wondering whether . . . I mean, some people reckon they can only love one man and if that was . . .' Without realizing it, he was crushing his cap against his chest.

Clare watched him with a wary expression on her face.

'The thing is, Miss Wishart, you might one day find someone else.' There, he'd said it! 'You being an attractive lady and still young.'

Her eyes widened. 'Why, thank you, Jimmie,' she said, obviously surprised but flattered.

'I mean to say, you might be tempted to marry after all. Then you'd have someone to . . . to lean on, so to speak. To share the worries. Do you think you might?'

Now she looked a little flustered. 'Well, if the right man came along I dare say . . .' A faint colour came into her face and she said softly, 'I think Simon might wish me to find love again.'

'I'm certain of it! Of course he'd want you to be happy. How long ago was it? When he died, I mean.' Jimmie held his breath. She seemed willing to talk about it so there might be a chance she would consider someone else.

'How long? It was right at the beginning of the war which makes it nearly six years.' She sighed.

Jimmie nodded. 'I reckon he'd want you to be happy.'

She nodded, deep in her thoughts and seemed to be only half listening. Then abruptly she straightened up and said briskly, 'So, we've decided on three days' rest for Jonty. I can leave you to see to him, Jimmie. Give him a lot of love and attention. Make a fuss of him.' She smiled. 'I shall be late if I don't make a move. Thank you for letting me know about him.'

Disconcerted, Jimmie made no move to delay her further. He didn't know whether to be pleased or sorry with the way the conversation had gone. She hadn't given him time to say exactly what was on his mind, but on the other hand she had said she would be prepared to find another love and that was worth knowing. Meanwhile Jonty awaited and with a hopeful heart and a skip in his step Jimmie set off towards the stable.

Sunday morning came and Molly refused to get out of bed, claiming that she was feeling too sick to go to church.

'Your pa's not going to wear it,' her mother warned, standing beside the bed with her arms crossed and a determined look on her face. 'You know what he's like, Molly, so make the effort.'

'I'll be sick in the church!'

'Course you won't.'

'I will . . . and then everyone will know.' Molly closed her eyes.

'You ought to eat something. A piece of dry bread will do the trick. You can't starve yourself just because you feel sick.'

'I can't face dry bread. I don't want anything. Just leave me alone.'

'Well, on your own head be it! Don't say I didn't warn you.'

Downstairs her husband sat at the table hunched over his plate. He had used a slice of bread to wipe up the remains of the egg and bacon and now glanced up at his wife.

Annie said, 'She can't get up. If she moves she feels sick and she says she doesn't want to be sick in church because then everyone will know she's . . .'

'I know! Don't go on about it.'

She sat down. 'Another cup of tea?'

He nodded, sunk in gloom. 'D'you reckon that Mrs Parks has guessed? A right gossip she is.'

'You don't know that, Tom. You don't even know the woman.' She poured the tea, hoping he would give in over Molly and let her stay where she was. 'You and I could go together,' she suggested, 'and say Molly has twisted her ankle – if anyone asks.'

'And the chap what did it will be laughing at us! Knowing what he's done.'

'Maybe he doesn't go to church.'

'If he sets foot in that holy place after ruining our girl . . . I hope the Lord strikes him down. I'd like to see the blighter drop dead and that's the truth!'

'Fat lot of good that would do for our Molly. Drop dead indeed! We'd never get them to the altar then. Not if he was to fall down dead. Better to pray that the chap has a change of heart and does the decent thing.'

'If he has any decency in him – which I doubt.' Tom Jenner banged his mug down and pushed back his chair. 'You can go without me. I can't face it. You say your prayers and one for me – see what good it does.'

Shocked, she stared at him. 'But you're already dressed in your Sunday suit.'

'Then I'll take it off again. If Molly's not going then neither am I.'

Without waiting for her inevitable protests, he went back upstairs and Annie sat in a miserable silence. She felt as though dark clouds were closing in around her and was suddenly fearful and indecisive. *Damn them both! Perhaps I should go but how will it look? Odd, that's how, and anyone in the know will be sniggering at our family. And how can I stand in God's house and tell downright lies?*

She was still struggling with her options when Tom came downstairs in his working breeches and faded shirt. Ignoring her obvious unhappiness, he strode past her and went outside, headed towards the pigsty.

So, that's it, Annie thought bitterly. I shan't go! A shame, but there was nothing else for it. She would have to say her prayers at home. It was also a shame because church on Sunday was the only chance she had in the week to wear her one good outfit – a dark blue dress and jacket and a grey velour hat with the dark blue ribbon – and look half decent. No point now in changing into her Sunday best. Sighing, she got up heavily from the table, wishing, not for the first time, that she had chosen Albert Best instead of Tom Jenner all those years ago.

On Monday, a blast on the horn and a screech of brakes alerted Clare to Steven Flint's arrival, and she hurried down the steps to greet him. The weather was fine, the hood was down and Steven sat proudly at the wheel of a smart green car with yellow trim. He drove a Spyker, Clare recognized, determined not to reveal her ignorance of all things mechanical. At least she would get the car's name right.

Steven was resplendent in a tweed jacket with matching cap, and a scarf was draped nonchalantly around his neck. Clare smiled with pleasure – he had gone to a lot of trouble to impress her, she thought, and was glad that she, too, was looking her best.

He climbed down and shook her hand warmly. 'My dear Miss Wishart, this is such a pleasure.'

'It is for me, too,' she replied. 'I've been counting the days.'

Steven was a sturdy man, maybe around ten years older than she was, but with a cheerful face and bright blue eyes. His hair was touched with grey and he could never be described as slim, but he was certainly not fat. His handshake was firm as he regarded her with evident approval.

She said, 'What a handsome car. A Spyker?'

His smile broadened. 'Yes, this is my favourite toy! A great motor.'

Together they walked round it, admiring it from every angle. Steven overloaded her brain with details and she nodded in a way that suggested she understood. Motor cars were obviously a passion with him. Most of the details passed over her head.

'Dutch,' he told her, 'but they're very popular over here

now.' He held her hand as she climbed into the front passenger seat and settled herself with a flutter of unexpected nerves. 'The company want to enter her in another race to prove her mettle. Have you ever heard of the Peking to Paris motor race? Something along those lines would be perfect.'

Steven had promised that he would keep his speed down for Clare's benefit and he drove through the village at a respectable twenty-five mph, watched by several villagers who blinked once at the car and again at Clare, who felt a small thrill of satisfaction that the news would soon be all over the village. However, once they left the houses behind the speed increased and she found it rather alarming as she clung to her hat with one hand while the car bounced and shuddered along the narrow country lanes and turned corners with what seemed to Clare to be disconcerting speed. The phrase 'dicing with death' popped into her mind. He glanced across at her. 'It seems much faster than it is, trust me!'

'Does it. That's good to know. I will . . . trust you, that is.'

'We're going to the Unicorn Hotel,' he told her. 'It's tucked away somewhere just this side of Hastings. I hear good reports about it. Wonderful fish straight from the sea. Do you like fish, Miss Wishart?'

Before she could answer that she did, Steven was telling her more about the Peking to Paris race.

'It took place in 1907. From China through Siberia, through Moscow, on to the Gobi Desert, through Europe to Paris! Must have been amazing. I wish I had been there.'

Clare sneaked another look at him and liked what she saw. He seemed to have an eagerness and enthusiasm for life that was rather endearing. His carefree style was somehow liberating and as the miles sped by she felt herself relaxing. Perhaps she could eat slowly and make the meal last as long as possible. She was certainly enjoying his company.

As though reading her mind, he said, 'We'll chat about your book over lunch. We're in no hurry, are we? There's a very pleasant lounge, I'm told, and we can make ourselves comfortable. I'm looking forward to hearing your ideas.'

During the last ten minutes of the journey Steven explained that Bell & May was a family run business started by his grandfather on his mother's side. That was Dennis Bell. When recently the firm needed to expand, Steven's brother-in-law, Benjamin May, also put money into the company.

'So today we have myself, Ben May's son Harold, and my uncle Austin. A board of three. We have a very talented editor, Mrs Everts, plus a few juniors, the company secretary and an accountant.'

'And Miss Birch?'

'Good Lord, yes. My secretary, but she's due to be married soon so I expect she'll leave us. It's a small firm in this day and age, but we like it that way.' He grinned. 'You'll soon get to know people – if you decide to join us. We have a small party at Christmas so that the authors can meet one another. It's more friendly that way. More intimate. We have fourteen authors at the moment, but, of course, I'm hoping to sign up more – and you are one of them!'

They pulled up outside a large hotel. Clare felt a little overwhelmed now that reality was setting in. She had never expected to belong to what seemed to her a large organization and the thought of a party in London was daunting. 'I hope you like my ideas,' she offered anxiously.

Steven stopped the car and hurried round to help her out. 'My dear Miss Wishart, I would never have approached you unless I was quite certain. I shall most definitely like your ideas – I know the way you write – and I know we shall work well together.' With exaggerated courtesy and a reassuring smile, he linked her arm through his and they walked together into the Unicorn Hotel.

From an imposing menu Clare chose lemon sole with parsley butter and creamed potatoes. Her companion, who looked as though he might be a hearty eater, decided on roast beef with Yorkshire pudding and a variety of vegetables. Steven asked if the gravy was 'substantial' before ordering because he hated 'that watery stuff that some hotels serve'. While they waited for the food to arrive he apologized for boring

her about his car and Clare insisted that she had not been
bored but rather bemused.

'I can see I have a lot to learn about motor cars,' she told
him.

'But now it is your turn,' he said, smiling. 'I only caught
a glimpse of Merle Place which is quite amazing. Will you
tell me about it, please?'

'I will with pleasure, but I can do better than that. When
you take me back I will show you round, if you have the
time.'

'I shall make time,' he assured her.

Clare told him about the early family rift when a quarrel
between her grandfather and his youngest nephew, Frank,
brought about an end to family relations between them.
'Frank's brother and father both took the nephew's side
so my grandfather never spoke again to any of them again.
My grandfather was the eldest of two brothers so left it to
me because I had cared for him when he was ill.'

'There's a storyline for you!' Steven laughed.

Clare shrugged. 'It didn't end happily,' she warned. 'When
my mother died, my father sent me to live with my aunt
and uncle and Donald. *We* didn't get along at all well. Just
one of those awkward families, I suppose, a few rifts and
resentments. At the moment Donald lives with me at Merle
Place so you may well meet him later.'

'But you ended up with the property. A great joy for
you,' said Steven, 'but a huge responsibility. And then came
the war.'

At that moment, the food arrived and they busied themselves with the lunch, but still found time to talk between
mouthfuls.

'Merle Place is beautiful – or was,' Clare conceded, 'but
there was nothing else in the bequest except a small amount
of money and I cannot possible maintain such a large place
especially as it has been sadly neglected. But, yes, I had
only owned it for two years when the war started and it was
soon requisitioned by the government as a hospital for the
troops. It has slowly decayed throughout the war and is now
desperately in need of care and attention. In desperation I've

put it on the market, but so far only one potential buyer has been to view it.'

The waiter appeared and refilled their glasses and Steven waited politely for Clare to finish her food before putting his own knife and fork together.

He said, 'We must look at the desserts menu. I have a very sweet tooth. Whenever I go home my mother makes treacle tart especially for me.'

Clare laughed at the vision and thought how lucky his mother must be to have a son who had turned out well. It sounded like a happy family.

He grinned. 'My mother keeps insisting that I'm lonely, which I'm not, and I keep telling her that when I *am*, I shall either find a woman who can make treacle tart or else buy a dog!'

The dessert trolley arrived and Clare chose apple pie and Steven satisfied his sweet tooth with honeyed apricots and cream.

When the meal ended they moved into the bright, spacious lounge area and ordered a pot of coffee. It was time, apparently, to discuss Clare's novel.

Steven said, 'Earlier in the week I reread one of your recent serials – 'The Longest Road' – and I think I could see why you gave it that title. Your pampered heroine is overtaken by a debilitating illness and has to come to terms with her changed lifestyle. It's a beguiling plot, Miss Wishart, and Edina told me that the magazine had hundreds of letters from readers who found it inspiring.'

Clare nodded, flattered by his attitude. 'That was the longest road of the title – the long road back from the depths of despair.' She frowned suddenly. 'Now that you mention it, I think a similar theme often appears in my stories.'

'But not consciously?'

'No,' she admitted. 'To be honest I usually make the stories up as I go along and discover the theme at the end! If there is a theme. Probably not the best way to work, but it suits me.'

'It certainly does. I suppose life is a bit like that. We don't fully understand our lives until it's nearly at an end.

Then we see it more clearly – both the good and the bad. You might say that life itself is the longest road we ever have to tread.'

Clare nodded, but she was suddenly beginning to feel unsure of herself. She had never consciously sat down and thought about why she wrote the way she did. Perhaps now she would have to take it more seriously. 'I think perhaps I take my writing too lightly,' she said anxiously. 'Maybe I *should* think the story through before I start.'

At once his expression changed. 'Oh, Miss Wishart, you mustn't think that way. You are doing all the thinking subconsciously and that's why your work is so seamless. It seems effortless. You mustn't get self-conscious about it. I should be upset if I in any way influence your work adversely.'

'I'm not averse to criticism,' she said quickly. 'There must be a lot I can learn.'

'Writers learn by writing,' he said with a smile. 'That's the way it happens, believe me.'

Relieved, Clare asked him if he had ever attempted to write a novel and he laughed aloud. 'Never! I know my limitations! No, my skill is in finding new talented authors and now I've moved into the family firm I'm discovering them for Bell and May. I'm rather like a sheepdog, rounding up authors and guiding them into our pen – no pun intended!'

His laugh was infectious and Clare joined him, though she thought it would be sad if he ended up with nothing but a dog for company.

During the ride home Clare told Steven a little more about Donald and explained the set-up at Merle Place. It was as well she did for Donald was waiting on the steps to greet them. He had gathered from Mrs Parks that Clare was going out to lunch and might bring a gentleman back to see the house and possibly sit over a pot of tea.

To Clare's relief, Donald was on his best behaviour. He greeted them both with a cheerful smile and shook hands with Steven after Clare had introduced them.

'I expect Clare will show you round the old place,' he said breezily. 'It's a shame we can't keep it in the family,

but that's the way of it, I'm afraid. Oh, by the way – ' he
turned to Clare – 'that chap rang while you were out.
Latimer. Alan Latimer. He wants to talk to you about something important so I suggested he rang back tomorrow. I
hope that was the right thing to do.'

Surprised, Clare said, 'That's fine, Donald. Thank you.'

He said, 'I'll leave you two to your tour, but maybe I
could join you for a cup of tea later. I'm going to take a
look at Jonty. Jimmie thinks there's something seriously
wrong and I telephoned for the vet, Mr Gratton, but his
housekeeper says he's been away for a couple of days and
won't be back until tomorrow. A family funeral.'

Clare's excitement faded at once at the disturbing news.
She was at once consumed by guilt because, buoyed up
with the excitement of her meeting with Steven Flint, she
had forgotten about Jimmie's anxiety on Jonty's behalf.

'We'll all come down and take a look,' she said, trying
unsuccessfully to hide her agitation.

The three of them hurried to the paddock where they
found Jimmie leaning on the gate, trying to persuade the
old horse to eat a handful of grass. Jonty was standing still
with his head down and his eyes closed. Jimmie looked up
at their approach and Clare saw the worry in his eyes and
the angry set of his jaw. He glanced at Steven, but said
nothing. He turned to Clare. 'Poor old boy's not going to
last much longer. I came up to tell you, but you'd gone off
somewhere.'

His tone was accusing and Clare's guilt deepened. Jonty
had been so much a part of their lives for so long she had
taken him for granted, and now it looked as if he would
die. She had been neglectful and the delay in telephoning
the vet may have contributed to his deterioration.

Donald, true to form, gave her a meaningful look but, to
Clare's surprise, Steven laid a hand on her shoulder. 'You
mustn't blame yourself, Miss Wishart. These things happen
to all of us – and if the vet has been away for two days
you wouldn't have been able to change things.'

Jimmie said, 'I've been thinking. There's another vet over
at Staplehorne – or there was some years back. He might

come if he's still there. Mind you he was getting on a bit
then, but . . .' He shrugged. 'Reckon his name's Spencer or
something like that. Starts with S as I recall. If not Mr Jenner
might know a thing or two. Molly's father. He's a farmer.'

Donald said, 'Molly's father? Why drag him into this?
He's not a vet. He doesn't want to trail over here.'

Clare said, 'It might be worth a try.' She looked hopefully at Donald who shook his head firmly.

'Don't look at me, Clare. You know what they say about
Tom Jenner – he's mad as a hatter. Goes round threatening
to kill people.'

Jimmie said, 'Suppose I coax Jonty back into his stall
before it gets dark. We don't want him out here all night.
It might rain and he could catch a chill. That would be the
last straw.'

'That's a good idea, Jimmie. Whatever would we do
without you?' She turned to throw a warning look in Donald's
direction, but he was already on his way back to the house.

Steven said, 'Miss Wishart, I could drive you to the farm,
to Molly's father's place, if it helps at all.'

'It would – and thank you.' She watched as Jimmie
urged the old horse in the direction of the stables and as
soon as she was satisfied that Jonty would soon be back
in his stall, she and Steven made their way to the car.
Minutes later they had pulled up in the farmyard and Steven
remained in the car while Clare approached the farmhouse
door. She was surprised when Tom Jenner opened the door
instead of Annie. He looked tired and hadn't shaved for a
day or two.

Without inviting her in, he said gruffly, 'The wife's having
a bit of a sleep. Not feeling too bright. What is it?' She
explained and he said, 'How old is the horse, this Jonty?'

'We think he's about twenty, but nobody's sure. He could
be older.'

He shrugged. 'On his way out most likely although some
horses live to be thirty. I dunno. Nothing you can do if it's
old age 'cept keep him comfortable. A rug will keep him
warm.' He frowned. 'My father kept horses all his life. Now
what would he 'ave done?'

Clare said, 'Jonty isn't eating anything.'

'Something warm then, mebbe, like a bit of boiled barley and a handful of linseed simmered in water for an hour or so. Mix it into the barley mash.'

Clare was desperately trying to remember this information and wishing she had thought to bring something on which to write it down.

Warming to his theme, Tom said, 'An apple might tempt his appetite likewise a carrot. Not much more I can tell you.' He rubbed his stubbled chin and shrugged again. 'Reckon that's it.'

She said, 'You've been so helpful. Thank you, Mr Jenner.'

He considered her, his eyes screwed up. Then he said, 'If you don't get the vet and . . . well, let me know in the morning and I'll pop across.' He smiled faintly. 'Glad to help. You've been good to my Molly.' At the mention of his daughter, he swallowed hard and his face crumpled.

To Clare's embarrassment she saw tears in his eyes, but before she could say any more he stepped back and closed the door sharply in her face. Sobered, she returned to the car and was driven home.

As if sensing her change of mood, Steven changed his mind about the tour of Merle Place and asked her if they could make it some other time and she agreed thankfully. He drove off after making her promise to invite him down again. Clare agreed and waved him off, but her day was spoiled. She went straight down to the stables where she and Jimmie carried out Tom Jenner's suggestions and Clare made a great fuss of Jonty in an attempt to make up for what she saw as her earlier indifference.

She went to bed early and cried herself to sleep.

Eight

Mrs Parks looked up in surprise next morning when Molly came into the kitchen ten minutes early instead of fifteen minutes late. 'Gracious. Pigs might fly!' she said. Molly remained standing, clutching her coat close around her body. She faced Mrs Parks defiantly. 'You've got to help me,' she declared. 'It's no good. I can't go on like this with Ma and Pa rowing all the time about me, and the baby's father wants nothing to do with me. If you don't help me, I'm going to jump in the river and drown myself. I mean it and I can't swim so that'll be the end of me.'

Shocked, Mrs Parks sat down heavily and pointed to another chair. 'Sit down, girl, and don't talk so daft.'

'I mean it. Then they'll all be sorry, but it'll be too late.' Her mouth quivered.

'Sit down, Molly, before you fall down. You look dreadful. White as a sheet.' She stood up again and busied herself with making the tea, partly because she thought they both needed a cup of tea, and partly because she could not bear the young housemaid's stricken face. 'And no more talk of drowning yourself, d'you hear me? I won't listen to such things.'

Molly sat down, hunched into her coat with the collar turned up as though it was midwinter instead of early summer. She glared at the housekeeper. 'So, you won't help me?'

'It's not a case of won't, but of can't. What do I know of such things? I had two children but none that I didn't want to keep. I'm surprised at you.'

'You don't even know what I want you to do!'

'Course I know. You want to get rid of the baby and you think I know how to go about it, but I don't. And if I did

I wouldn't tell you. It's murder, that is – killing your child before it's even born, poor little mite.' She made two mugs of tea and sat down again. 'Drink your tea, Molly, and pull yourself together.'

'I jumped off the table six times, but nothing happened – except that I hurt my ankle. Nothing happened to the baby. It's not fair.'

Now she looked more like a sulky child than a stricken woman and Mrs Parks wavered. Poor girl. Just seventeen, but she looked younger. Always had looked young for her age. Was she really old enough to be a mother and run a household? Mrs Parks sipped her tea thoughtfully. Would the girl really drown herself? It seemed unlikely but if she did . . .

She said, 'Does your ma know how you feel?'

Molly shook her head, reached for the sugar bowl and stirred three spoonfuls of sugar into her tea. Then she added a fourth and then a fifth.

'Molly!'

'Who'd miss me? Not my folks, they're both mad at me. And Do—?' She stopped, a hand over her mouth.

Mrs Parks said,' Oh it's Do?, is it? Do? who? The sooner you tell someone who he is, the sooner we can sort things out for you. He's to blame as much as you, so he ought to take some responsibility. If he's any kind of a man – a decent man – he would.' She knew most of the villagers and was racking her brains to come up with a young man starting with Do that knew Molly. She said, 'Do I know this man?'

Molly sipped her tea, saying nothing, her eyes downcast, refusing to meet the housekeeper's gaze.

Mrs Parks changed tack. 'Your father has a right to know, Molly. He could talk some sense into the chap. That's what you want, isn't it?'

Molly said, 'There's something you can take that makes the baby come loose and it's not painful or anything. If you know what it is you should tell me because I mean what I said. I can't swim so once I jump . . . that'll be it! All over.'

'A chemist might know, but then he might report you to

the police.' Mrs Parks sighed. 'Look, Molly, I did hear of a man who gave his young woman a few grains of chloride so that may be what you're thinking of. But – and it's a big but – it didn't work. She didn't lose the child, but she was *very* ill. Very, very ill,' she amended hastily as Molly started to look curious. 'I really don't think you should try it – and what would happen if the chemist asks why you want it? He might guess what you're going to do and call a policeman. You could be in trouble. You could be arrested – and then what would your folks say?'

'Serve them right. They could die of shame for all I care!' She blew on to her tea to cool it. 'I'm already in trouble. If I have to go away until the baby's born, Miss Wishart will get someone else and I'll have no job to come back to. Then I'll be in more trouble.'

Mrs Parks could see her point. 'Look, Molly, tell me who this chap is and . . . Look, I'll talk to him for you. How's that? He might listen to me, an outsider, so to speak, where he won't risk talking to your parents.'

Molly lowered her mug and regarded the housekeeper with wide eyes.

'Would you?' she whispered. 'Would you really? I mean he might listen to someone else, someone not important, like you.'

'Not important! What's that supposed to mean?' Mrs Parks's good intentions wavered.

'I mean, you're not someone he might be afraid of. I mean the mistress would be no good because he's her cousin and I had to swear not to let her—'

'What?' cried Mrs Parks. 'He's her cousin? Who's her cousin? You've lost me completely.'

'Donald. He's her cousin so she mustn't know. I had to swear not to tell her. I don't want to lose my job.'

Mrs Parks stared at her, her mouth open. *Am I hearing this? It can't be true. Not in a million years! Donald Wishart and Molly Jenner? Never!* She took a deep breath. 'Are you telling me that the man you love . . . the man who got you . . . ?' Her voice rose. 'This chap is *Donald Wishart?*'

Molly nodded. 'But don't shout it out,' she begged. 'She might hear.'

'Donald Wishart? *Donald Wishart?* Oh, Molly!' She laid
a hand over her heart. 'You silly, *silly* girl! I . . . I don't
know what to say.'
If this is her idea of a joke, I'm not blooming well laughing!
Lordy! Please don't let it be true. The mistress will go mad.
Molly was struggling with her emotions. 'How can it be
silly to love someone? When you talk to him . . .'
'What? Talk to Donald Wishart? I'm certainly not going
to talk to him.' She felt breathless.
Molly said, 'You just said you would. You promised.'
'I did not promise anything. Anyway, I didn't know who
it was then.' She put a hand to her head. 'Well, you certainly
have got yourself into a right pickle, Molly Jenner!' A feeling
of faintness swept over her and for a moment she covered
her eyes with both hands, waiting for it to pass. The sound
of chair legs scraping the floor tiles alerted her and she
uncovered her eyes in time to see Molly disappearing
through the back door.
'Molly, come back here!' She levered herself from the
chair. 'I didn't mean it. Maybe I will . . . Yes, I will talk to
him, but Lord knows what I'll say. I'll have a think about
how to go about it.' She stumbled to the door. 'Molly! Come
back here! I mean, someone like me telling him what his
duty is – he won't be very happy. He'll probably get me
sacked. Oh Lordy!' She stepped outside into the garden but
immediately someone rang the front door bell and she went
through to answer it. She found a man on the doorstep,
someone she vaguely recognized but couldn't name.
'I've come about the horse,' Tom Jenner told her. 'Still
alive, is it?' Mrs Parks, he thought, was a fine figure of a
woman and looked as though she would stand no nonsense.
'The horse? You mean Jonty? What's wrong with him?'
'Your mistress knows. You'd best give her a shout. I
haven't got all day.'
She stared at him confused, but then she invited the
farmer to wait in the hallway while she found Miss Wishart.
Tom shook his head. 'I can't hang about. I'll find my
way to the stables,' he told her and set off around the side
of the house.

She called after him. 'Find Jimmie. He'll know.'

He nodded without answering. He'd heard about Jimmie from his daughter. He sometimes wondered how they made ends meet at Merle Place. A shame that. His father remembered it from when he was a boy and then it was grand and they had big parties at the weekends in the summer with posh people coming down from London.

He came upon a broken-down greenhouse, but there was no sign of life. Frowning, he walked on, peering in all directions for a glimpse of Jimmie. He wondered if he knew the man. Might have met him in the pub without knowing his name . . .

'Ah, the stables,' he muttered.

A man was leaning on the half-door of one of the stalls. He turned at Tom's approach. 'Thanks for coming so quickly,' he said, 'but I reckon we're too late.' He stepped aside to allow Tom to look past him.

The horse was already on his side but making pathetic efforts to get up. Tom shook his head. 'Kinder to put the old fellow down,' he remarked. 'It worries them to be on their sides. They're never at ease like that and he's too old to try and get back on his feet.' He looked around. 'Where's Miss Wishart? She'll have to give the go-ahead.'

The man frowned. 'I suppose she can't face it but you're right. I'll go and find her. Shall I say you're going to put him down? That that's what you recommend?'

Tom shrugged. 'Reckon it's best for the old fellow. No point in letting him suffer any longer. She needn't be here if she doesn't want to be. It'll be quick – a bullet to the head. No pain at all.'

Clare came downstairs feeling annoyed with herself. It was rare for her to oversleep, today of all days. In the kitchen, Mrs Parks was preparing breakfast.

Clare said, 'Molly not here yet?'

'Been and gone,' said the housekeeper, who seemed to be avoiding eye contact.

She's probably broken something, thought Clare, but let it pass for the moment. 'Been and gone? How do you mean?'

'I mean she was in a funny mood . . . Flew off the handle at me and then rushed out into the garden. Talking about throwing herself in the river and suchlike nonsense.'

She began to slice mushrooms but Clare said, 'We'll eat breakfast a bit later, Mrs Parks. I'm very worried about Jonty. He's terribly ill.' Her voice shook a little. 'I'm going down to see him now. Tom Jenner might come by. He offered to help last night, but doesn't hold out much hope.'

'Ah! I thought I recognized him from somewhere. That's what he meant. He's already here and he's gone on down to the stables. I told him to talk with Jimmie.'

Clare quickly headed for the back door but then paused and swung round. 'Talking about *what*? Throwing herself in the river? I hope she was joking!'

Mrs Parks shrugged. 'I couldn't say, ma'am. She's a bit scatty at the moment. I try to make allowances for her condition but . . .' She threw up her hands in a helpless gesture. 'She'll come back, no doubt.'

'Well, let me know when she does and I'll try and talk some sense into her.'

Clare met Donald coming back to the house to find her. He explained that the vet had offered to put the old horse down. 'Painlessly,' he added. 'He won't suffer. 'He turned and walked back with her towards the stables. 'Look, Clare, if you can't face it, I'll stay and give him a hand if he needs someone. He seems a decent bloke.'

'Would you, Donald? I'd be really grateful. I don't think I want to see Jonty die.' They skirted the rose bed.

'He had to die some time, old girl!' Donald glanced at her stricken face. 'His time has come. Better to die than live on and suffer. Horses are luckier than people in that respect.'

'You're trying to cheer me up, but it won't work. I blame myself, Donald. I should have realized earlier. I should have done something.'

'You can't turn the clock back.'

They came in sight of the stables and Clare said, 'Where is he?' There was no sign of the vet or Jimmie.

'Probably in the stall with Jonty.'

At that moment Tom Jenner appeared in the doorway and Clare said, 'Oh, Tom Jenner is here as well. You didn't say.'

Donald stopped in his tracks, startled. 'Tom Jenner! That's not . . . That is, I thought he was . . . Isn't he the vet?'

'Of course not. It's Tom Jenner, Molly's father.'

Donald took a step back. 'I thought . . .'

Clare walked on and greeted the farmer. 'I'm so sorry. I overslept. I had a bad night. Couldn't sleep, worrying about Jonty.' She glanced round. 'Isn't Jimmie here? I thought he'd be up early . . .'

Tom stared. 'He was here just now. He went to fetch you.'

'That was my cousin, Donald.' She turned, but he was nowhere to be seen. 'Jimmie is bigger altogether. Sandy hair.'

'Bit of a mix-up, seemingly. Still, not to worry. If you could just sit with the old boy and distract him with a few kind words . . . You needn't watch. It'll all be over in a tick.'

Reluctantly Clare stepped past him. Why on earth had Donald taken himself off? Just like him – offering help, then weaselling out. Unwillingly she settled herself on the straw beside Jonty who was obviously dying. His breath came as shallow, irregular sighs and his eyes were closed. Feebly he gave an occasional kick with his legs in a futile attempt to stand.

'There, there, Jonty. You're a good lad. A very good lad,' Clare said gently, stroking his neck. While Tom slipped a bullet into his pistol she tidied the horse's mane, ran her hand lovingly over his soft warm mouth and leaned down to press a kiss on to his head. 'You've been a lovely friend,' she told him. 'Much loved and . . . and much . . .' She swallowed hard and blinked back tears. 'You were one of the family, Jonty, and much appreciated and . . .'

Tom Jenner said, 'Best get your head out of the way, Miss Wishart.'

She jerked her head back, clutched a handful of mane and closed her eyes. The pistol shot was muted and at once the horse's head dropped slightly to one side. He lay still and silent on the hay beside her. Briefly she felt Tom Jenner's comforting hand on her shoulder then he busied himself putting his things away. 'Nothing more you can do. I'll send someone to collect him later,' he said gruffly.

Clare heard his retreating footsteps as tears came thick and fast. She was full of anguish, sick with remorse and dulled by a deep sense of loss.

Donald rushed back to the house, utterly confused. So that man was Molly's father! God! That could have been a real disaster! He let himself in at the back door and prepared to rush past the housekeeper, but she said, 'Oh, Mr Wishart, could I have a word, please?'

He hesitated fatally.

She said, 'I'm rather worried about—'

'I'm sorry. I'm in a hurry.'

'Wait, please!'

He turned back and was surprised to see how pale she was. Mrs Parks was clutching her apron, her eyes were wide and . . . frightened? She looked as if she'd seen a ghost. He frowned.

'Is it important? Only I have rather a lot—'

'It's Molly, Mr Wishart. She's gone running off in a great state. Very agitated.'

He felt his heart begin to thud. 'Run off? Where to?'

'That's it. I don't know. She said . . . She threatened . . .' Mrs Parks took a huge gulp of air. 'She says she can't go on.'

'Well, you should speak to my cousin. It's her job to see to the staff, not mine. Now, if that's all . . .'

'No, wait! You don't understand. I don't mean she can't go on here. I mean she can't go on with her life. She says she'll kill herself.'

Donald felt a jolt of fear. 'Kill herself,' he whispered. 'You must be mistaken. Not Molly. She's not the type.'

'I mentioned it to the mistress but she was in a hurry and I don't think she took it in. I mean . . . The girl is in a wild state. She's very young and she can't talk to anyone because she refuses to say who the father is. That's set her father against the man and against Molly. She's getting desperate and someone needs to talk some sense into her. Suppose she does kill herself. She's pretty upset.'

'She wouldn't,' he insisted, but his heart was pounding now with fear. A sense of looming disaster seized him. He said again, 'She wouldn't know how to kill herself!'

'I hope not but suppose . . .'

'She hasn't got a gun, has she?'

'A gun? I should hope not – but her father has guns.' The housekeeper's eyes widened. 'He's a farmer. They all have guns, don't they? But no, she's saying she'll jump in the river and she can't swim. What can I do? I tried to stop her . . . she'll drown and everyone's going to blame me if anything happens to her.' Abruptly she put a hand to her head. 'Oh, dear! I feel dizzy. I'm going to faint . . .'

Donald rushed forward and managed to catch her. He held her upright until she came to, then sat her down carefully. 'I'll fetch the doctor.'

'No!' She clutched his arm. 'I don't need a doctor. It's just the worry. Oh, dear! Could you get me a glass of water? All these goings on . . .'

When Donald returned with a glass, she sipped from it while he watched anxiously. 'If only this young man knew how much she loves him,' Mrs Parks murmured. 'He could put an end to all this. She's such a lovely girl. Very sweet and trusting and she adores the fellow. Can't think why, the way he's treated her.' She sighed but her expression was brighter and he decided she was recovering. 'But there – it happens all the time. Some other man might come along and marry her. It wouldn't be the first time.'

Donald raised an eyebrow. 'What – marry a woman who has . . . er . . . who is expecting another man's child? Not very likely, in my opinion.'

'Well, you're wrong there, Mr Wishart, because it happened to my niece's friend only last year.' She leaned forward confidingly. 'The chap wouldn't wed her, but she kept the baby and before the child was a year old she'd had an offer of marriage from someone else. He was a really decent man, the second one, and they're so happy. She's had another child since then.' She smiled. 'Best for everyone, that was. The first chap did her a real favour by abandoning her. He couldn't have been much of a catch. Very immature and selfish. But back to Molly.' She stood up with an effort. 'I'll ask Miss Wishart to send Jimmie to look for her. If she reaches that bridge, in the state she's in!'

Mrs Parks drank the last of the water he had given her. Donald had already left the kitchen without a word and she watched him race off across the lawn in the direction of the bridge.

'That's right. You go and find her,' she whispered. The whole household seemed to be in uproar, but she had done her bit. *I think that went rather well. Especially the bit about my niece's imaginary friend. And all on the spur of the moment. It's time to make myself a well-deserved pot of tea.*

Badly shaken by Jonty's death, Clare retreated to the study and shut herself in with her thoughts. Almost immediately, the telephone rang and Mrs Parks called her downstairs to speak to the estate agent.

'Good morning, Mr Yates,' she said. 'I'm sorry to keep you waiting but we have had a family . . . er . . . problem this morning and I'm rather at my wits' end. But how can I help you?'

'I'm sorry to hear that, but my news might cheer you up. I've had an enquiry from a middle-aged couple – Mr and Mrs James Souter – who are looking for a suitable place to open as a centre for psychic studies. That is, somewhere students can spend a few months at a time researching what they call "the other side" and gathering information on the spirit world. They are currently writing a book on the subject, which will be their third, so I assume they are genuine researchers and not "crazies".'

Clare was taken aback by the prospect, but common sense warned her not to reject the offer out of hand. 'I suppose there's no reason why they shouldn't do that,' she replied. 'I don't actually know that I share their beliefs but . . .' She hesitated. 'What exactly are they? Mediums? Do they hold seances or look for ghosts?' It occurred to her that she might learn something from them for her proposed novel.

She heard him laugh. 'I didn't ask. They seem quite ordinary and are keen to visit Merle Place. They need somewhere spacious and private. Quiet seems to be essential, too. I told them Merle Place might fit the bill. I said I'd speak to you first because – and this might be the snag – they want to rent it for the first year to see if they can make a success of the venture. If it works out they'll buy it.'

'Rent it? Oh, but . . .' Clare frowned. 'I don't know,' Clare told him frankly. 'Maybe we should let them see the place first. No point in discussing financial arrangements if they don't like the look of the house. What do you advise, Mr Yates?'

'I agree. But from their point of view there is no point in them seeing it if you are definitely not prepared to consider renting. How do you feel about that aspect, Miss Wishart?'

She hesitated, thinking as rapidly as she could. 'Could we talk later today? I don't want to make a wrong decision in the heat of the moment and at present I have things that rather urgently need my attention.'

'No problem at all, Miss Wishart. I'll let them know we'll have an answer for them tomorrow. Would that do?'

'Perfectly. Thank you.'

'There was one other interested party, but he refused to meet the asking price. When I asked him to make a serious near offer it was twenty-five per cent below what you want.'

'Twenty-five per cent below? That's outrageous!'

'Exactly and I told him so. I suggested he think again in case he could improve on the offer, but I've heard nothing since. It is a large property and I did warn you that it might be difficult to find a buyer.'

'Yes, you did and I understand completely. But perhaps we should allow them to come and see round the place. They might fall in love with it.' She laughed, a little embarrassed. 'I suppose there's not much chance of that. It's just me being naïve.'

'Not at all. I'll pass on your comments to them. There's nothing lost if they say no.'

Clare tried to regain what she saw as 'the upper hand'

in the conversation. 'It's early days yet, so I'm happy to wait and see what else comes along. I hope the next few months will bring more viewings because Merle Place looks its shabby best with a glow of sunshine and summer is almost upon us.'

They parted on this note and Clare stood for a few moments in the hall, wondering what to do next. Mrs Parks came out of the kitchen and Clare asked, 'Where is everybody?'

Mrs Parks rolled her eyes. 'Here and there and nowhere!' she exclaimed. 'Molly hasn't come back, your cousin went dashing off somewhere and I haven't seen Jimmie this morning. I assumed he was busy in the garden.'

'That's odd. He wasn't at the stables and I thought he would be. Didn't he come in for breakfast?'

'No.' She waited awkwardly at the foot of the stairs.

Clare said, 'Is something wrong? You look somehow distracted.'

'Me? No!' Her voice rose. 'Don't worry about me. I'm just trying to do the housemaid's work as well as my own!'

Mortified by Mrs Parks's irritated tone, Clare said, 'Oh, poor Mrs Parks. Forgive me. I'm a bit distracted myself. Jonty had to be put down. Did you know?'

Mrs Parks shook her head. 'Still, he was getting on a bit and he had a good life.'

'Mr Jenner came.' Clare blinked rapidly and brushed her eyes quickly with her handkerchief. 'Just leave the upstairs, Mrs Parks. We won't worry over a bit of dust. Molly can make up her hours when she comes back. Just see to lunch, will you?'

She watched the housekeeper return to the kitchen, but a small suspicion remained that all was not quite as it should be. For the moment, however, she didn't have the heart to pursue the matter.

It will all come out in the wash, she thought with a faint smile. That had been one of her mother's favourite sayings and at this moment Clare found it comforting.

It was just one of those mornings! She had intended to start making notes and researching for the novel she and

Steven Flint had agreed on – the solitary lady living in a haunted house, but now her inspiration had deserted her as problems crowded in and she wondered what to do first.

She set off in search of Jimmie and looked in all the usual places; the potting shed, the greenhouse and the shed that housed the mower and other paraphernalia. There was a stiff breeze but no sign of rain and she was warm enough without her jacket.

When her search proved unsuccessful, she retraced her steps to the stable and went up the wooden stairs, calling his name. Silence greeted her; she took a few moments to check round the room for clues, but there was nothing out of the ordinary – except his bed. This, she realized with a frisson of alarm, had not been slept in. So where had he been? It came to her. He had probably stayed with Jonty, although if that were the case, why wasn't he around when Tom Jenner arrived? Where had he gone? She went down the stairs and out into the stable yard, her mind racing uneasily. It was so unlike him to 'go missing' without letting her know. Biting her lip with growing anxiety, she decided to take one more look round the garden. If she didn't find him, perhaps she should call in the police – or was that overreacting?

'Calm down, Clare,' she said to herself. 'Nothing's wrong, but where on earth are you, Jimmie?'

She was passing the corner where the earliest rhododendrons were already blooming, when she heard a sound that made her turn her head sharply. Was it a groan? 'Jimmie? Is that you?'

Pushing her way through the dense foliage of the rhododendrons she almost fell over him. He was on the ground, crawling towards her, his usually ruddy face ashen, his features twisted in pain.

'Jimmie! Oh my God!'

He tried to speak, but his voice shook so much that the words were unintelligible. His hands and lips were blue and sweat beaded his face. In addition he seemed very confused and helpless.

Kneeling beside him, she cried, 'What's happened to you?'

Her first thought was that he had been attacked. 'Can you get up if I help you? Who did this to you?'

She put an arm round him and he struggled to get to his feet, but it was at once obvious that he was too weak. 'I'll find Donald,' she told him desperately. 'And we'll manage between us.'

Donald was nowhere to be found so it was Clare and Mrs Parks who eventually raised Jimmie to his feet and somehow coaxed him step by step back to the house. Clare made him comfortable on the sofa with a pillow and blanket while Mrs Parks made him a drink of warm milk thickened with a little oatmeal and laced with honey.

'That'll give him some strength,' she told Clare, who was hovering in the kitchen after telephoning for the doctor. 'And comfort his stomach. He's had a bad shock, that's for sure, and if he's been out there all night he'll be chilled to the bone. Must have been anxious, too – afraid of dying in the night.'

Clare nodded, grateful for the housekeeper's help. For once she was longing for Donald to come back. 'Just like Donald to be missing when he's needed!'

Mrs Parks gave her a strange look and seemed about to say something, but then changed her mind. She handed the milk to Clare and said, 'I'll be around if you need me. I've got some cold ham for lunch, but I'll get Jimmie a bit of fish when the chap calls, if that's all right with you? He'll need something light.'

'A good idea. Thank you, Mrs Parks.'

Clare took the drink into Jimmie, who was still in a state of shock and very pale, but as he sipped the thick sweet drink, a little of his colour returned and by the time he had finished it, he was able to speak more clearly.

'Nobody did it . . .' he whispered. 'It was a pain in my heart and my arm. I think I passed out . . . I found myself on the ground next to Jonty.' He stopped, breathless, and closed his eyes.

'Next to Jonty? What time was it?'

'Don't exactly know. I was going to stay with him all night, but I got frightened when I came to . . . thought I'd best let you know. I was coming to the house to tell you when it got worse and I collapsed . . . when I woke up again it was dawn.'

'Oh, Jimmie! How dreadful for you! I'm so sorry I couldn't help at the time. You might have died,' she said. 'I've sent for the doctor. Until he comes you are not to move from that sofa. If it's your heart we'll take good care of you.' She gave him a cheerful smile to hide her fears. 'Are you feeling any better?'

He nodded.

'Better not tire you with idle chit-chat. Try to sleep now. You obviously need some proper rest. Mrs Parks is going to steam some fish for your lunch. I'll bring you down a small bell that used to belong to grandmother and we'll leave the doors open. If you need anything or you feel a bit anxious, ring it and one of us will come.'

He said something about avoiding being a nuisance.

'When have you ever been a nuisance, Jimmie?' she demanded. 'You've always been an absolute rock. I'm just glad you are safe and here with us and we can look after you.'

Ten minutes later, back in her study, Clare sat down and tried to calm her nerves. One catastrophe after another, she thought, and uttered a brief but heartfelt prayer that Jimmie would survive what had obviously been a heart attack.

Nine

Just before seven that same evening there was a distinct chill in the air; the persistent drizzle outside was not entirely responsible. Molly stood at the sink peeling potatoes and trying not to listen to her mother, who was nagging her about yet another day's work missed at Merle Place.

'You can't expect her to put up with your tantrums for ever,' she told Molly. 'And what about Mrs Parks? Is she supposed to do your share as well as her own? I never took you for selfish or thoughtless, Molly, but I'm beginning to wonder.'

'I've got things on my mind, haven't I?' She turned to glare at her mother.

'And whose fault is that?'

'Mine. Everything's my fault!' She turned. 'Everything in the whole blooming world's my fault according to you and Pa. OK. I've said it. Blame me for everything!'

'All I'm asking is where you were all day if you weren't at work? It's a fair question.'

'I was . . .'

'With him, I suppose.'

'Yes. And why shouldn't I? We have things to talk about.'

'Such as?'

Molly threw the potato she was holding across the room and swore under her breath.

'Molly, Wash your mouth out with soap!'

'Well, leave me alone. I'm doing my best.' She glanced at the clock. 'If you must know he's coming here.' She retrieved the potato, which, after rebounding from the wall, had rolled back towards her.

'Coming here? Who's coming here?'

'Who d'you think? Him! You want to talk to him so you'll get the chance.'

'Him? When?' Her mother's horrified gaze darted round the kitchen, taking in the breakfast crumbs still on the table, muddy boots in the corner, grubby dishcloths draped above the stove to dry off.

'This evening. He wants to talk to Pa.'

Her mother's mouth opened and shut like a fish gasping for air and Molly noted it with satisfaction. *Serve you right, both of you. On and on – nag, nag, nag. Now he's coming. Panic all you like, Ma. Don's coming and he's going to stick up for me.* At least she hoped so.

'This evening?' Her mother snatched down the dishcloths, swiped them across the table to gather up the crumbs, and threw them into a bucket under the sink.

Molly watched relief mingling with anger in her mother's expression, but all Annie said was, 'And what's he going to say when he gets here?' She glanced nervously out of the window.

'Don't ask me. He says it'll depend on what sort of welcome he gets.' Don had come after her to the bridge, his face pale and creased with worry. She had told him she'd thought better of drowning herself. 'Because that means killing the baby and it's not his fault and I love him already. Or her.'

'What sort of welcome he gets?' her mother echoed. 'What's that supposed to mean?'

'If Pa bawls him out he won't want to join this family.' This wasn't exactly true. Don had said they would go away together if her family were unhappy because he didn't want to be perpetually at war with his in-laws.

'You'd best warn your pa, then. He's with the pigs.'

Molly shrugged and began to peel another potato. She felt good being in control in this way, but deep down she was still cautious. Don could easily change his mind if the meeting was a disaster.

'Molly! I said go and warn your pa that your chap's coming!'

'You warn him. I've warned you.' They wouldn't be able

to tell her what to do once she was married. She mouthed the words, 'Please, God, let it happen!' If it all went wrong now she didn't think she could bear it.

Her mother sat down heavily. 'So, since he's coming I suppose you can tell us his name.'

'It's Don.'

'I mean his full name. What's his surname?'

Molly hesitated. She had wanted to see the look on their faces when Don turned up, but now she couldn't wait. 'It's Wishart. I've done eight potatoes. Is that enough?'

'No, it isn't enough. Do another three.' Annie frowned. 'Wishart? What are you talking about? I asked what's his surname.'

'And I said Wishart. Donald Edgar Wishart.' She picked up three more potatoes from the sack.

The silence lengthened and Molly struggled to keep her face straight.

Her mother said faintly, 'Donald *Wishart*? You don't mean . . .'

Molly added water to the potatoes and set the pan on the hob. 'He knows Pa said all those horrible things about him and threatened to kill him so he's not exactly looking forward to meeting him. He doesn't approve of violence.'

A heavy silence descended as Molly continued to peel potatoes.

'You are joking, Molly, I hope.'

'I'm not joking, no.'

'You and Donald Wishart!'

'Yes. Me and him. Why not?'

There was another silence and Molly imagined her mother's thoughts whirling crazily.

'You didn't tell him about what your pa said – not about shooting whoever it was.'

Molly nodded, salted the potatoes and put them on to cook.

'For heaven's sake, girl! That was just talk, you know it was.' Mortified, Annie shook her head, staring at her daughter who simply shrugged. 'Your pa's not a murderer! Wouldn't hurt a fly and you know it. You should never have said . . . Your pa . . .'

Molly glanced past her mother to the rainswept yard beyond the window. Don had just arrived and was dismounting from a rather rusty bicycle. 'Here he is now.' As though scalded, her mother leaped from the chair and they both watched as Tom Jenner came round the corner from the pigsty and lifted a laconic hand in greeting. They heard Tom say, 'I been thinking about Miss Wishart's horse . . .'

Molly's mother gave a strangled cry and slammed a hand over her heart, and in a sudden panic Molly's new-found self-confidence faded away. With an anguished gasp, she fled upstairs to the sanctuary of her bedroom and locked herself in.

Donald interrupted him. 'Not now, Mr Jenner, please. I have to talk to you about something else. Is there somewhere we can go, just the two of us?'

'Come into the barn.' He led the way into a small barn half-filled with hay, sacks of animal feed, bins and boxes and a large selection of farm utensils of various shapes and sizes. Looking at them, Donald wondered if he would ever get the chance to learn what they all were and how they were used. Now that he had made a decision about Molly, he was feeling less fraught and the thought that he was doing the decent thing pleased him. In a small way he felt almost heroic. Molly had thrown her arms around him and it had felt good. No one had ever shown him such passionate affection and he realized he was enjoying the sensation of being responsible for someone's happiness.

They sat down on two bales of hay and Don took a deep breath before his courage failed. It had taken an effort to cycle over. He would have preferred to arrive in the pony and trap, but now that Jonty was dead that was out of the question. Now he felt somewhat bedraggled and ran his fingers through his wet hair.

'I haven't come about Jonty,' he said firmly. 'It's about your daughter. I have to tell you, Mr Jenner, that . . . that I'm the father of her child and I'd like your permission to marry her.'

Open-mouthed, Molly's father stared at him. 'You?' he gasped. 'You're the one that . . . *You?*'

Donald nodded warily. This was not exactly how he'd imagined the scene. Surely the man would see that he, Donald, was a good match for his daughter. 'I'm sorry about the way things . . .' He faltered to a stop.

The expression on Tom Jenner's face was not encouraging.

'You're the chap that ruined my Molly? My God!'

'As I said I'm terribly sorry . . .'

He was unprepared for the fist that caught him under the left side of his chin and knocked him off the bale of hay on to the muddy floor. It hurt like hell but Donald wasn't going to let Jenner know that. Afraid to stand up, Donald stared up at his assailant from the floor.

'You had that coming to you,' Tom cried hoarsely. 'That's for my girl – for taking advantage of a girl of seventeen. What sort of man are you?' He glared at Donald who was picking himself up and rubbing his chin. 'Would you want your daughter to marry a man like that?'

Surprised by the unexpected reaction and the pain in his jaw, Donald was silent, wondering whether he dared sit down again on the bale, but he decided he might still be within reach of Tom's right arm. He decided to stand just out of range. 'I'm sorry,' he stammered, scrambling upright again. 'I–I know it isn't . . . that is, I understand how you feel . . .'

The fist flew out again and caught him below the ribs and sent him sprawling backwards.

'And that was for putting me and Annie through all kinds of hell! And no, you *don't* know how I feel. How could you?' He pointed to the bale of hay. 'Sit down.' He rubbed his knuckles. 'I won't hit you again. And thank your lucky stars my heart wasn't in it or I'd have put you in the hospital! I'd have broken your bloody jaw if I'd been serious and a few ribs for good measure.'

Winded and trying to hide his fear, Donald sat. His grand, well-chosen phrases had all flown from his mind and he felt at a loss to know how to proceed. Probably he should take offence and storm out of their lives but on a bicycle it would look pathetic. He also ached all over and didn't think he'd make it as far as the bike.

Tom Jenner said, 'My answer is yes – you can marry her if she still wants you. Can't see what she sees in you, but there's no accounting for taste.'

'She says she wants to marry me.'

'More fool her, but that's her business. Look, Donald, I married Annie for the same reason – Molly was on the way. Annie is eight years younger than me. That's how I know how these things happen. Her parents never forgave me, they forbade her to marry me and when she did marry me, they refused to have anything to do with us. Never visited. Not once. Never wrote. Not even a Christmas card. They've never set eyes on their only grandchild – Molly. It caused deep unhappiness for Annie . . . So, I don't want that for our girl. I swore that I'd never behave like that, no matter how badly I feel about what's happened. I'll talk to Molly and if she wants you, that'll do. My wife will agree with me on this.'

Donald frowned. Aggrieved, he felt somehow cheated out of his big moment, robbed of his grand gesture. There had been no arguments for him to win and no final handshake. He said, 'There is something else. About my income. At the moment I'm between jobs . . .'

'You don't want a job, Donald. You'll have plenty to do at Frenchies. For a start you can do up the cottage. We'll give it to you as a wedding present, but it's in a state so don't get too excited. It needs a lot of work, but it's roomy enough. If you start tomorrow you can make part of it habitable by the time you're wed. And there's plenty of work on the farm. Hard work in all weathers – and in return you'll have eggs, veg, meat and so on but I shan't pay you more than a pittance because I can't, though you'll have no real overheads.'

'Oh, I see.' Overwhelmed by the idea of becoming a property owner, Donald could think of nothing to say except to stammer his thanks.

Tom Jenner went on. 'You'll have your own life and your

poor cousin will be well rid of you.' He grinned suddenly. 'Good news for all concerned, eh?' He stood up. 'Let's go and talk to the women. We'd best get you and Molly to the church as soon as possible.'

Trailing behind his future father-in-law, one hand on his aching jaw, Donald felt dazed by the speed of events. Had he done the right thing, he wondered. What were the snags? There must be some . . . He wondered how close the cottage was to the Jenners's home – would his in-laws be breathing down his neck? On the other hand he wouldn't have so far to go to work if the weather turned nasty. Mrs Jenner might be the interfering type, but at least she would be around to help Molly with the baby if there was a crisis of some kind. He'd never done much restoration work but how hard could it be to whitewash a ceiling, paint a door or stick up wallpaper?

Donald smiled as he thought of Molly's shining eyes and imagined them in bed together in their own home. He saw her busy at the stove, cooking him a well-earned dinner. He'd have to tell her that he didn't like bloaters or meat with gristle or . . . Could Molly cook? Probably she was learning a bit from Mrs Parks. He thought about the baby and decided he would make a swing. All children liked swings.

He laughed as he imagined Clare's face when he broke the news to her. Mr Jenner was right – she would be glad to see him go and, strangely enough, the idea didn't trouble him at all. All things considered, he thought he'd come out of it rather well.

Tom Jenner turned as they neared the kitchen door. 'Did I hurt you?'

'You did, rather.'

'Good. Now we'll call it quits.'

The unhappy doctor turned up at Merle Place at twenty minutes to midnight, having been delayed by his horse casting a shoe in the middle of nowhere, and the farrier having to be fetched from the nearest pub. He was in a foul mood because of the interruption to his drinking and charged them extra for the inconvenience.

Jimmie had dozed off by the time he arrived and Clare was able to talk to the doctor before he woke him. He then gave his patient a brief examination that confirmed their suspicions that it had been a heart attack. The doctor advised that they leave Jimmie to sleep on the sofa rather than move him to a bedroom in the middle of the night. The doctor gave him a sleeping draught to make sure he didn't become restless during the night and promised to call in again around ten the following day.

Clare was exhausted, but she lay in bed when the doctor had gone and reviewed the day with a sense of wonder. So much had happened in such a short space of time! Poor Jonty was dead and would soon be buried. Jimmie had had a heart attack. And Donald! She didn't know what to make of the twist in the tale of Molly's undoing – or had it been the making of her? At first Clare had refused to believe that Donald had behaved so badly or that Molly had been so unwise as to allow it to happen. Clare didn't know whether to be pleased or sorry for the girl.

Clare asked herself how *she* could have been so blind? Her own cousin and the housemaid! Donald had been Molly's mystery lover and she, Clare, had never had the slightest inkling. Too wrapped up in your own problems, she reminded herself regretfully. She hadn't had a chance to say much to her cousin after he broke the news about the wedding because he had rushed off to spend the rest of the evening at Frenchies Farm, but tomorrow she would congratulate the couple and let none of her doubts show.

Molly obviously loved him and he was prepared to marry her, for which everyone must be thankful, but she wondered how Donald would find life on the farm. She could only marvel at his courage. Up in the morning early, out in all weathers. It was going to be a great shock to his system. But perhaps that was what he needed – responsibilities and someone who adored him. It was a potent mix, she admitted, smiling up at the ceiling and crossing her fingers for him.

The other question was whether he could make Molly happy. Clare would have gone to the other side of the world to escape being married to Donald, but there was no accounting for taste and Molly obviously found him wildly attractive. Clare saw him as unreliable and a scrounger who delighted in tormenting the people he didn't like or of whom he didn't approve. It was hard to think of his good points although she knew he must have some. Was it possible that Molly could bring out the best in him? Clare sincerely hoped so but only time would tell.

The clock on the church tower struck two thirty. Wearily she tried to stop analysing all that had happened and prevent herself from worrying about what tomorrow might bring. She finally fell asleep at about three a.m.

The next day Jimmie, at his own request, would be moved to his own quarters (where he claimed his cat would be pleased to see him) and it was arranged that Jimmie's meals – a suitably light diet – would be taken to him at intervals. His condition appeared to be stable, for which Clare was deeply thankful.

She had hired two of the church's gravediggers to bury Jonty on a spare patch of ground behind the shrubs where no trees grew and Clare had ordered a small stone plaque with the horse's name on it. It didn't make her feel less guilty, but she told herself it would be a reminder in future that she should be less self-centred. It would be strange not to see the animal around and she would miss him.

She vaguely remembered him as a very young foal when her grandfather had first bought him, and had watched him grow up. She had ridden him from time to time during various visits and recalled he had been a willing and biddable horse. Jimmie would miss him, too, and they would have to find a replacement, but that could wait a while. The idea of another horse in Jonty's stall sat uncomfortably in her mind.

Donald arrived home in time for breakfast and Clare greeted him with a congratulatory kiss. She found herself wondering if the Jenners had allowed him to sleep with his bride-to-be, but as Molly was pregnant there was no reason now for the Jenners to keep them apart.

'You astonished us all,' she told him with a smile, indicating the pan of scrambled eggs. 'Help yourself before they go cold.'

He gave the food a distracted nod. 'We sat up talking until the early hours so they asked me to stay overnight. I thought you'd guess where I was.'

'I did. I hope you'll both be very happy. Molly's a very sweet girl.' She watched him help himself to his breakfast and poured him a cup of tea. 'The truth is, Donald, we're all astonished.'

He gave her a lopsided grin that made him look very young and uncharacteristically vulnerable. 'I astonished myself,' he said. 'It's all a bit sudden, but the fact is I know I'm doing the right thing. And Molly's father is a decent old stick. Very fair.'

'I thought you said Tom Jenner was mad?' She kept her face straight.

'Did I say that? I daresay I was confused. Molly was telling me he wanted to shoot whoever it was. He didn't know it was me, of course. It must be a relief for him – I mean, I'll be a more than decent son-in-law. Mrs Jenner's taken to me already. She calls me Don.' He grinned. 'She says we'll have very handsome children!'

Clare shook her head, dismissing her doubts. This was no time for carping or criticism. The main point was that Molly thought Donald was wonderful and maybe he would grow into her vision of him as the years went by. Her mother had always said that a good woman could be the making of a man. She said, 'You haven't taken much egg. Aren't you hungry?'

'Hungry? Er, not really. Too much on my mind.'

'Keep your strength up!' she said. 'Lots of work to be done. Plenty to think about. A wedding, a house, a wife and baby! It's exciting, isn't it?' She spoke lightly, gently teasing him, but as she spoke she realized that, in fact, it *was* exciting. Something to look forward to. She began to think how she could be involved. Her cousin was going to live nearby so she would see the child grow up – if she stayed at Merle Place, of course. If she was fortunate enough to sell the house, she might be miles away and in a way that would be a pity.

In-between mouthfuls of toast and marmalade, Donald

told her about the cottage. 'It will cost a few pounds,' he said, 'so I've decided to tackle the bank manager. See if I can get a loan. Molly and I went round the cottage with her father last night and it's not bad at all. Doesn't smell damp like some places when they've been empty for years. He didn't rent it out because he wanted it for Molly when she got married. Some paint, a few rolls of wallpaper. Molly's got expensive tastes! Wants wallpaper with roses on it!' He laughed.

'She must be very happy.'

'She is. Talking about a bedroom for the baby. We both want a boy, but her mother says twins run in the family. Can you imagine that?' He rolled his eyes in mock despair.

Clare said, 'I suppose Molly won't want to work here any more. I'll have to—'

'Oh, but she does want to. At least she wants to carry on so she can save a bit of money. Just until the baby's born, of course. Then she'll have too much to do.'

For a moment, Clare could only nod. Once she had visualized a home and family of her own but that had been denied her.

Donald said, 'Would that be all right with you? I thought maybe she could come in an hour later when she's over the worst of the sickness and leave an hour later in the afternoon.'

'That will be fine with me.'

Clare explained her plan for the little headstone for Jonty, but she had the impression that Donald had already lost interest in the affairs of Merle Place. As he chattered on about his coming marriage, Clare considered his predicament. Would any bank lend him money? He would have such a small income it seemed unlikely, but without it, he would be hard-pressed to make the cottage habitable.

Impulsively she said, 'Donald, don't bother with the bank. I'd like to give you some money as a wedding present.' She plucked a sum out of the air. 'Fifty pounds – to spend on the repairs to the cottage. If I manage to sell Merle Place – and it's a big if – I'll give you another fifty immediately.

And of course you will get something extra when I sell Merle Place.'

He stared at her. 'Clare! That's so generous. Thank you.' A broad grin spread across his face and, leaning across the table, he took hold of her hand and kissed it. 'Gosh! A hundred pounds! That's . . . that's really wonderful. You can't imagine what a difference . . .' His eyes rolled joyfully. 'Wait until I tell Molly! She'll be thrilled.'

He looked like the cat that got the cream, she thought. She was touched by the kiss. This was a new Donald. Perhaps Molly's magic was already working on him.

'Will you show me round the cottage?' she asked. 'I'd love to see it before you . . . Oh! Excuse me.' She broke off as the telephone rang and jumped up to answer it.

It was Mr Yates.

'Good morning, Mr Yates.'

'You'll be pleased to know that the Souters have decided they might be willing to buy – a step in the right direction – but say they must come and view the property before they can go any further. They want to come down this afternoon. It's very—'

'This afternoon? Good heavens! They don't—'

'Give much notice?' he agreed. 'No, they don't, but they apologize and say they have to visit someone in the family – they describe it as a small disaster! – and could come here afterwards as they wouldn't have to come far out of their way.'

'Would you be here with them?'

'I'm afraid that's not possible. But I'm sure you can deal with it. Simply tell them that all financial matters have to come through me. Don't be tempted to do deals on the price. That's my job. If they want to proceed in any way, they must reach me by telephone or come into the office.'

'I understand.' Clare paused. Did she feel up to this? She wasn't altogether happy, but was rather curious to meet two psychics. Perhaps she could pick their brains. If she mentioned her new novel maybe they would be keen to help with researching the book. Perhaps she could ask about their previous books and buy one or two if they appeared

to be suitable. Maybe they were hoping that Merle Place
was haunted. A ghost would really intrigue them.

'Miss Wishart? Are you still there?'

'Oh! I'm sorry. I was distracted for a moment. Yes, send
the Souters over this afternoon. I'll do my best to inspire
them.'

She returned to the dining room, but Donald had already
disappeared so she couldn't tell him about the prospective
buyers' visit. Probably in the kitchen with Molly, she
thought, and poured herself another cup of tea. 'What's
next?' she wondered aloud, trying to plan the day ahead.
'Ah, yes, Jimmie.'

Jimmie was to be moved back to the stables so she would
have to catch Donald before he dashed off on whatever
errand he had planned.

Forty minutes later they had, not without some difficulty,
transferred their patient to his own lodgings and he was
obviously relieved to be back in his familiar room. The cat
rushed to greet him and he smiled weakly.

Donald said, 'You'll be in good hands. My cousin was
a nurse, you know.'

Clare said, 'A ward maid, not a real nurse, but I'll do
my best.'

Jimmie smiled up at her. 'I have great faith in you, Miss
Wishart.'

Donald hovered, anxious to be off.

Clare said, 'I can manage now, thank you, Donald. I'll
pop along later to the farm, if I may, to see the cottage.'
To Jimmie she said, 'It's great news, isn't it, Jimmie, about
the wedding? We shall soon be rid of him!'

Donald threw a playful punch in her direction.

Jimmie said, 'Am I invited?'

Donald said, 'Only if you recover in time. We're going
to see the vicar in a day or two to arrange the date.'

'The sooner the better, eh?'

Clare wondered if it was a thinly disguised barb about
the coming child. If so, Donald either missed it or couldn't
trouble himself to acknowledge it. Clare was relieved when
he took his leave and left her with Jimmie.

'Is there anything you want?' she asked him. 'There's no way you can communicate with us, but we'll pop down from time to time. The doctor isn't coming again until this evening. His wife rang to say there's been an accident at the crossroads.'

'I'll be fine in a day or two,' Jimmie insisted. 'It was a bit of a flutter, nothing more. I feel so damned useless, pardon my French! I need to be up and about.'

'Not until the doctor says so.' She smiled. 'Rest, Jimmie. The more you rest, the quicker you *will* be up and about.'

Walking back to the house, she was aware of a frisson of alarm. She knew that his recovery could take a long time. She would give it a week and then, if necessary, she would ask one of the boys in the village if he wanted to earn a bit of extra money doing some gardening. That would put Jimmie's mind at rest. And they would have to look for another horse to pull the mower. Never a dull moment, she thought. When was she going to start her writing? If Mr Flint rang she would have to pretend she was already immersed in her research and making pages of notes. She hated to lie after he had been so good to her, but she didn't think he would properly appreciate the number of demands she currently had on her time.

The Souters were a very ordinary couple and Clare felt vaguely disappointed. She didn't know exactly what she had expected though. Probably tall, thin people with haunted eyes, maybe with wary expressions and hushed voices. Almost certainly eccentric.

They arrived at ten to three in a small Ford motor. James Souter was thin but shorter than average, with round spectacles and a mild manner. When he removed his hat he revealed a balding head and Clare guessed his age at around fifty. Geraldine, his wife, was taller, heavier, with fluffy ginger hair and plenty of freckles – a cheerful soul.

'I'm so pleased you could see us at such short notice,' she told Clare. 'We've seen so many properties and Merle Place is the latest on our list.'

Both Souters stepped back and retreated to the other side

of the motor car in order to gaze up at the frontage of the house.

James Souter said, 'Maybe we should see round the outside while the sun is still shining.'

His wife laughed. 'James swears by his seaweed! He brought it back from a weekend in Southend years ago. Today it has apparently forecast rain.'

Her husband shrugged good-naturedly. 'You must tell Miss Wishart how often it is accurate!'

'More than I'd expect,' she admitted.

They began the tour of the grounds. The decrepit green-house, it seemed, would have to be replaced if the Souters bought Merle Place.

'Maybe a summer house would look nice there instead,' Clare suggested.

'Oh, yes! The students would love that.' Geraldine stopped, obviously trying to visualize it, while her husband moved on.

The stables also would be removed if they bought the property. 'Because no one would ride,' she told Clare, 'and we would hire in a firm of gardeners to keep the lawn in trim.'

They caught up with Mr Souter.

'I see you own a car. Have you been driving long?' Clare asked.

'About a year,' he answered. 'I fear the days of horse transport are numbered. Very sad but life moves on, as they say.'

Geraldine said, 'I certainly prefer the motor to the trains.'

Inside the house, the couple's opinion appeared to be reasonably positive.

'Plenty of bedrooms for the students,' said Geraldine, 'while James and I would have our own private flat above them in the attic rooms and the ground-floor rooms would be for meetings, the kitchen, dining room, group work sessions and so on.'

'It would be ideal,' her husband agreed thoughtfully.

'Ideal apart from the price,' his wife suggested.

Clare realized they were hinting, but remembering

Mr Yates's warning she told them she was not prepared to discuss terms as that would be best dealt with by the estate agent.

Undeterred, James Souter asked, 'But would you reconsider our initial request to rent for the first year? Your agent was very firmly against that idea, but I feel sure we might come to an agreement.'

Clare thought rapidly. 'I don't think so. I can't understand how it would help you because even in the first year you would need to make changes to the place which I may not approve or allow. It would cost a lot of money if I did agree to changes, but you would lose the investment if you did not go ahead with the purchase.'

They were both silent, regarding each other unhappily. What was the real problem, Clare wondered. Shortage of money or the suspicion that they would not succeed with the project as a whole.

James Souter cleared his throat. 'The problem is most of our capital is tied up in India where we have lived for fifteen years. It will take time to get it all out – there are various restrictions on the movement of capital sums. We wanted to go ahead with our plans right away.'

Clare nodded. 'I can see that is difficult for you, but when I sell I shall need to buy another home for myself and rent coming in would not be satisfactory from my point of view.'

They moved on a little gloomily and eventually sat down for refreshments. Clare at once brought up the subject of haunted houses and explained about her novel. They were immediately cheered by the chance to forget the difficulties and discuss a subject which interested them.

'It would be wonderful if Merle Place were haunted!' cried Geraldine, her eyes gleaming. 'I don't suppose you have a resident ghost, do you?'

Clare shook her head.

'But it must be possible,' Geraldine insisted. 'Possibly no one has ever seen a ghost, but that doesn't mean there isn't one. Apart from your family members who lived and died here, there must have been military personnel during the war who did not recover from their medical treatments.'

She leaned forward. 'You see, with respect, you may not be a perceptive person, Miss Wishart. There may be ghosts of which you are unaware. If my husband or I were to spend a night here we might very well be reached by someone from the other side! We would understand the various manifestations – such as a sudden and distinct lowering of the temperature. That is often a first sign of paranormal activity.'

'Or a strange odour. Or certain sounds.' Her husband's face lit up. 'We could hold a seance for you. Now if it were a poltergeist . . . We visited one house, I recall, in mid-Sussex, where furniture was seen to move about without visible means of propulsion. It slid along the floor and—'

'Stop, James!' Geraldine interrupted him. 'We mustn't frighten poor Miss Wishart.' She turned to Clare. 'You must please forgive us. We take these things for granted, but others with less understanding sometimes feel unnerved at the prospect.'

Clare was not about to deny that she was one of these people. She was already worrying about being in the house alone after Donald moved out and was pleased at the woman's awareness of her nervousness. 'I don't think I should care for it,' she confessed with an attempt at a light laugh. 'Perhaps I could buy one of your books instead and simply read about it.'

'That would be a good idea. You could then avoid making any mistakes in your novel. Time spent on research is never wasted.'

Later, Clare saw them leave Merle Place without regret. They were nice enough, but they would not be ideal purchasers. Mr Yates would never approve their request and neither would her bank manager. And if there *were* ghosts at Merle Place, Clare preferred that they should rest in peace.

Ten

It was the following day before Clare managed to make a visit to the cottage which Donald and Molly had been given to live in once they were married. It stood on the outer edges of the farm that Tom Jenner owned and was a small building with a slate roof underhung with tiles. A small garden enclosed it that was itself surrounded by a picket fence in need of repair.

'The fence can wait,' Donald told her. 'I want to concentrate on the inside. Molly is determined to have a little room for the baby so we have to make good a kitchen, bedroom and nursery. Once they are habitable we can move in. Not bad, is it?'

Clare said, 'Not bad at all.' The neglected garden was no worse than could be expected. An apple tree sprawled in one corner, there were a few foxgloves, a brick path which could be greatly improved by weeding, a sagging clothes line and a tangle of brambles mixed with wild roses. 'It faces south. That's good,' she said.

Donald produced a key and, with a self-conscious flourish, let them into the cottage. It smelled dry and dusty but not damp. The door led straight into the front room, which had a broken window, a small fireplace, and faded wallpaper of an indistinct pattern.

Donald said, 'Soon we'll smarten it up with a lick of paint and some wallpaper, but that can wait. There's no electricity, of course, but we'll manage with oil lamps.'

'You can make it very cosy,' Clare agreed, 'and it has a pretty view over the garden and beyond.'

The kitchen needed more attention. The big sink was cracked and discoloured, the built-in dresser had lost its shelves and the rusting range was extremely old-fashioned. Clare couldn't imagine Molly cooking anything on it. The floor was just well-trodden earth covered in part by a large decaying jute mat.

Donald said quickly, 'We shall have a brick floor – or maybe quarry tiles. With the money you're giving us we can afford a little luxury.'

Clare watched him as he poked around in the walk-in larder and a sudden lump came to her throat. How was it that she had never seen the good side of him before? Why had she taken him at face value for so many years? She felt ashamed of all the wasted years when they might have been good friends and was glad she was able to help him now. A hundred pounds would go a long way towards making a cheerful, comfortable home for the young couple.

'It's going to be a very attractive property, Donald,' she told him. 'I'm sure Molly's going to love it here. A very nice place for the baby to grow up in.'

He positively beamed. 'And with his grandparents so near. Ma Jenner is counting the days.'

The stairs were in good condition and they made their way up to the bedroom. Here the floor sloped a little, but he explained how that could easily be remedied by putting small wedges under the legs of the furniture where necessary. Tattered curtains framed the small window, but the catch still operated and when the window was opened the room was filled with the sound of the farmyard: the rattle of a wheel-barrow, grunts from the pigs and a contented clucking from the hens.

'And this will be the baby's room!'

It was hardly larger than a broom cupboard, thought Clare, but she was envious nonetheless. She imagined the baby's cot and a small chest of drawers full of baby clothes. *If I could change places with Molly, would I do it? Could I be a farmer's wife? Why ever not if it meant I could have a family of my own? Would I give up Merle Place or my chances of a literary career? Yes, I think I would . . .*

Forcing back unhappy thoughts of her own lost chances, she stared down into the back garden where the privy stood in splendid isolation, its door hanging on by one hinge, the wooden roof shingles warped by years of harsh winter weather.

Following her gaze, Donald said, 'Molly's pa is going to make it bigger so there's room to hang up the tin bath and a few tools and things. Oh! And a new bucket and a new wooden seat.'

'Molly must be so happy!'

'She is. And her ma is teaching her how to cook a few good meals although at the weekend we might eat with them. Her ma claims that it's cheaper to cook a meal for a family of four than two families of two! Makes sense to me and it will take the heat off Molly while she gets used to managing the baby.'

Donald told her the wedding had been fixed for the twelfth of June and Molly was borrowing a dress from a girlfriend who had married a year ago.

'She'll tell you all about it,' he promised. 'Cream lace or something like that. And her grandmother's giving her a prayer book to carry down the aisle.' He gave Clare a lopsided grin. 'It's all a bit of a daze, to tell you the truth, this wedding thing. Takes a bit of adjusting to.'

'I expect it always is.' Clare's tone was unconsciously wistful.

Donald put an arm round her in a brief and uncharacteristic hug. 'It's never too late, Clare.'

Clare wondered at his words. For a long time she had given up all thoughts of marriage and had resigned herself to a solitary future. Now, seeing Donald's shining eyes, she felt the first stirrings of hope. Maybe he was right. Maybe it was not too late. Donald Wishart was living proof that sometimes miracles did happen.

Steven Flint stood at the window of his London office, staring down into the small area of park that was one of the capital's greener areas. His hands were thrust into his pockets and he was whistling tunelessly. Miss Birch, his secretary, recognized that, despite his casual manner, he was thinking deeply.

He had recently returned from a prolonged lunch with

an agent. A regular meeting that took place on the last Monday of each month. The agent frequently introduced promising new writers to him, so Miss Birch assumed that something of interest had been discussed during lunch.

Smiling, she said, 'When will I get to hear about this latest discovery, Mr Flint?'

'Mm?' He turned distractedly. 'What was that?'

'I'm enquiring about this new writer you've been discussing. I take it that's what is absorbing your thoughts.' Carefully she withdrew her latest letter from the typewriter and separated it from the carbon sheets.

'Then you'd be wrong,' he told her, abandoning the window and moving to stand beside her desk. 'I was actually thinking about Miss Wishart and wondering whether or not she is making any useful progress. She seems to have rather a lot on her mind, poor soul.' He shrugged. 'Always difficult to persuade a new writer to buckle down. Hard to convince them it's a job, not a hobby.'

'I thought the lunch was about the new man, David Something-or-other, that writes horror.'

'David Galloway. Yes, it was.' He picked up a paper clip and began to twist it out of shape. 'Harold thinks we should take him on, but horror's not something we do – not a genre I'm keen on. But according to Harold he's got potential and there's a growing market in Europe for the stuff. I said I'd think about it.'

'Did you have a nice lunch?'

'Nice enough . . .' He tossed the ruined clip into the saucer of her teacup and she flinched. 'I'm thinking I should go down again to see Miss Wishart. I want to give her a deadline for November, but I don't want to scare her. If she's not pressing on I could make it next March and slot her in for publication at the end of the summer – maybe October.' He returned to his place by the window and his hands slid back into his pockets.

He turned back to her. 'Do you know anyone who reads horror stories?'

'I don't think I do.'

'That was my point exactly.' He sighed. 'I shall have to

take a look at it, I suppose, since he insisted on giving me a copy of the manuscript.'

'It sounds as though I won't be meeting Mr Galloway!'

'Possibly not.' He pushed up the lower half of the window and leaned out.

Watching him from the corner of her eye, Miss Birch allowed herself a small smile. He had been restless ever since he returned from the visit to Merle Place and she suspected that he had taken a shine to the woman and wanted an excuse to see her again.

And about time too. You can't stay free as a bird forever, Mr Flint. If you get much older you might never take the plunge and what a waste that would be.

If she did not already have an admirer of her own, Miss Birch would have been interested in Steven Flint herself, but her own gentleman friend had recently proposed and she was thus otherwise engaged.

She fed more paper and carbons into the machine and adjusted the roller. 'Why not pop down to Kent and call in on her? Pretend you are in the neighbourhood and wanted to see if she was coping or needed some encouragement.' She kept her tone impersonal.

Steven brought his head in from the window so quickly that he banged it on the frame and cursed mildly. 'Pop down again?' He pretended to think about it.

'Better to be on the safe side, Mr Flint. The poor soul might be floundering.' She gave him a quick smile and turned to the next page of her shorthand notes.

He said, 'D'you know, I think you're right, Miss Birch? I shouldn't neglect her. I might even go tomorrow.'

'I could telephone her on your behalf and ask if she'd be at home.'

'Thank you. Splendid plan. I'll have a word with Harold to check he'll be in. Can't leave poor old Austin to steer the ship alone.'

Five minutes later Harold had confirmed that he would be in the office the next day and so would Austin so Miss Birch reached for the telephone.

* * *

While Steven Flint was talking to his secretary, Clare was having a disconcerting conversation with the doctor. It was not at all reassuring. He suggested bringing in a heart specialist to check Jimmie's condition.

'It won't be cheap but it may be necessary. Your gardener may have had a fault in his heart since he was a child,' he explained. 'He remembers having measles very badly and the fact that his mother worried about whether or not it would affect his eyesight. She obviously didn't understand that it could also affect his heart.'

'But he's always seemed so strong,' Clare protested. 'I always saw him as indestructible.' She sighed. 'Maybe gardening wasn't the best job for him.'

'Who can tell? Everything seems clear with hindsight, Miss Wishart. We can all be wise after the event.' He began to close up his bag. 'I'll telephone and let you know if and when the specialist will see him. Try not to worry. Your Jimmie is a fighter. If will power helps, he's got a strong chance of recovery – providing he doesn't have another attack. It is possible at any time. I would have preferred him to be in the big house so that he could alert you in an emergency.'

Clare followed him outside and watched him clamber into his pony trap. 'He refused point-blank, doctor, to stay in the house with us and when he became agitated we thought it best to give in.'

'Fingers crossed, then, Miss Wishart.' With a brief smile he urged his horse forward and with a wave disappeared along the drive.

Worried, Clare went into the kitchen and passed on the doctor's comments to Mrs Parks.

'Well, Jimmie's a grown man,' she replied. 'He made up his mind and we just went along with his wishes. He has to take the blame if anything goes wrong.'

'Oh! Don't talk like that, please. We have to take care of him.'

Mrs Parks took a warmed dish from the back of the stove and set it on the table. 'This soup has turned out very well,' she said with a nod of satisfaction. 'I puréed the potato and leeks and added a little milk. I could grate a little cheese on top. What do you think?'

'A good idea. I'll take it down to him.'

Mrs Parks added the cheese and placed a plate of thin brown bread and butter on to the tray. 'There we go,' she said, pleased with her efforts. 'Tell him I said he did well to eat most of his breakfast. He must keep up his strength and my mother always made us coddled eggs when we were poorly.'

Clare covered the tray with a cloth and carried Jimmie's lunch carefully through the garden and up the steps to his room.

He was already propped up, by doctor's orders, but accepted the tray with less enthusiasm than Clare had hoped. The cat sat nearby and it crossed her mind that if Jimmie wasn't hungry he might be feeding the cat as well as himself. Clare passed on Mrs Parks's message and pulled up a chair, determined to see that he ate it all.

She mentioned the heart specialist and Jimmie groaned.

'A lot of fuss about nothing!' he said. 'Waste of money these so-called specialists. I'll be up and about in no time.' He waited, the spoon poised. 'There's no need for you to stay,' he said. 'I'm sure you're busy. Better things to do than—'

'I'm staying to see that you eat it all,' she told him. 'So please make a start. A light vegetable soup with a sprinkling of cheese. Very easy to digest, Jimmie, and Mrs Parks is trying very hard to look after you. She's very knowledgeable about invalid food.'

He began to spoon up the soup and nibble at the bread and butter, but Clare could see that he had no appetite.

She said, 'Should I notify any of your friends or family that you are ill?'

'I'm not ill! A mild heart attack is nothing. Happens all the time.'

'Jimmie, please! I want you to see the specialist. I don't . . . I don't want anything bad to happen to you.'

'But they charge the earth and do no good!'

'I don't care what they charge. I want him to examine you and to tell me you're going to get fit again.'

'They're all quacks!'

'They're *not.*' She forced a smile. 'Anyway, you have no say in the matter. I've decided. You're in my power now!'

He stared at her for a moment. 'Miss Wishart, there was something I wanted to ask you, but it must wait until I'm better. You know how much I think of you. You mean more to me than anyone in the world and—'

'Jimmie! Don't – I mean, this is not the time . . .' She felt her face burn with embarrassment. She knew intuitively what he was going to say and was afraid to let him continue. His devotion touched her. It always had. But if he was about to propose she would have to turn him down and that, in his present weak state, could not be helpful.

'I just wanted you to know,' he began, 'if I should die and you didn't know . . . didn't know how much you meant to me . . .'

The forgotten tray leaned precariously and she reached out to steady it. 'I think I've always known,' she told him, 'but I've never wanted to find another man. Simon was . . .' Agitated, she stood up. 'This is not the time,' she repeated helplessly. 'I know you are fond of me and I appreciate your wonderful loyalty.'

The cat crept closer to the tray and with great daring began to lick the butter from the bread. She leaned down and picked the cat up and put it on the floor.

Ignoring her actions, he said hoarsely, 'So are *you* fond of *me*?'

What could she say? Instinctively she shied away from hurting him. 'Of course I am, Jimmie, but . . .' She hesitated. She mustn't destroy his hope and yet she didn't want to lie. 'I need time. I'm not sure about anything really. Maybe some day . . .'

He smiled, apparently delighted with her half-hearted answer. 'Thank you.' His face lit up. 'Thank you, Miss Wishart. You've given me hope.'

I have to escape from this conversation, Clare told herself, as panic crept in. She had gone too far. She had been too weak. She should have told him the truth.

He glanced up as he resumed his meal. 'I shall eat all

this,' he said with a smile. 'Thank Mrs Parks. Tell her I'm feeling better already!'

He took the triangle of bread and butter that the cat had licked and removed it from his plate. He folded it in half and put it on his bedside table. 'The cat can have it later,' he told her.

She said, 'Doesn't it have a name?'

'Doesn't need one. He knows he's my cat.' Jimmie grinned.

Go, thought Clare. Go while he's happy. 'I'll leave you to it then, Jimmie. I'll collect the tray later. You rest.'

Turning, she hurried away. As she walked back through the garden, she muttered angrily to herself. 'Idiot, you've given him false hope. Oh Lord! You bungled that.'

She had confessed to feelings for him that she did not have and at some point he was doomed to disappointment. Not that she didn't like and respect him – Jimmie was a decent man and should have been married long since – but she didn't love him as he needed to be loved and that was what she should have told him. But what else could she have done in such difficult circumstances? With a weary shake of her head, she admitted that she had no idea how to deal with the situation. Saying no was much harder than she had ever imagined.

The phone call from Miss Birch a few moments later was short and to the point. 'Mr Flint wonders if he could pop in on you tomorrow morning as he will be in the area. He has an appointment in the afternoon, but could spare an hour before lunch.'

Clare's first reaction was entirely pleasurable. She was going to see him again, recalling the excitement she had felt on their first meeting. Almost immediately, however, doubts crept in and she frowned.

'Tomorrow? But why? That is, it's only a few weeks since we met and nothing much has changed.'

'It's just a friendly call, Miss Wishart. Nothing to worry about. Most of our authors would welcome a personal visit from their editor.'

A personal visit from the editor! Something must be wrong. And she thought she had detected a steely note in the secretary's tone.

'I'm not saying . . .' Clare wondered what she *was* saying. Did she want Steven Flint to call in or didn't she? She could say no, couldn't she? He could hardly insist on coming . . . But did she really want to put him off? Perhaps she could delay the evil hour by saying it was such short notice. 'I am rather at sixes and sevens,' she stammered. 'It's really not the ideal time. Perhaps . . .'

'He is looking forward to seeing you, Miss Wishart. He'll be very disappointed if he misses this chance. Most weeks he is tied to London. I do advise you to try and see him. A good editor like Mr Flint can be a great help if you have any problems. Early difficulties can be sorted out before they develop.'

Early difficulties! She was very persistent, thought Clare. Miss Birch seemed to be saying that if she missed this 'chance' she might not get another when she needed it. So what on earth was Steven Flint worried about? Had he had second thoughts? Suddenly the effort of refusing seemed too great. 'Well, then I will see him and I'll give him some lunch. But please ask him not to arrive before ten o'clock. I have someone under doctor's orders.'

'Ten thirty, then. And thank you so much.'

The phone call upset Clare and she began to panic in earnest. In the midst of her other concerns, her editor was coming down to check up on her and she had made next to no progress. This was pressure that she had never expected and had never experienced before. Her serials for *The Ladies Own Journal* had been written when she felt the inclination and not before, and no one had been breathing down her neck, demanding to learn of her progress. Edina had expected and received her chapter on a regular basis and it was understood that Clare would present her with suitable material. Now she had an entire novel to write and Steven Flint, whom she had initially liked very much as a man, was proving to be a rather demanding editor. For the first time Clare wondered if promising a novel had been a mistake.

*   *   *

Closeted in the study for two and a half hours that afternoon Clare struggled to produce a credible synopsis, and the more she pored over it, the more she became convinced that it was quite beyond her. She snapped at Mrs Parks when the housekeeper interrupted her to bring in a cup of tea and some cakes warm from the oven and received a well-deserved glare in return. At five to five she ripped the paper from the typewriter, crumpled the pages and tossed them into the waste paper basket beside the desk.

Rushing from the study, she hurried downstairs and snatched up the telephone. Dialling the London number with a trembling finger, she waited for Steven Flint to answer.

'Miss Birch – Steven Flint's office. Can I help you?'

'Oh! Miss Birch! I have to speak with Mr Flint. It's urgent!' Even to her own ears, she sounded hysterical.

'I'm afraid he went home early today. He has a manuscript to read so he . . .'

'But this is very important.'

'If you would like to leave a message . . .' There was a pause. 'Who is this?'

'Clare Wishart. I have to speak with him. I've . . . I'm afraid I have changed my mind . . . about the novel. I can't do it. It won't come together.' Her voice was rising. Soon, she thought, she would be in tears. Whatever would the secretary think of her? She would tell Steven Flint and they would laugh at her.

'But Mr Flint will be able to help you. That's the whole point of his visit. It's not unusual for him to guide new authors. He always says—'

'Does he have a telephone at his home?'

'I'm afraid we don't pass on personal numbers, Miss Wishart. Please believe me that you will find Mr Flint very helpful and patient. You really have nothing to worry about.'

'But I do! I have a lot to worry about. I have a gardener who is ill with a heart attack and a large house I can't afford but can't sell . . . If you would explain to Mr Flint I'm sure he would understand.'

'But I can't disturb him at home, Miss Wishart. It's one

of his rules. He hates to be interrupted when he's reading a manuscript.' Clare heard someone speaking to Miss Birch and then she came back on the line. 'I have to go. It will be fine, I can assure you. Don't worry.'

The line went dead. 'Damn!' Clare almost never swore, but Miss Birch had tested her patience to breaking point. Hanging up the phone, Clare turned to find Mrs Parks waiting and wondered how much she had overheard. Too much, probably.

The housekeeper said, 'I could make Jimmie a light sandwich – minced chicken, perhaps. Or do you have any other ideas?'

'No. None.' She was horribly flustered. 'Minced chicken sounds light yet nourishing. Would you mind taking it down to him, please? Just before you go home.'

She realized that she had not told Mrs Parks about the need for the heart specialist and decided to keep that news until tomorrow. All she wanted to do now was get back to her writing. Despite her best endeavours, Steven Flint *was* coming tomorrow morning and she must have a synopsis of some sort ready to discuss if her request to be allowed to abandon the novel was not going to be accepted. To date, she had not signed anything but she had agreed verbally to write the book and the editor may have slotted her book into the coming year's list of publications, in which case cancelling would make it awkward for him.

Clare had found Steven so agreeable that she had no wish to create problems. In fact she had found him more than agreeable – he had been kind and funny and his enthusiasm had been infectious. She had enjoyed their meeting more than she would admit to herself – Steven Flint was very good company.

So why am I being so stupid? I really did like him. He made me feel appreciated and light-hearted and I want to see him again but not about the novel. Just as a friend – but that's not going to be possible. He comes as part of a package! Would that offend him? Being regarded as part of a package was hardly a compliment. To him I'm just another author on the Bell and May list. For me he's just my editor.

She sighed. Tomorrow he would be here and they would spend a few hours together. She would make a big effort with her novel today and would try to think of an idea – or a rough synopsis. Miss Birch had hinted that he was making a special effort on her behalf. She wondered whether he liked her as a person or whether he was just worried about her ability.

Her mind was in such a whirl as she went up the stairs that when she tried to remember what she and Mrs Parks had decided on for tomorrow's lunch her memory failed her. 'Pull yourself together, Clare!' she whispered fiercely. 'One way or another you have to impress him, so stop worrying and get on with it!'

Mrs Parks returned from the stables next morning after delivering Jimmie's breakfast tray. There was a light rain falling and she had been forced to cover the food with two clean cloths in an attempt to keep the smoked haddock warm.

Clearing away the table in the dining room, Mrs Parks gave Clare an odd glance.

'What is it?' Clare asked. 'Why are you looking at me like that? Donald was very late back last night so is probably going to miss breakfast. Serves him right if he doesn't get up in time.'

'It's not him, ma'am, it's you!'

'Me?'

'Well, I got a very strange story from Jimmie – about you and him. Mind you, he still looks dreadfully pale but in himself he seems much brighter. He's even talking about getting up.' She stacked the tray with expert hands and weighed the teapot as she lifted it. 'There's another cup in here if you want it.'

Clare shook her head. 'He can't get up,' she protested, 'At least, not until the specialist has seen him. Why, what has Jimmie been saying?' She braced herself for bad news.

'Funny sort of hints. About you not being alone for much longer. About him looking after you, Miss Wishart. Things like that.' She shrugged. 'Seemed to be saying that you and him . . .'

'Oh Lord! It won't ever be a case of me and him, but however gently I put it, he twists my answers to fit what he hopes for. He's not at all well and I was trying not to upset him. The doctor said to keep him calm, but it's not easy to refuse a man who's ill.'

'I can imagine. But poor old Jimmie. If you'll pardon me saying so, he's always had secret hopes about the two of you. Not that he's ever spelled it out to me – he wouldn't do that, ma'am – but you know how you can sense these things. I guessed ages ago that he was a bit soft on you!'

'That's probably why he wants to get up and about – to prove that he's a fit man. But he isn't fit. He's had a heart attack and the doctor thinks he may have had a weak heart for years. Undetected. He's arranging for a specialist to examine him. Getting up is the last thing he should be doing.' She regarded the housekeeper helplessly. 'I honestly don't know what to do for the best, Mrs Parks. Break his heart or keep up the pretence – not that I was pretending exactly, but I couldn't say an outright no.'

If she was hoping for some useful advice it was not forthcoming. Mrs Parks swept the crumbs from the tablecloth into the little pan and picked up the tray. 'Rather you than me,' she said firmly. 'I should have said no to my young man when he proposed but I didn't. Just couldn't wait to be wed – to anyone! He turned out to be a lazy wretch, but what can you do? He'll never change.' Halfway out of the door she paused. 'Not that Jimmie would be like that. I didn't mean that about Jimmie.'

'I don't know why he didn't marry when he was younger.'

'Oh, but he did. Married and had a little boy but two years later she left him. Ran off with a man twice her age and took the kiddie with her. He never mentions either her or the boy. I heard some gossip about it from someone else.' The tray wobbled and she steadied it. 'Not that I let him know that I know. He obviously wants to put it all behind him.

Startled, Clare was staring at her. 'So, he's married! How can he talk to me about a future if—?'

'Not any more. She's dead. The boy was brought up by his grandparents. On her side.'

'How did she die – his wife I mean?' Clare was trying to readjust to this new Jimmie – a man with a past she had never suspected.

'Childbirth after the second child – she'd found herself another man. There were some complications or other. You know how it is. One said it was the birth itself, but the others reckoned it was the fever that followed. Childbed fever. One of our neighbours went that way.' Shaking her head, she carried the tray out of the room.

Complications of childbirth? No, Clare didn't know about the complications of childbirth. She knew nothing about that side of marriage. And she hadn't known that Jimmie knew. All this time, sympathizing with her on occasions over Simon's death, he had never said a word about his own sad past.

'Poor Jimmie!' she said softly. If only she could make it up to him by falling in love with him, but so far she felt nothing but firm friendship.

She was still sitting there when the housekeeper returned to remove the tablecloth.

She said, 'Don't forget you've got that London chappie coming at ten thirty – whatever his name is.'

'Oh! Mr Flint!' Clare leapt to her feet with undignified haste. 'What am I thinking of? Thank you, Mrs Parks.' She hurried upstairs and into her bedroom. She had stayed up late into the night and had done all she could to the synopsis, but now she must decide exactly what to wear for her meeting with Steven Flint – a meeting that might well be the last one they would have.

Eleven

Steven Flint arrived promptly and, seeing him from the window, Clare was on the steps to meet him as he stepped from his motor. Clare smiled but her hands were clasped tightly and her heart thumped with anxiety.

To her surprise he hurried forward and took both of her hands in his. He looked agitated, less composed than previously, and she supposed he was dreading the meeting as much as she was.

'Miss Wishart, I owe you an apology,' he stammered.

At the same time Clare said, 'I'm truly sorry, Mr Flint. Your secretary must have told you that . . .'

He released her hands. 'You must forgive me! Please. It was crass of me. Springing it on you that way. I spoke to Miss Birch before leaving London and she told me you were worrying about your work.'

'I have so many problems at the moment – I realize now that I may not be able to meet the commitment . . .'

He laid a gentle finger against her lips. 'Please,' he repeated. 'This is my fault.'

He removed his finger and Clare was surprised to find that the small personal touch had thrilled her. It seemed an age since any man had touched her and she had reconciled herself to the loss of a kiss or a hug or even a walk hand in hand.

He went on earnestly. 'The truth is I wanted to see you again. That's all it was. There is no problem with you or the speed with which you write or what you write. None at all. I admire your work, Miss Wishart, and I'm a stupid, insensitive beast.'

'Oh, no! Not at all.' She struggled to keep her voice

steady. 'I have tried again with the synopsis, but I dare say you won't like it.'

'Miss Wishart, you're not listening to me,' he said gently. 'Forget about the manuscript. I suddenly wanted to see you again. Just like that. I enjoyed meeting you. We had such a wonderful time – at least, I did and I thought perhaps you did. I hated to think we might not meet up again for weeks or even months. Miss Birch suggested I call in on you again.'

'She did? Well, it makes sense since you are in the area.'

'Ah!' He stared at the ground, disconcerted. 'Actually . . .' He looked up. 'That was a lie. I don't have another appointment. I've come down especially to see you, but I see now how selfish that is. Descending on you without waiting for an invitation especially when you have someone sick in your home.'

The relief was enormous. So enormous that Clare's face broke into a broad smile. He was not dissatisfied with her in any way. There was no pressure on her. She let out a great sigh. 'I feel a lot better. Thank you.' The fact that he admitted his sole reason was to see her again had not yet dawned. 'Then let's go in and have a pot of tea. I may have to make it myself. Our gardener is ill in bed and we are taking it in turns to minister to him. The biscuit tin may be empty, too, but we'll see.'

She left him in the drawing room while she made the tea. When she rejoined him, she explained about Jimmie's heart attack.

'That's a worry for you,' he agreed. 'Will he have to go into hospital?'

'I hope not. He's sure to refuse and that will be very embarrassing after the doctor has arranged a visit from a specialist. Mrs Parks popped in to see him on her way home yesterday and felt uneasy about him. He certainly looks ill to me. But you didn't come here to talk about Jimmie. Since you are here, you may like to read through my synopsis and tell me how I can improve it. A little help wouldn't come amiss!'

Without waiting for his answer, she went up to the study in a rush of enthusiasm and picked up the four pages that made up the synopsis. Was it any good? Would he like it?

To calm her nerves she sat down, closed her eyes and took several deep breaths, thoroughly ashamed of her stupid panic the day before when she spoke to Miss Birch. It had all been a misunderstanding. Steven Flint had said that there was nothing wrong with her writing.

Clare smiled and began to relax. That was when it came back to her – Steven Flint's admission when he first arrived and took hold of her hands. What exactly had he said? She frowned. '*I suddenly wanted to see you again . . . we had such a wonderful time together . . .*'

'Good heavens!'

He had been so keen to see her again that he had invented another appointment in the area. Which meant that he was impressed by her! She was cheered by the notion. But she would not mention it, she decided. Better to say nothing.

But he likes me, she decided. He likes my writing and he likes me!

Feeling distinctly more confident than of late, she went back to the drawing room and handed the synopsis to him.

'Aha! The synopsis. Your very first synopsis. Was it too difficult?'

'No – that is yes! Very difficult, but only because there is so much happening in the rest of my life. It's hard for me to concentrate. My cousin is getting married shortly as well as everything else.'

He smiled. 'It does get easier, I promise you.'

'I certainly hope so!'

The rest of the morning passed in a cheerful way and they enjoyed a simple lunch of cold chicken pie and salad. For dessert they had raspberries from the garden with warm rice pudding. Steven Flint offered some advice on her plot that Clare accepted gratefully. When it was time for him to go, she came outside to say goodbye. 'Maybe we should meet up again in a month's time,' she suggested. 'Or . . . or less?' She hoped she wasn't blushing.

His eyes lit up. 'What about once a fortnight – give or take a few days?'

Clare nodded. That would give her two weeks to improve

the synopsis as he had explained – and it was something to look forward to. Nothing more was said by either of them about the very real attraction that seemed to be developing between them, but after he had gone Clare went back into the house feeling more cheerful than for some time past. She longed to know more about her editor but had not asked and he had volunteered very little. They seemed to have spent a lot of time talking about her and the work in progress.

'Next time,' she promised herself and set off to the kitchen to ask Mrs Parks, in a casual way, what she had thought of the visitor.

'Mr Flint?' Mrs Parks pursed her lips thoughtfully. 'He seems a decent sort. Nice looking. Smart dresser. I do like a man to wear well-polished shoes. Not that that proves anything, mind you. My mother used to say, "You can't tell a gift by its wrapping." He might be a devil worshipper or an axe murderer – but I wouldn't think so.'

They both laughed.

Mrs Parks cocked her head enquiringly. 'Married, is he?'

'Really!' Clare protested. 'But, no, he isn't.'

That same afternoon, as soon as Mrs Parks removed Jimmie's lunchtime tray, he decided to test out his theory. He thought that the sooner he was back on his feet, the sooner he would recover. He found being confined to bed intensely boring and was unable to sleep during the day as instructed. Bed rest and more bed rest the doctor had said, but Jimmie had rejected the idea without actually putting it into words. He had worked all his life and had looked forward most mornings to the challenges of the day and now he thought about the uncut lawn with dismay. He should be with Clare as she inspected various horses to replace Jonty. Instead she would have to go alone. Unless she took Donald with her – but what he knew about horses would fill a postage stamp! What did Donald Wishart know about *anything*? God help Molly, married to him. That was all he could say about that fiasco.

Time to go, he told himself and with an effort he pushed back the bedclothes. For a moment the effort exhausted him

and he sank back against the pillows Mrs Parks had plumped
for him. He waited until he could breathe easily again and
then sat up straight. Another pause while he recovered. He
admitted to himself that he was a bit out of sorts. It wasn't
surprising, he thought, as he'd had a heart attack.

The cat at the bottom of the bed woke up and stared at
him indignantly. Jimmie slowly swung his legs round so
that they dangled over the edge of the bed. From that position he was staring at the commode and he swore under
his breath. Being lifted on to it and knowing that one of
the women was going to have to empty it, made him curl
up inside with desperate embarrassment. Today he had
sworn to reach the lavatory, which was situated beyond the
far side of the tack room and easily available for the various
grooms and stable lads who had once frequented the stable
yard in the dim, distant heyday of Merle Place.

He eased himself forward. There was nothing to cling
on to so he was going to have to get his balance. He slid
down, allowing his weight to fall on to his knees and was
astonished how weak his legs were after so little time in
bed. The cat, watching him, stretched and meowed.

'What are you looking at?' he growled. 'I can do it!' He
shook his head. Even the cat was fitter than he was.

At last, after a great effort, he stood semi-erect. For a
moment his head swam and then he fell back on to the bed,
panting for breath. It took two more attempts before he
succeeded in standing upright and unaided and then he gave
a small cry of triumph and smiled with satisfaction. 'Heart
attack be damned!' he muttered. It had been a bit of a faint,
that was all. Trust the women to make a song and dance
about it and drag the doctor along to prod him about.

The cat meowed, jumped from the bed and ran ahead of
him to the door. 'Want to go out, do you? That makes two
of us!'

Slowly, carefully, a few inches at a time, Jimmie shuf-
fled his way towards the door. When he reached it he sank
gratefully against it. He was gasping for breath and there
was sweat on his face and in his hair.

Clutching the latch, he lifted it and pulled the door open.

The cat slithered out, ran across the cobbled yard and disappeared.

Fifteen minutes later Jimmie was on the way back to his room when he slipped on the cobbles and sprawled headlong. By this time he was becoming more than a little nervous. His heart was beating erratically and he found himself unable to rise again. Instead he crawled painfully back up the steps into his room and across the floor to his bed. Hardly able to breathe, he summoned strength from somewhere and, ignoring the rumpled bedclothes, struggled back into bed and lay there in a cold sweat. Fear sliced through him as his heart fluttered wildly and common sense told him that he had overstepped the mark. In his eagerness to erase Clare's perception of him as a helpless invalid, he had taken a huge risk and was now suffering the consequences.

Thoroughly frightened, he whispered, 'Don't stop!' to his heart and waited. Was this what they meant by being at death's door? Closing his eyes, he willed himself to stay calm. Only when he could breathe comfortably again did he admit to himself that perhaps his adventure had been a mistake.

In the kitchen, towards the end of the afternoon, Molly surveyed the dessert with pride. 'And you say Don likes this?' she said for the third time.

Mrs Parks bit back a sharp reply. Molly had requested to be allowed to help with the cooking so that she could expand her repertoire and impress her husband-to-be. Today, Mrs Parks had chosen to make Italian Cream and Molly had assisted.

'Very light and suitable for invalids,' the housekeeper explained.

'It's simple to make, but you must have a cool larder or an ice house where it can set. Miss Wishart likes it, too, and it will be easy for Jimmie to eat. It slips down easily even if you have a sore throat.'

Molly read aloud from her notebook that held the small collection of recipes she had so far learned to make. 'Italian

Cream – heat cream gently, sprinkle on gel powder and stir. Add van ess and sugar. Pour into dish and cool until set. Serves four.' She looked up. 'Is that right?'

'Show me.' She cast a quick eye over Molly's efforts. 'What's van ess?' she asked. 'And gel powder? Vanilla essence and gelatine powder. You should write it properly. And you've spelt Italian wrong.'

'I was in a hurry.'

'Italian only has one t.'

Molly scowled. 'It Talian. That's two.'

'Italian. One word. One t. Don't argue.'

Molly pulled a face and with a loud sigh amended her recipe. 'So if there's only two of us . . . ?'

'Halve all the ingredients – but it makes more sense to make it for four and keep half in a cool place for the next day.' She scooped some into a small dish and handed it to Molly. 'You can take this down to Jimmie before you go home. Cover it with a plate and find a spoon. And don't dawdle on the way or it'll go runny.'

Molly unlatched the stable door and let herself in and arrived at Jimmie's bedside to find him resting against his pillows. His face was very pale, his eyes were closed and his lips were an unhealthy blue. Frowning, she watched him. So this was what people looked like when they were ill, she thought. He certainly didn't look right – not like the usual Jimmie. Usually he was cheerful and sometimes he told them jokes. He had told them a really funny one about a Scotsman, an Irishman and an Englishman who were on an island somewhere . . . and . . . She gave up. She could never remember jokes, but it had been a very funny one. Even Mrs P had laughed and then she had thrown the tea towel at him and said, 'Get along with you, Jimmie. You and your jokes!'

She smiled at the memory and then realized that she would miss being around in Merle Place with Mrs P and Jimmie once the baby arrived . . . She might even be sorry to leave Miss Wishart, scribbling away in that study of hers, even if she did nag a bit and fussed about the tea leaves for the carpets which Mrs P said was a bit old-fashioned.

Yes, she would miss them all. But then she, Molly, would have Don and the baby. Her face brightened.

While Jimmie's eyes were closed, Molly helped herself to a spoonful of the jelly cream. It was delicious.

She wiped the spoon on her apron and said loudly, 'You awake?'

Opening his eyes seemed to be a slow business. He stared at her blankly.

'You all right? It's me, Molly.'

'Yes.'

'I've brought you some of this stuff I've made,' she told him eagerly. 'A special recipe, good for invalids. It's called Italian Cream and I've put it in my book for when I'm married. I can also make cheese toasts, orange rock cakes and coconut layer pudding.' She peered at him. He seemed to be falling asleep again. 'Jimmie! Italian Cream. Don loves it and Mrs P said you can eat it easily because it slips down.' She removed the covering plate, placed the spoon in his right hand and held out the dish for his inspection.

He lifted his right hand a few inches and dropped it. His eyes *had* closed again. Molly tutted.

'Not . . . hungry,' he murmured.

Mortified, Molly said, 'Not hungry? But I made it especially. Well, I helped Mrs P. Just taste a bit. Here . . . Open your eyes.' Was he being difficult on purpose, she wondered. She offered him a spoonful and he opened his eyes and mouth obediently. 'You'll like it. It's good, isn't it?'

He swallowed.

'Have some more. Mrs P says it's nourishing – whatever that means.'

He shook his head then screwed up his eyes as though in pain.

'No-o!' he whispered.

'Yes, Jimmie.' She wasn't going to take it back half eaten. 'It's good for you.' She pressed the next spoonful against his lips and reluctantly he allowed the jelly cream to go in. 'There you are! You like it.'

He seemed unable to resist and after more coaxing the dish was finally empty.

'I told you it was easy.' Smiling, she put the dish down for the cat to lick and fussed with Jimmie's bedclothes, pulling them up around him and tucking them in. She thought that if Don was ever ill, which he might be sometimes, she would know how to look after him.

She looked at Jimmie doubtfully. His eyes were closed again. Had he forgotten she was there? she wondered. Ungrateful pig, she thought crossly. He hadn't thanked her for the Italian Cream or complimented her on her cooking skills, but perhaps he was tired.

Jimmie had never congratulated her on her forthcoming marriage, but Mrs Parks had said that the two men weren't really on good terms so maybe that was why he was being mean to her. Maybe he was jealous because she was getting married and he had nobody. Some people were like that. Maybe he thought she was marrying above herself – which she was, but that was none of his business. 'Good luck to you, Molly!' That's what the woman in the post office had said. She was nice.

Molly tried again. 'Ma's made me a big cake for my wedding. You're invited, Jimmie.' He might not come because he didn't get along with Don but the food and drink would be free so maybe he would. She wondered if he would give them a wedding present. Probably not. Her aunt on her mother's side was giving her a mixing bowl and a wooden spoon and Mrs P was going to give them a matching milk jug and sugar bowl painted with flowers and bees which had belonged to her mother. Molly had a bottom drawer containing two pillowslips she had made and a neatly hemmed tablecloth embroidered with white daisies. Don was going to buy a table. Molly felt quite faint with excitement.

'And we'll have ham and chutney,' she told Jimmie. 'Some from Mrs P and some of our own. I helped Ma make it – pear and ginger chutney off our big pear tree. We got them down before the wasps got to them. Bit of luck, that, because last year – Jimmie? Are you listening?'

He had closed his eyes again. Probably he was listening, she thought, but pretending he wasn't interested. Mrs Parks said he'd been married ages ago but his wife had run off and left him. Poor old Jimmie. Still he could be a bit of a misery – like now.

She pushed the cat away and retrieved the dish. 'You sure you're all right?' There was no answer. Maybe he'd fallen asleep. 'I'm off then. Bye.'

Back in the kitchen Mrs Parks was filleting mackerel – a job she hated.

Molly smiled brightly. 'He loved it,' she told the house-keeper. 'At first he said he wasn't hungry, but then he ate it all.'

'How did he look?' The housekeeper narrowly avoided cutting her finger and cursed under her breath.

Molly shrugged, pulling on her jacket and preparing to go home. 'He's had a heart attack. What d' you expect? He looked awful. Half awake most of the time and then he fell asleep.'

'What did he have to say – anything?'

'No. Not even thank you! I told you – he fell asleep. His bed was a mess so I tidied it.'

'Good girl. Get along then.' Distracted, she turned to check the oven and Molly made good her escape.

Clare awoke next morning to a feeling of dread and re-membered that the specialist was coming to see Jimmie at 2 p.m. or thereabouts. His name was Robinson and the doctor had assured her he was the best in the area. Just before eleven, when Mrs Parks told her Sarah was at the front door, she was not too pleased but hurried to greet her.

Sarah was elegant, married to a wealthy man who worked in London as an accountant. Her family had lived in the village for generations and before her marriage she had been looked up to as one of the Braithwaites – Braithwaite & Co being the most expensive local building firm in the Maidstone area, with an excellent reputation.

'Come in,' Clare told her with a smile. 'I've tried to see you several times during the past few weeks but—'

'I was away. My mother was ill again and my sister tends to panic so I had to go up to London.' She followed Clare into the drawing room and they settled themselves. 'My sister can deal with the day to day care,' she confided, 'but I go willingly when called because Mother lives with my sister and for that I'm immensely grateful. I just don't have the patience with old people, not even my own relations.'

Clare had asked Mrs Parks to bring in a tray of tea and some biscuits and while she busied herself with the teapot she told her friend about the dramatic happenings which Merle Place had seen. 'First poor old Jonty and then Don getting engaged to Molly Jenner – and then poor Jimmie had a heart attack.'

'I heard about that from the postman. Is he going to be all right?'

'To be honest I'm not sure, but the specialist is coming this afternoon so I shall have a better idea then. When I saw him last thing last night he was asleep but looked very grey and this morning he looked no better. He won't accept that he is very ill and does too much. He will insist on making his way to and from the lavatory but he shouldn't. That's why he's got the commode. He shouldn't be walking about.'

'I expect he's afraid of his muscles wasting away while he's in bed. I expect it reassures him. I wouldn't worry too much, Clare. People know their limitations.'

'I suppose so,' she said, still unconvinced.

Sarah sipped her tea. 'So Molly's seducer is your cousin!' she said bluntly.

The choice of words took Clare by surprise and for a moment she was lost for an answer.

Sarah grinned. 'You do know the village is agog!'

'I imagined it would be.'

'I'm surprised it isn't splashed all over the local paper! Quite a twist on the traditional outcome where maid is abandoned by heartless younger son!' She laughed lightly to show that this was kindly meant.

Clare recovered her poise. 'The strange thing is it seems to suit Donald. He's totally smitten, as they say. Involved heart and soul now! And Molly's thrilled, of course. She genuinely loves him for all his faults. It's quite touching in a way.'

'She'll be an interesting in-law!' Sarah raised her eyebrows.

'Hardly an in-law,' she corrected her. 'He's my cousin, not my brother. She'll be related but only distantly.'

Sarah nodded. 'The Jenners are a nice family. I hear the newly-weds are moving into the old cottage.'

Clare nodded, wondering uneasily if Sarah was fishing for news with which to regale the rest of the villagers who naturally thrived on gossip. She didn't mind – she was quite willing to listen to gossip herself, but she suddenly felt defensive and decided to change the subject.

She talked about the people who had shown an interest in Merle Place and at once she felt that she had Sarah's undivided attention.

'People are very worried,' Sarah told her. 'There's a rumour about it being turned into a study centre for the paranormal. People are nervous. Some of them are rather superstitious. I think they imagine weird investigators summoning evil spirits who will rampage around the village at midnight whenever the moon is full!' She rolled her eyes. 'Hard to believe this is the twentieth century and people still cling to these old beliefs and superstitions!'

'They needn't worry,' Clare assured her. 'It's most un-likely they will buy it. There are problems with that particular offer but I won't bore you with them. I have another potential buyer who wants to turn the house into an expensive boarding school for boys under eleven. Not that there's any hurry.' She wasn't going to admit that she was becoming desperate for money. 'It's early days yet and the estate agent is very hopeful.'

Clare wanted to talk about her book and her new editor but so far Sarah hadn't asked about her writing. In any case Clare felt she had given up enough of her time. She glanced at the clock on the mantelpiece and Sarah took the hint and rose to go.

'I can see you're busy,' she said. 'I hope the news is good about Johnnie.'

'It's Jimmie but thank you. I must talk to Mrs Parks about his lunch and then send down some clean pyjamas.' She smiled. 'Must have him looking his best when the specialist comes!'

'He's very lucky to have you taking care of him.' She stood on the front steps. 'Please give my congratulations to your cousin. Say I wish him well. When is the wedding?'

'The twelfth of June.'

'I'll try to be there to throw some rice.'

Clare watched her go with relief. Could she call Sarah a close friend, she wondered, or was she simply an acquaintance? Did she have any close friends? She sometimes thought that being part of Merle Place set her apart from the rest of the village in more ways than one.

Angus Robinson, the heart specialist, was not at all how Clare had imagined he would be. He was plump, his round face was partly hidden by a curly beard, and his eyes twinkled behind small, round spectacle lenses. He followed her down to the stables, talking non-stop in a strong Scots accent, interrupted only by short attacks of coughing.

They called out to Jimmie as they went up the steps, but, receiving no reply, Clare said, 'He was asleep when Molly brought him his pyjamas so we let him sleep. The bed rest is so important – but hopefully he's awake now.'

One glance toward the bed, however, and Clare felt a immediate frisson of alarm – a sense of impending trouble. Her steps faltered, she gave a faint cry and hurried forward.

'Jimmie?'

Behind her she heard the specialist gasp as she crouched over the still figure in the bed. Jimmie stared sightlessly at the ceiling and his mouth hung open.

'Let me see him!' snapped Mr Robinson and Clare moved quickly aside and stood watching while he set down his bag and bent over the still figure.

'I think we're too late,' he said grimly.

'No! He can't be . . .' she protested, but already she knew the specialist was right.

'Much too late.' He straightened up, his plump features drawn into a shocked mask of dismay. 'Poor fellow! This is terrible! I'm afraid there's nothing I can do for him.

He's been dead for maybe an hour, I should say.' He sighed, there was no twinkle now in his eyes and his expression was downcast. 'Could we have saved him?' he asked no one in particular. 'Doubtful. From what the doctor told me it was advanced. Went too long undiagnosed. It's often the way of it. I shall write "heart failure" on the death certificate.'

'You think he had another heart attack?'

'Almost certainly. It would have been very quick. Not painless, mind, but very quick.'

Jimmie's cat appeared round the door and took a few steps towards the bed then paused. His ears flattened slightly and his tail stiffened. Before either of them realized what he was intending, the cat ran forward and leapt on to the bed. For a moment he seemed to sniff the air with his head up enquiringly. Then he turned and raced for the door.

'Do you think he knew?' asked Clare.

'Aye, I would say so. Animals are very canny. You'll see nor hide nor hair of the creature again.'

Still in a state of shock Clare stammered, 'Jimmie was always so fit. I don't recall him ever having a cold. He was always working. Loved the garden . . . he was so proud of it.'

'Sounds as though he enjoyed life.' Mr Robinson opened his bag. Extracting a loose-leafed folder, he sat down on the bedside chair and made a few jottings on a clean page. He took out a half-hunter watch, checked the time and slipped it back into his waistcoat pocket.

'I think he did enjoy it.' Clare nodded, her voice trembling. 'His life, I mean. Oh! I do hope so.' She moved to the foot of the bed and stared at Jimmie and tears filled her eyes.'

'There was nothing you could have done, my dear Miss Wishart. Sometimes the Lord is merciful. This may have saved him from becoming a permanent invalid. Would he have liked that, do you think?'

'No. He'd have hated it.' The tears began to run down her face.

Slowly she edged round to the side of the bed and took one of Jimmie's hands in hers. Softly she rubbed it as if the friction might somehow bring him back to life. Time passed but she seemed cocooned from reality. She saw nothing through her blurred tears and heard nothing but the fierce beating of her own heart. Eventually she felt a hand on her shoulder.

'Try and face up to it, my dear,' the specialist told her gently. 'It's all over and you can do nothing to help him. The poor wee man has been taken from us. God has called him to His side.'

'He did too much,' she sobbed, dabbing at her eyes with a handkerchief. 'He wouldn't listen. Insisted he was fit. Insisted that he was recovering. He wanted to prove . . . Oh, Jimmie!'

'We must send for an ambulance to take him to the mortuary – to the hospital, in other words. We must use your telephone.'

'Oh! Must you? I mean . . . Do you have to take him away?' She remembered how much Jimmie had hated hospitals.

'I'm afraid he cannot remain here. They will bring a stretcher and we must let them do their job. We'll go back to the house and your housekeeper shall make us a pot of tea. You've had a bad shock. Come along. You can achieve nothing by staying here – nor would he want you to.'

Within minutes Mrs Parks was in tears and it was Clare who made the tea, while Molly, suitably crushed by the news, was sent to the cottage at Frenchies Farm to inform Donald of Jimmie's death and to ask him to come back to Merle Place to lend moral support.

Clutching the cup tightly to steady her hands, Clare sipped the sweet tea gratefully but it offered no relief. Nothing could reach the pain of grief somewhere within her that had turned the whole world dark.

Twelve

Jimmie's funeral on the following Monday was a lonely affair and took place in the local church. Clare, in touch with his sister, Dorothy, had offered to arrange for Jimmie's funeral and she had agreed willingly, insisting only that they would later pay for the erection of a headstone. Dorothy and her son had travelled down by train from Hornsey. Dorothy wore a grey coat with a black armband and her grey felt hat was trimmed with black feathers. The son's reddened eyes expressed his grief and he held his mother's arm, guiding her carefully to her seat in the church. Molly and her parents and Mrs Parks were there and Clare and Donald, naturally. Three or four villagers resplendent in black sat together halfway back and Clare knew that they attended all funerals whether they knew the deceased or not. The choir of six young boys sang dutifully – their voices thin and reedy – and the bell was duly tolled. The vicar read the service in a way that suggested he cared, and Clare spoke a few words about Jimmie and what he had meant to the household at Merle Place. Then, unexpectedly, Jimmie's nephew asked if he could say a few words.

His name was Edmund and he was thin with very fair hair. He made his way to the front of the pews with a sheet of paper in his hand and began a search for his glasses. Unable to find them he crushed the paper and stared out across the silent congregation.

'Uncle Jimmie was someone I remember from when I was a boy,' he began. 'He used to come and see us and was always laughing and joking and he called me "the nipper" and always brought me a toy animal for my farm – a horse and cart, two pigs, a few chickens . . . sometimes a few pieces of fencing. I think he enjoyed the farm as much as I did, if not more. But then we moved away north for Dad's work and Uncle Jimmie moved to Kent so we didn't see him. Once he brought a horse and cart. That was for my birthday.' He glanced at his mother for inspiration, but she simply gazed at him, red-eyed, and said nothing.

He caught Clare staring at him and she gave a nod of encouragement.

'Anyway I know he loved my family,' Edmund went on, 'and we loved him. He had a son who never knew him and now he never will and . . . Well, sadly, that's his loss. He doesn't know what he missed. We'll never forget Uncle Jimmie.'

His voice broke on the last few words and he returned to his place and fumbled for a handkerchief. He blew his nose, glanced round and added, 'There was a black and white cow, too. I've still got them all.'

Clare had listened in astonishment and was at once filled with a deep regret that she had never thought to ask Jimmie about these few members of his family. They could have visited Merle Place, she thought. Jimmie would have liked that. She turned to smile at the young man, but overcome with emotion he covered his face with his hands.

Back at the house they all drank sherry and enjoyed cold meats and a selection of stewed fruit and syllabub. Clare was amused to see that the four villagers ate more heartily than everybody else. Afterwards, she sought out Jimmie's sister and told her how much they had all valued her brother.

'I don't know what we'll do without him,' she confessed. 'We shall miss his cheerful ways and it won't be the same without him.' She wondered what the sister would think if she knew how fond Jimmie had been of his employer but decided not to speak of it. Instead she said, 'It's a long way for you to visit his grave, but if you ever do come down from London, let us know and come and visit. You'd all be very welcome. If we're still here, of course. And we'll keep the grave trimmed and put flowers on it regularly. Even if we sell Merle Place, Donald and Molly will be around.' It was the very least she could do, she thought miserably, for a man who had cared so much for her. She wished again that she had been able to return Jimmie's affection. Love, however, could not be forced, no matter how convenient it might have proved. At least Jimmie had died with a hopeful heart and had never had to face a final rejection.

Later the same afternoon, when everyone else had gone, Clare received a phone call from Mr Yates. The estate agent sounded his usual cheery self and Clare found the call a welcome break from the unhappy tensions of the day.

'Some mostly good news,' he told her. 'The Souters want to offer for the house on one condition.'

'Does that mean they have offered the asking price?'

'Yes, that's right, but they still insist on renting the premises for a year first. That's the not so good news.'

Clare drew a deep breath. 'The answer's still no, Mr Yates, and the more I think of them, the less I want them to take over Merle Place. It doesn't feel right. In fact, I think – yes, I definitely want to withdraw the house as far as they are concerned, in case they suddenly decide to buy immediately.'

'There would be no excuse to refuse them! I see where you are going with this, Miss Wishart. Which leads me to some better news. A man called Adrian Latimer – no, it was Alan Latimer – has been in to see me and is obviously interested, but he says he wants me to keep his enquiries from you.'

'Keep it from me? But why?'

'It sounds odd but his reasons are very admirable so I feel free to break my word. He claims to be an acquaintance and doesn't want to put you in an awkward position if he cannot come up with the money. I told him the price and he has gone away to think it over and see what can be managed.'

'I liked Mr Latimer.' She thought rapidly. 'Did he say how he would use the property?'

'He did. He wants to open Merle Place, or somewhere

like it, as a retreat – that's the word he used – for artists, writers, musicians . . . A kind of haven, I suppose he meant. Not a religious retreat. Somewhere quiet where creative people can escape from their daily grind and concentrate on their work. It sounds very different, but quite suitable, don't you think?'

'Very suitable. But I suppose I shall have to pretend ignorance until he sees fit to tell me his plans.' She smiled. 'I won't betray you, Mr Yates.'

After she had replaced the telephone, she longed to talk it over with someone, but Donald had changed his clothes and had rushed back to the cottage to finish some wallpapering so she was on her own. For a moment she was tempted to try and reach Steven Flint but reluctantly abandoned the idea. It would be too presumptuous, she decided. But it did now appear that Merle Place might soon change hands and she would be free to find herself a new home. But where would she go and what would she do? Suddenly it seemed she must now face up to her uncertain future. No Jimmie to consult with. No Merle Place (if Alan Latimer bought it) and no Donald. She was entirely on her own and for a moment or two the thought frightened her. It was a lonely prospect – the rest of her life stretching ahead into the unknown.

But I'm only one of millions of women, many of them in straitened circumstances who would envy me my opportunities. I have assets and a God-given talent and I have to find a satisfactory way to spend the rest of my life.

'Clare Wishart!' she said aloud. 'You have a lot of hard thinking to do!'

Clare was touched the next day when Donald sent Molly in to work with a note inviting Clare to inspect the work he was doing on the old cottage. At half past ten precisely, as instructed, she knocked on the cottage door and stood on the step, admiring the possibilities of a future garden. Already there was a picket fence which leaned drunkenly towards a rustic sundial and an overgrown rockery bordered with rose bushes which had long since returned to their original state with briar-type leaves and thorn-studded stocks.

'Bang on time!' Donald beamed at her. 'Come in. Sorry about the paint smell but I've opened all the windows. Molly can't bear the smell so she won't be coming along later today. I do get on much quicker when I'm alone.' He pointed to the front of the door. 'That old bell is going to go. I've bought a brass knocker but it's a surprise for Molly.' He tugged at the knotted string and the old bell jangled discordantly.

Clare, still fascinated by the change in him, followed him meekly around the house, saying all the right things. 'Oh, Donald, the stairs have been scrubbed . . . and the landing window looks so pretty. What a difference a new pane of glass makes! And who made the flowery curtains?'

'Molly's ma. She's quite a decent sort actually. We get along very well.' He patted the banister. 'I'm going to rub this down and Molly's going to polish it. It should come up.' He jerked a thumb toward the ceiling. 'There was a large damp stain there but I've whitewashed over it. You'd never know if I hadn't told you.'

Clare admired the ceiling.

'Now for the pièce de résistance!' Donald threw open a door. 'Our bedroom!' He watched her face for a reaction and Clare obligingly widened her eyes and gasped.

'Donald! How clever you are! New wallpaper! I had no idea!'

He did his best to look modest but failed. 'Neither had I!' he told her. The wallpaper clung bravely to the wall, with only an occasional bubble to hint at the struggle Donald had had with it. The paper itself was of a white trellis with assorted flowers peeping through. It was obvious where each strip of paper joined its fellow, but the overall effect was charming and somehow innocent.

Donald was describing the room as it would be shortly when the young wedded couple took up residence. 'With the bed against that wall and a chest of drawers there. The wardrobe will have to stand on the landing but no matter. What do you think?'

'I think it's marvellous, Donald. You have transformed the cottage. I imagine Molly is going mad with excitement.' Surprising herself, she reached forward and gave him a brief hug. 'Molly is so lucky – and so are you! I can't wait for the wedding.'

'Only three more days!'

They grinned at each other. Then, abruptly Donald's expression changed.

'I'm sorry . . .' he began.

'About what?'

'About . . .' He swallowed uncomfortably and stared past her. Eventually he said, 'About poor old Jimmie. Molly says I was unkind to him. She heard things, she said, from Mrs Parks. I suppose he hated me. I wouldn't have blamed him. I don't know why I . . .' He scowled unhappily, not meeting Clare's eyes. 'I was rough on him, poor devil.'

She hesitated. 'I'm afraid you were. But it's all over now. It's in the past.'

'But that's just it. It's too late to undo it.'

No use pretending otherwise, thought Clare and remained silent. If he wanted to ease his conscience she would let him try. She prompted him gently. 'I never did understand why you didn't like him.'

Donald shrugged. 'I just couldn't get over it. I suppose I was jealous.' He scuffed the floor with his foot. 'Molly said I had to face facts . . .' He risked a glance in her direction. 'Because you all liked him. Good old dependable Jimmie could do no wrong. Nobody liked me.'

'Oh, Donald . . .' Clare searched for the right words, knowing that there was no way to make him feel better about his behaviour.

'I didn't want him to die, Clare.'

'Of course you didn't. I expect he understood – that you didn't mean him any real harm.'

'He had a soft spot for you, Clare. That riled me, too. I thought maybe you and him . . . It drove me mad.'

'No. It was never going to end that way.' She didn't want to say any more. 'But there's nothing to be gained by making yourself unhappy, Donald. It can't be changed. And despite the bad feeling between the two of you. I think all in all Jimmie was happy here. He loved Merle Place.'

'Molly says that if he were here now and I apologized . . .' He grinned suddenly. 'She's so earnest, that girl! And God-fearing. Her ma and pa did a good job bringing her up.' He sighed deeply and then shook off his regrets. 'Come and see the kitchen!'

Fifteen minutes later Clare returned home where Mrs Parks was waiting for her, a gleam in her eyes which Clare didn't understand.

Mrs Parks said, 'I've something to show you,' and, without another word, led the way upstairs. Wondering what she was going to find, Clare followed her into her cousin's bedroom.

Without a word the housekeeper approached the bed and lifted the mattress. Three silver spoons were revealed. 'This is where he hid them,' she exclaimed, 'when he tried to pin it on us!'

Wordlessly Clare reached in and brought out the spoons. With a sigh she straightened up and Mrs Parks allowed the mattress to fall back into place.

'Oh, dear!' Clare regarded the housekeeper. 'So now we know. Another mystery solved.'

Mrs Parks shook her head. 'Strikes me we'll have to button our lips!' she remarked. 'Too late now to stir things up.'

Clare nodded gratefully. 'But if we return them, Molly might ask where we found them.'

'She will, I'm sure. She was that upset at the time. Best keep them out of sight until Molly leaves. Say nothing.'

They regarded each other uneasily. At that moment the telephone rang and Mrs Parks retreated to the kitchen.

'Clare Wishart here.'

'Miss Wishart, it's me, Alan Latimer. I've been thinking about Merle Place and would like to talk to you about a plan I have – perhaps plan is not quite accurate – shall I say an idea that might or might not interest you. May I come down to discuss it with you?'

'Of course. I'd be delighted to hear it.'

'Possibly Friday or Saturday?'

'Friday,' she replied swiftly, eager for some cheerful company. 'But only if you promise to stay for lunch. It sounds very intriguing. Are you going to give me a hint about this idea?'

He laughed. 'Certainly not, it would spoil the surprise! But I'll accept your invitation to lunch. Would twelve o'clock be suitable?'

'Wait!' she cried. 'Whatever am I thinking? On Saturday my cousin is getting married in the local church. Come to lunch Friday and stay overnight. Then you can come to the wedding. The more the merrier.'

'If you're sure I won't get in the way of all the preparations.'

'You won't do that – but you might be given something to do,' Clare told him. 'In fact, the bride's parents have insisted that the reception is at their home – the farmhouse. The bride, by the way, is Molly, our housemaid.'

'Well I never!' He was trying to hide his surprise. 'I remember her. She is marrying your cousin?'

'Yes. We've all been taken by surprise but everyone's happy about it. Do say you'll join us. I know Molly's parents won't mind.'

'Then I shall bring a little gift with me. Can you suggest anything?'

'Household linen is always acceptable. Maybe a table-cloth or some towels.'

'Hmm . . . I always feel that linen is rather uninspiring.' Seconds passed while he thought about it. 'I have the very thing,' he said. 'I shall give them a carriage clock.'

That evening Clare made her way over to Frenchies Farm secure in the knowledge that Donald and Molly were hard at work in their cottage. Tom had decided to go to the pub rather than listen to the women talk about the wedding 'breakfast'. Clare belatedly asked Annie's permission to invite Alan Latimer and it was given without hesitation.

The two women settled round the kitchen table. They sipped tea to the accompaniments of the dog's snores and the sound of a barn door creaking in the wind that had sprung up during the day.

Clare asked, 'How's the cake coming along?' and it was immediately fetched from the larder and displayed in all its glory – a large round yellow Madeira cake bursting with cherries.

Annie smiled proudly. 'Turned out a treat. Some folks like sultanas and mixed peel, but my husband can't abide them. Nothing like a sweet cherry – that's his opinion, so Molly said I was to make one that her pa would like.' She rolled her eyes. 'Since Tom gave your cousin the thumbs up, he's been Molly's hero! Real funny it is.'

Clare consulted her notebook about the small contribution she had been allowed to make. 'I've ordered the beer and a small barrel of cider and Mrs Parks is making lemonade for the children . . .'

'Children?'

They looked at each other. Clare said, 'Won't there be any?'

'Only the two little bridesmaids – that's the two girls from next to the post office. Janice and Margie, the younger sisters of Molly's friend Stella.'

'Oh, well, I like lemonade. I'll drink some of it, but I'll warn her not to make too much!'

'There'll be maybe fourteen or sixteen in all,' Annie told her. 'Just a few close family and friends. Tom hates fuss, but he reckoned sixteen would satisfy our Molly. The wedding cake should feed twenty so let's hope we don't get any gatecrashers.'

The farm was providing a ham and a big game pie and Annie would conjure up salads and home-made breads. Mrs Parks had offered two large bowls of her best chutney as a wedding present, which Annie (who had shelves full of her own famous pear and ginger chutney) had reluctantly accepted.

Clare said, 'Is your husband going to give Molly away?'

'Of course – although he's terrified. Hates being dressed up. Well, don't bother then, I told him. Come in your old moleskins and muddy boots. Let your daughter down in front of the whole village!' She grinned at Clare. 'Who's the best man?'

Clare blinked. 'Best man? Good heavens!'

Annie's jaw dropped. 'Don't tell me you haven't got a best man. The wedding's on Saturday!'

'I . . . er . . . I don't know. I didn't give it a thought. I suppose that's up to Donald. It should be his brother or best friend, but he doesn't have a brother.' This is ridiculous, she told herself. Of course we have a best man. Donald must have asked someone to support him. Had she been told at some time and since forgotten? 'I'll check with him on the way home,' she promised. 'I know he's been busy.' Does he actually have a close friend, she wondered. Did he have *any* friends, close or otherwise? If not, who else did she know who would step in at the last moment?

Annie said, 'She looks a treat in the dress. Real lace, and for her hair she's made herself a little circle of silk daisies and white ribbon threaded in and out. She's very clever with her hands. My mother used to say she could be a florist when she grew up. She's got an eye for decorations and things.' She sighed. 'It's upstairs, the dress I mean, but I daren't show you. Molly made me promise. But she didn't say anything about the bridesmaids.'

Clare hadn't been paying much attention but now she jumped to her feet and followed Annie upstairs. Two identical dresses hung from coat hangers on the end of the wardrobe. They were pink edged with white ribbon and the necklines were decorated with white daisies to match the bride's circlet. 'They're twins,' she told Clare. 'Six-year-old twins. Molly says they're little terrors most of the time, but they've been threatened with Lord knows what if they play up in church.'

'We're going to have some lovely photographs,' Clare assured her. Tom Jenner had decided a photographer was a waste of time and money, but Clare had insisted and had hired a man from Maidstone who had been recommended by Sarah Tennant.

An hour and a half later, on the way back to Merle Place, Clare had tried to speak with Donald about his best man.

The door, however, was firmly shut and locked and, glancing upwards she thought she glimpsed a face at the bedroom window, but although she waited patiently nobody came down to answer the bell. Clare suddenly guessed what might be happening upstairs in the privacy of the new bedroom and, her face flaming with embarrassment, she slipped quietly away.

On the way she had a brainwave. She would telephone Alan Latimer, explain the situation with regard to the best man and ask him if he would step in if it proved to be necessary. It would be a big test of his friendship but she could think of no one else.

When Alan arrived, they settled in comfortable armchairs in the drawing room, while a fierce but warm wind blew dust and leaves across the terrace outside the French windows. Clare could see how excited he was and how eager to share his great idea.

He leaned forward. 'I think I suggested once before that Merle Place would make an ideal retreat.'

Clare nodded, mindful of her promise to Mr Yates to pretend ignorance of the scheme.

He went on. 'I still think that would be a splendid idea and I've been making a few enquiries among friends and relations. I'd like to be part of a group – a consortium, if you like to call it that – that owns Merle Place.'

She was genuinely delighted. 'That would be wonderful!'

'I don't have nearly enough money to buy the house outright nor the expertise to organize it, but I have a small nest egg from an aunt, due on her death, and she might be prepared to advance me some of it. My uncle is also interested and I shall see my bank manager next week. What I need to know, and I've spoken to your Mr Yates, is whether or not there is any room for negotiation?' He sat back, watching Clare's expression. 'I can see you like the original idea. My suggestion is that you retain a stake in the house as a member of the consortium.'

'Indeed I do like the idea!' She hesitated. 'I wish I could see a way of joining your proposed consortium, but I don't think it's possible. You see I will need the money from the house to buy another smaller one and subsidize myself for the future.'

'Very understandable,' he said. 'But my idea is this. You needn't break off your contact with the house altogether, because you are a writer and you might well come back from time to time to use the place as somewhere you could write in peace. If you lowered the price the difference would be your contribution. It would need to be carefully organized by a good solicitor but it might work.'

'That's a wonderful idea. I hadn't thought about it that way. Let me think about it, Alan, and take some advice.'

'I already have several friends who are keen to take advantage of the place – not as investors but as artists. A London friend who runs an art gallery would definitely come down to Merle Place and he has another friend who might. He has offered to recommend us – if we go ahead, that is. And I have an old school friend, Gerald, who composes music for performance on stage. It's mostly for quartets or quintets – often chamber music. I went to a performance of Christmas music two years ago and was terribly impressed. He's been quite successful over the past few years.' Alan rolled his eyes. 'Poor old Gerry has five children and he positively leaped at the idea of a few weeks without them!'

They both laughed.

When the discussion seemed to have run out of steam, Clare brought up the subject of the best man role and at first Alan was hesitant.

'It's not that I won't do it,' he said, 'but could I do it well enough? I've never had to speak in front of an audience.'

'You'd be better than no best man!'

'I don't even know your cousin very well.'

Clare had prepared herself for this perfectly valid argument. 'I could write a short speech for you to read,' she offered. 'And I could explain that none of Donald's family can be present. I know it's an imposition and I won't take against you if you don't feel able to do it.' She felt that he

was wavering and after a few moments of anxious reflec-
tion he agreed to read the speech and a weight was at once
removed from her shoulders.

'Mother, I have a request to make.' Steven Flint drew a
quick breath.

Margaret peered at him over the top of her spectacles,
then continued with her sewing. 'What is it, dear?'

Steven regarded her nervously. 'I was wondering . . .'

She lowered her embroidery. 'If you want me to go with
you to Agatha's, the answer is no. It will always be no. I can't
abide that woman. She knows it. I know it. We have nothing
in common – except you, of course – and she bores me.'

'It's nothing to do with Agatha, Mother. I shall go alone.'

'I'm pleased to hear it. Your godmother has tried my patience
once too often and at my age I feel able to be ruthless.'

She resumed her sewing, screwing up her face as she
drove the fine needle through the linen. She was reluctantly
embroidering a handkerchief sachet for Agatha's birthday
– a present her son would duly deliver. To make best use
of the daylight Margaret always sat beside the window which
was a pity, Steven thought, because that meant the rest of
the large high-ceilinged room looked emptier than was
necessary. His mother lived in a large first-floor flat in the
most expensive part of Chelsea and since she had renounced
the Victorian idea of heavy furniture and dark drapes, she
had bought very little in the way of replacement. She looked
small and vulnerable, he thought, haunted by the knowledge that she would not live for ever. Vanity made her lie
about her age and he suspected she was nearing eighty. If
she had any medical problems he was not permitted to share
them. Unlike most of her contemporaries, being ill was
considered 'not quite the thing' by his mother, and Margaret
replied to his occasional enquiries as to her health with,
'Fine and dandy, thank you, dear,' and a look that dared
him to enquire further.

'I was wondering if you were planning another dinner
party in the near future, Mother, because I'd be grateful if
you would invite—'

'Not another young hopeful?' She stopped sewing abruptly and stared at him. 'Not that strange man that writes those dreadful horror stories. If you are going to ask me to invite him, save your breath, dear. A horror writer is hardly the sort of man I would want to inflict on my other guests . . .' She continued with her sewing.

'It's not him, Mother. You're talking about David Galloway who incidentally is a charming man, but I'm talking about—'

'Horror writers are a breed apart, dear, in my opinion. How do they sleep at night, I wonder, with their minds full of evil and satanic rites and all sorts of wickedness. I blame their parents.'

Steven regarded her affectionately. His mother was a small, frail-looking woman with a will of iron. She had once been very beautiful, but now she reminded him of a rapidly fading flower.

He said mildly, 'David Galloway is a perfectly normal young man who happens to be an excellent writer. He simply has an inventive mind and a fascination for all the things that terrify us. But what I wanted to ask you is—'

'As it happens I shall be having a few friends round to dinner in a week's time to celebrate.' She frowned. 'To celebrate something! Now, what was it? Oh yes!' She rolled her eyes. 'How could I forget to celebrate the date when I came out all those years ago?' She sighed heavily and her face took on the faraway expression which her son recognized.

Steven was mortified to discover what the dinner was to celebrate. His mother's coming-out ball in London had been the highlight of her life and she had celebrated the date every year since without fail. It seemed that her two marriages and the birth of her only child had jointly come a poor second to the occasion.

Margaret smiled wistfully. 'I was the belle of the ball – or so they told me. I took London by storm!' She glanced at a large photograph of herself when she was in her twenties – a photograph which, framed in an ornate silver frame, stood on the grand piano. As usual her grey eyes filled with nostalgic tears for the days when she was young and beautiful but almost immediately she blinked them away. 'That's when I first set eyes on your father,' she said cheerfully. 'God bless his dear memory.'

Steven hid a smile. 'I'm sure Father was quite bowled over,' he suggested. He was rewarded with a dazzling smile.

'He certainly was, dear. He wanted to dance every dance with me, but of course I couldn't allow it. He often reproached me in later years. He complained that, since he had immediately recognized me as his future bride, I should have recognized him!' She shook her head fondly at the memory.

Steven forced himself to ask his favour. 'About the dinner party – I was hoping you might have room to include a young woman at the dinner.'

'Ah!' She gave him a speculative look. 'When you say young . . . ?'

'Much younger than me, I'm afraid.'

'Good heavens, dear! Anyone would think you were in your dotage!'

'I'm forty-three, Mother.'

'I do know that, Steven. But what does that matter to a woman? You're still a very attractive man.'

'You're prejudiced.'

'Of course I am. Now let me think. I had planned on eight at table but the guest list isn't set in stone.' She put down her sewing. 'I've invited the Donaldsons, of course, and poor old Colonel Dickson – his wife died six months ago, I'm sure I told you. He was so devoted to her. The shock of her death almost unhinged him, poor fellow. You'll hardly recognize him, Steven. He's a shadow of his former self. I doubt he'll be the life and soul of the party but—'

'Then why invite him, Mother?'

'Because he needs feeding up, dear, and cheering up – and because he was there, all those years ago, at my ball. He and your father were friends. Well, acquaintances, shall we say, and he remembers me when I was in my prime. And Helen and Ivor Jefferys are coming and their daughter Alice.'

He groaned. 'Oh, I remember the ghastly Alice!'

'Don't be unkind, dear, she isn't that bad. She is certainly not ghastly.'

'She *is*! She's such a phony. All she talks about is her art and she can't paint for toffee – you said so yourself.'

'Did I really? Well, that was very tactless of me.'

'You didn't say it to her.'

'I should hope not!'

'Her work is only found in galleries because the owners are friends of hers and they're too kind to refuse her.'

His mother was no longer listening. 'So, counting me, that's seven . . . Oh, yes! Jack Lewis. He's been travelling in remote parts of Spain for more than a year and is writing a book in the form of a diary about his experiences.' She laughed at Steven's expression of sudden interest. 'Too late, dear! He's already been commissioned by one of your rivals. I forget which but for a reasonable sum. And he's delighted, naturally.'

She peered at her son, as her grasshopper mind retraced the conversation so far. 'This young woman you are bringing . . .?'

Was he imagining it or did Steven detect the usual hopeful tone in her voice when members of the opposite sex were mentioned.

'She's a writer,' he told her.

'You mean an up-and-coming writer? One of your lame dogs?'

'No, Mother, she's been published before – in *The Ladies Own Journal.*'

'Not a journalist, surely!'

'No, Mother, you're jumping to conclusions as usual. She writes fiction. But what's wrong with journalists?

'And her name is?' Margaret asked, ignoring her son's question.

'Clare Wishart,' he told her. 'You may have read some of her work. She writes under the pseudonym of Clarinda Hart.'

'Clarinda Hart?' Margaret's eyes opened wider. 'Of course I've read her. She frequently writes the serial and I do enjoy her work. If I include her I assume you will also grace our table? We could seat ten at table and still be comfortable.'

'I'd love to be there. Thank you, Mother.'

'I assume she is unmarried.'

'Yes, she is. Does that matter?'

She ignored the question. 'I've always rather liked the name Clare. Is it spelled with an "i"?'

'No, Mother.'

'Oh, well, no matter. Is she pretty?'

'I'm sure she's not as pretty as you were when you "came out",' he said carefully, 'but she's certainly attractive.'

'And you like her?'

He nodded.

'Then I shall like her, Steven. If you give me her address before you go home, I shall send her an invitation.'

Thirteen

It was finally the day of Donald and Molly's wedding. Clare was halfway through the speech she was preparing for Alan Latimer when the postman arrived and she ran downstairs to find an invitation awaiting her.

Mrs Margaret Hampden requests the pleasure of your company on Friday 25 June for dinner – eight o'clock for eight thirty. Dress: formal. RSVP.

'How very odd!' she said, handing it to Donald for his inspection. 'I don't know a Margaret Hampden. There must be some mistake.'

'You must know her. She knows you. Your name is on the envelope. Think, Clare.'

'I tell you I *don't* know her. I don't recognize the address either. Dorchester Terrace? No.' She shook her head. 'It sounds very grand and it says formal dress.'

'I see I'm not invited. Perhaps it's someone you've met who doesn't know me.' Donald sounded rather hurt.

'I can't think who. I never meet anyone.'

'It's addressed to you so you'll have to answer it.' With a shrug, he propped the invitation on the mantelpiece. Dismissing the problem, he asked, 'Are these socks and shoes all right?'

She glanced down at his feet. 'Perfectly all right. Nice polish to the shoes!' She smiled at him. 'Hard to believe you will soon be a married man with a wife and a house and a baby. I'm so pleased for you, Donald. I never expected such a day to come.'

'Neither did I!' He swallowed hard. 'The Jenners have

been very good – even if he did knock me down!' He grinned rather sheepishly.

'Knocked you down?' She stared at him, shocked. 'Tom Jenner knocked you down?'

'When I went to ask for Molly's hand. He sent me sprawling with a right hook! I thought at first he might have broken my jaw. When I got up he did it again.'

'You didn't mention it.'

'It's not the sort of thing you boast about, is it? And it was no less than I deserved after . . . Well, I did take advantage of his daughter. I can't deny that. Molly half expected him to shoot me.' His voice softened. 'You know, she really does love me.'

'And you love her,' she prompted then hesitated. 'You do, don't you?'

'Yes, I do.'

'You have to keep telling her that you do.' She wondered suddenly if he had any understanding of young women and the way their minds work – their strengths and weaknesses, their vulnerabilities. 'Young wives need a lot of reassurance.'

'And you'd know that?'

His retort came quickly, unguarded, and Clare realized that deep down, somewhere within him, the old Donald still lingered. But her cousin, it seemed, had already regretted the words.

'Sorry, Clare, forgive me,' he stammered. 'I shouldn't have said that. I didn't mean it. I know you and Simon . . .'

She forgave him instantly. It was his wedding day and nothing must spoil it. 'We'll pretend I didn't hear it! I have to get back to this little speech that Alan has agreed to give. He's been very kind, to step in at the eleventh hour.'

'Very kind.'

It occurred to her suddenly that Molly's parents would be giving their daughter kindly advice about her forthcoming marriage, but Donald had no one to offer any support – except her. He was very much alone, she realized guiltily, and might well be suffering an attack of pre-wedding nerves.

She said quickly, 'I'm sure it's never all sweetness and

light, being married, Donald, but I envy you. I know you'll
be very happy . . . you just have to take the rough with the
smooth.' That sounded very trite, she thought, but rushed
on. 'That's what my grandmother used to say and I'm sure
she was right. She once said the trick is . . . er . . . to quickly
forget the bad times and always enjoy the good times.' In
fact her grandmother had said no such things, but Clare
wanted Donald to trust someone's words – someone who
was wiser and had more experience than she, Clare, could
claim to have on the subject of marriage.

Recognizing the little homily for what it was, Donald said,
'Yes, ma'am! Thank you, ma'am! I'll remember, ma'am!'

They both laughed.

She said, 'I'll miss you.'

'Will you? That is . . . I can be difficult at times.'

'So can I. I'm glad you have somewhere to go when
Merle Place is sold – a home and a family and a whole
new life. Everything has worked out for the best and by
this time next year you'll be a proper family.'

He gave her a long look. 'You can share the baby, Clare.
We're going to ask you to be godmother. How about that?'

'I'd be honoured, Donald.'

Before she could return to the best man's speech the telephone rang and Donald wandered off, leaving Clare to
answer it. It was Steven Flint.

'Clare! How are you? Blooming, I hope.'

She smiled at the thought of him. 'I'm well, thank you,
but very busy. We're in the middle of a wedding.'

'Not yours, I hope!' He pretended to be anxious but, of
course, he knew that wasn't true.

'Good heavens, no! My cousin, Donald.'

'Oh, yes! Of course. I'd forgotten. So it's today . . . Well,
you have nice weather for it. I won't keep you, Clare, but
I want to warn you. Probably tomorrow you'll receive an
invitation to a—'

'A dinner party? I've already received it. It came this
morning but I have no idea who sent it.'

'All is about to be revealed, Clare. It comes from my
mother. She would like to meet you.'

'Your mother? Oh, no, I don't think so. This one's from a Margaret Hampden . . .'

'That's it. My mother married again when my father died. I didn't think the invitation would reach you so promptly. This telephone call was to warn you to expect it. Will you be able to come? I do hope so.' There was a long pause. 'Clare? You're very quiet. I very much want you to be there.'

'Oh, Steven, I don't know.' She was aware of a creeping panic. 'I'm very much a country mouse to be honest. Why does she want to meet me? I'm not famous or anything.' She frowned. 'It's not a literary dinner, is it? I really don't think I could—'

'It's just a few friends sharing a meal. That's all. The fact is my mother likes to know my friends and she's heard so much about you from me – and none of it bad! Do say you'll come. I'll look after you, I promise. Mother knows how to entertain. She has a wonderful cook and interesting friends.'

Clare was torn. It all sounded very glamorous but she felt sure she would be out of her depth among London society. 'The truth is,' she began, 'that I'm not very good at sparkling, if you know what I mean by that.' Donald appeared beside her needing help with his cufflinks, but flustered she hissed, 'Ask Mrs Parks!' To Steven she said, 'I don't think we'll have much in common. I don't go to Ascot or Henley Royal Regatta or the opera. What on earth would I talk about? I'll be a fish out of water.'

'No, you won't, I promise. You can talk about your writing – that will impress them. They know I'm in the publishing business and the subject always crops up. And you have Merle Place. Selling property! Now that's of general interest – not to mention your experiences there during the war.'

His encouraging words went over her head as she continued to protest. 'And it says it's formal. If I pretend a previous engagement do you think she'd mind? She would never know.' The silence lengthened. 'Steven? Are you still there?' Even as she argued with him, she confessed to herself that the one thing in the dinner party's favour was that she would be with Steven again and that would be wonderful.

If it had been a quiet Sunday lunch for the three of them she would have felt differently about it. The truth was, she admitted to herself, that she didn't want to appear gauche or unworldly in front of Steven. Then it occurred to her that he may well have put the idea of the invitation into his mother's head. Did that mean that he wanted to see her again? How could she refuse him?

Mrs Parks appeared, saw that she was still on the telephone and disappeared again.

'Look, Clare,' Steven was saying, 'the truth is that Mother might survive the disappointment if you don't accept, but I certainly wouldn't. I would be heartbroken! I mean it, Clare. I had planned to come down in the car to bring you back to town and to put you up at a nice hotel for the night after the dinner and then drive you home the next morning – unless I could persuade you to have lunch with me and then come to a matinee. Then I would drive you home afterwards. So you see, Clare, you can't say no without making me utterly miserable!'

She shook her head. It was useless to protest. 'Then I'll say yes,' she agreed, 'but please telephone me tomorrow and convince me again. It's so hectic here and – oh, here comes Donald wanting me to fix his tie! Forgive me but I must go.'

Clare replaced the receiver, fixed the tie then sat down again to finish the speech. She had not changed her clothes yet and time was slipping away.

The ceremony was about to start and Molly knew she looked radiant. She had seen it in her mother's face as, adorned for the wedding, she turned slowly round for her parents to see her in her beautiful dress. She had seen it in the way her father's eyes had filled with tears – he had hastily brushed them away – and the way her ma and pa had exchanged looks without speaking. Was this the moment she wondered, when she should tell them the truth or was that better kept a secret. They seemed to have forgiven poor Donald, so was there any need to ruin their opinion of their daughter on this day of all days?

Her mother said, 'You look wonderful, Molly, and that's the truth although I say it as shouldn't.'

'Thanks, Ma.'

Tom drew his best handkerchief from his top pocket, blew his nose loudly and said nothing.

'Tom!' Her mother was horrified. 'Now I'll have to get you another one for your top pocket.' Grumbling, she dashed upstairs.

Molly regarded her father thoughtfully. How would he feel if he knew? He had knocked Don down for seducing his innocent little girl, not knowing that she had not been as innocent as he supposed. Her thoughts flashed back to the moment before she had decided to wed Donald Wishart. She had gone into the drawing room with a mop in one hand and a duster in the other. He was standing at the French windows with his hands in his pockets, staring out over the garden, and he hadn't turned as she entered although she knew he must have heard her.

'Penny for them, Mr Wishart!'

Without turning he said, 'They are for me to know and you to wonder at, Miss Pert!'

Miss Pert? It didn't sound like a compliment. Miserable old devil, she thought. Always moping about and being grumpy and here she was trying to cheer him up and he couldn't even be bothered to look at her. Slightly offended, Molly had studied him carefully. Mrs P reckoned he was a 'something vert' . . . oh, yes, an introvert – which means he couldn't get along with people. A bit of a loner, she'd explained. Well, he needn't take it out on her. On a whim she selected the mop and moved towards him, picking up the dust from the polished floorboards that surrounded the carpet.

When she reached the area where he was standing, she said loudly,

''Scuse me, sir, but I need to do the floor where you're standing.'

'Go round me.'

What do I have to do to make him look at me? He's just being cranky as usual. In a momentary fit of madness she pushed the mop over his shoes then stepped back, shocked by her stupidity. *Why on earth did I do that? He'll report me, sure as eggs is eggs! I'll get a telling off from Mrs P.*

He glanced down at his shoes. 'Thank you, Molly. They needed a bit of a polish.' At last he turned and amazingly he was grinning and he looked ten years younger and taller and his eyes seemed to be a deeper colour as they regarded each other in silence.

In some lights he might even be good-looking and maybe Mrs P is wrong about him. When he grins he's really quite sweet and compared with the lads in the village he might be a bit of a catch!

For a long moment they stared at each other, startled and then he said, 'I suppose I'd better push off before you mop the rest of me!'

Tongue-tied, she had tried to swallow but her throat was dry. 'I'm sorry, sir.' Molly was suddenly stammering. 'It was silly of me, but I dunno why I . . .'

But then he had wandered off as though he had forgotten her already and the moment between them, if there had been such a moment, died as he left the room.

Shaken and confused by her feelings, Molly had stared after him, her thoughts in turmoil but her decision made. She was going to wed Donald Wishart.

Today, twenty minutes later, standing beside him at the altar, waiting to marry him, she decided to keep her secret for ever. Donald Wishart had not seduced the Jenners's daughter – she had seduced him.

Snapping out of her reverie, Molly realized that the organ music had stopped, the congregation was hushed and the vicar had started to read from his book. Soon he was asking the important questions and both bride and groom spoke up bravely and were soon duly declared man and wife. Molly smiled brilliantly as her husband leaned down to kiss her. A satisfied murmur broke out among the wedding guests – and it was all over.

In no time at all they were back at the farmhouse, where the celebrations began in earnest. The bridesmaids behaved as well as small girls ever do – flouncing around in their frilly dresses and giggling at everything and nothing. Alan made a very dignified best man and gave his short speech with as much feeling as he could considering he hardly knew the groom. He had somehow learned it by heart and started with a few comments of his own which impressed Clare tremendously.

'I have been fortunate, ladies and gentlemen,' he said as the noise died down, 'to be allowed to be part of today's happy events and it is a great privilege to speak a little about today's happy couple – Molly and Donald. Or should I call them Mr and Mrs Wishart?'

Loud cheers greeted these remarks and the speech was also interrupted from time to time by the children's antics but nobody minded. After Alan's speech, toasts were made and the reception, in the Jenners's large kitchen, overflowed into the yard which had been tidied and swept for the occasion. Molly clutched Donald's hand as if her life depended on it and he beamed with pride as they chatted to their guests. Eating and drinking went on apace until the daylight began to fade and the numbers dwindled. Just before nine Donald scooped up his bride and carried her off towards their refurbished cottage.

Tom Jenner showed Alan round the farm, while Annie, Clare and Mrs Parks did the washing up. Later still Clare waved Alan off and then sat down suddenly, realizing just how tired she was.

It was almost dark when Clare made her way home and she was glad of Mrs Parks's company on the way back. They walked in silence most of the way and then Mrs Parks said, 'Well, that went off fine, ma'am, didn't it? No one can say they didn't have a good send off.' She turned to Clare in the darkness. 'D'you reckon they'll make a go of it?'

'Stranger things have happened,' said Clare. 'He wouldn't be the first man saved from himself by the love of a good woman!'

Fourteen

Clement Woodrow sat down in his chair in his office and yawned widely, grateful that none of his staff could see him. He had had a restless night after drinking too much port with the cheese and his insides still worried him. The men's lavatory was on the far side of the bank's offices and an upset stomach often meant an undignified rush past the staff.

Someone knocked at the door and Miss Petrie looked in.

'Good morning, Mr Woodrow,' she said, smiling. 'Even though it is Monday!'

He gave a little laugh to please her and she went on.

'It's my birthday today so I've brought in a cake – Madeira – your favourite.'

'Ah, happy birthday, Miss Petrie! And, yes, before you ask, I should love a slice of your Madeira cake. I assume you made it yourself with your own fair hands?' The bank manager liked to think of himself as a ladies' man.

'I did.' She beamed with pleasure. 'Right you are then, Mr Woodrow – a cup of tea and a slice of my cake.'

As soon as she had gone, his smile disappeared. He did wonder sometimes if he should put a stop to all this birthday cake nonsense and the office Christmas presents and unsuitable jollity that crept in from time to time.

Clement Woodrow was a small thin man of fifty-five, counting the years until he would have enough money to retire. He was a sober man with little sense of humour and his small dark eyes looked out on the world with apprehension most of the time. He certainly did not approve of his fellow bank managers who readily confessed to keeping 'a bottle of scotch' tucked away in the bottom drawer.

Clement clutched his rumbling stomach and groaned anxiously.

Another knock at the door brought young Mr Ben Griffiths, the assistant manager, to his desk with an open diary.

'Good morning, sir! I hope you had a nice weekend.'

'Yes, thank you, Mr Griffiths. And you?'

'Yes, thank you, sir. I've just had a call from Miss Wishart. She is rather anxious to speak with you this morning, although she doesn't have an appointment.'

'Hmm. Did she say what it's about?' He tried not to sound too reluctant.

'About the sale of her property, Merle Place.'

'Ah!' Clement nodded. 'I wonder if she has a buyer. Do I have any spare time today?'

'Yes, sir. One at ten thirty and one at five.'

'Offer her a choice, but I would prefer the morning session. I may be going home early this afternoon.' He smiled briefly at the younger man whom he considered to be the only member of his staff with a promising future in banking. Ben Griffiths, who was twenty-four years old, was bright and keen and had a wise head on his shoulders.

'Miss Clare Wishart,' he murmured, when he was once more alone. A pleasant woman. He had had a few dealings with the grandfather and remembered her as a young girl, clutching her grandfather's hand and smiling shyly at the 'important man' behind the desk. Much later she had been in and out of the bank when she inherited the property and occasionally news reached Clement about her activities. She had allowed Merle Place to be used as a hospital for returning servicemen and had also volunteered to join the medical staff in a minor capacity. Most unsuitable in his opinion.

He had advised against it, considering her too delicate a plant to survive in the hurly-burly of a military-style hospital. Clare Wishart came from good stock – a family he thought of as decent people – and he imagined her deceased relatives turning in their graves as she rushed to and fro emptying bedpans or changing soiled bedlinen.

'Very unsuitable!' he murmured. Years ago he had noted her in his file as 'Nervous. Can be difficult' and 'Sometimes inclined to be stubborn'.

And here she was about to sell Merle House, which had proved to be something of a white elephant. 'Where does the time go?' he asked himself aloud. Doodling on the edge of the blotter with red ink, he drew a cross and round it an apron with a pocket and inside the pocket, a watch. Nurse Clare Wishart, he thought, and found the idea unlikely. He tried to remember what she was doing now, if anything, to earn an honest crust. Like many women of her class she probably had very little to offer in the way of useful skills.

The pain came again and he wondered whether to take another of his pills. Of course he knew she had lost her fiancé during the early months of the war. She was one of millions of women who would remain spinsters through no fault of their own. All the more reason why they should learn to take advice. He tutted and shook his head and rearranged the objects on his desk – returning his pen to the red ink well, realigning a pencil sharpener, smoothing the leather-edged blotter with his plump fingers.

Yet another knock. Ben Griffiths poked his head round the door. 'Miss Wishart says she will be here promptly at ten thirty, Mr Woodrow.'

'Thank you. Remind Miss Petrie to bring in the tea and cake when she's ready.'

Distracted by the pain developing in the region of his stomach, he waved his assistant manager away.

Promptly at ten thirty Clare was shown into the bank manager's office. It was hot outside – what Donald called sultry and she called clammy. It had rained overnight and they had woken to find an uncharacteristic mist limiting visibility but it had quickly been dispersed by the sun.

After the polite preliminaries, Clare took a sip of tea and broached the subject of the meeting. She had made up her mind to sound confident. She would refuse to be intimidated.

'I have a small group of people interested in Merle Place,'

she explained. 'They want to develop it as a sort of resource for artistic people.' She waited for his response without much hope. She had never liked him very much, had found him rather negative, in fact, so she was not expecting him to embrace her plan.

'What kind of resource?' He regarded her suspiciously. 'A commercial venture of some kind?'

'Not exactly. A retreat.'

'From what exactly?' He raised his eyebrows.

'From the cares and pressures of the world – and from family life sometimes. A retreat offers accommodation for artistic people to live in peaceful surroundings while they compose music . . . or paint a picture or maybe write some poetry. That sort of thing. They might come for a week or a month or only a few days, but they are guaranteed to be among like-minded people. They forget their worries and—?'

'Are bank managers allowed into this oasis of calm?' He actually smiled.

Mr Woodrow was being humorous! Clare smiled with him then continued. She explained that it was unlikely the three or four members of the consortium could between them raise enough capital to buy Merle Place. 'They're currently exploring all avenues,' she told him, 'but I'm wondering if there is any way in which I could help by perhaps retaining a part of the house – either by raising money, most likely a bank loan, or by reducing the price accordingly so that I never sell the entire property.'

Mr Woodrow frowned and her hopes faded a little. He was going to find objections.

He said, 'What you are actually proposing is that you somehow become a member of the consortium. Am I right? You would be an equal partner in the scheme.'

'I suppose that sums it up, Mr Woodrow. The bottom line is I hate the idea of parting with Merle Place forever because it's been in the family for a long time. I know it's been left to me, but I am beginning to feel rather treacherous. I'd like to have one room, however small, that is reserved for me so that whenever I need a spot of tranquillity I can always go back.'

She wondered if his earlier doubts were disappearing and sat up straighter in her chair. 'I would like to discuss the idea with the other members of the group, but not before I know just where I stand financially. I will naturally discuss this with my solicitor when I have the necessary details. I have no intention of rushing headlong . . .' She stopped and regarded the manager with narrowed eyes. 'Are you all right, Mr Woodrow? You look rather pale.'

'I'm perfectly well, thank you, Miss Wishart,' he said firmly. 'You were saying?'

'Er . . . oh, yes. I have no intention of rushing headlong into anything.'

'I'm glad to hear it. If you are asking for my advice I'd have to say it does sound rather . . . vague. Rather unformed. Perhaps a shade risky.'

'Well, I agree it is unformed at the moment. That's why I have come to you and will go to my solicitor to collect the information I need.' She knew she sounded defensive but that was how she felt. 'I'm assuming you would be prepared to offer me a loan, Mr Woodrow.' She waited, still a little distracted by his expression. He was frowning, possibly at her comments, or possibly he was in pain.

He had screwed up his face and was almost doubled over.

He said, 'If you had sold Merle Place and were preparing to invest the money and live on it, what other security could you offer for a loan? How would you repay it?'

Clare stared at him. His line of reasoning came as a shock. 'Well, I don't know. I hadn't thought about it quite in that way.' She cursed herself for her stupidity. Her hopes were about to be dashed.

'There may possibly be a way round it, Miss Wishart, but an unsecured loan for a woman we would usually need a gentleman to act as guarantor.'

Clare felt her face colour with anger as the implications of his argument registered. 'Because I am a woman? Does that mean you consider me unreliable simply because I am not a man? Aren't there any men to whom you lend money who eventually prove unreliable? Men who default on the payments?' she demanded.

'Of course but that is a risk the bank has to be prepared to take. Women are—'

'And do you ever ask that a wealthy woman stand guarantor for an unreliable or risky man?' Warming to her theme, Clare rushed on, giving him no time to answer. 'Can you imagine how many widows this last war has created? Are they all to be denied help unless they can find a man to sponsor them? I think that's . . .' She swallowed hard. 'I think it's an outrageous attitude!'

For a moment they glared at each other.

He said, 'Many women have inferior jobs, Miss Wishart, and insufficient salaries.'

'So you assume I'm one of them without even asking how I might repay the money! I might find it very easy. In fact I have a publisher waiting for the book I'm writing – and I might put forward a very unsuitable man as my guarantor. Would that satisfy the bank?' Even as she argued, she wondered if she was ruining her chances of a loan by antagonizing him. She took a few deep breaths and told herself to calm down.

Mr Woodrow stood up abruptly and her hopes faded. Had she overstepped the mark?

'Excuse me a moment, please, Miss Wishart . . .'

To her surprise he stumbled towards the door, his face ashen, and she listened as his retreating footsteps quickened to a run.

Clare sat alone in the office for nearly ten minutes waiting for him to return. He must have either been taken ill or had forgotten all about her. Feeling abandoned, she ate three biscuits and poured herself a second cup of tea. Uneasily she wondered if she had so enraged him that he had had a heart attack.

She was still drinking her tea when a young man entered the room and introduced himself as Mr Griffiths, the assistant manager. They shook hands and he smiled. Clare thought she recognized a gleam of admiration in his eyes; it made her sit up straighter and gave her a little more confidence.

'I'm afraid poor Mr Woodrow has been taken home in a taxi,' he told Clare.

'He didn't look at all well.'

'No.' He hesitated. 'Between you and me, he has seemed unwell for some weeks now and hasn't consulted the doctor. I think now he will be forced to seek help.'

'I'm so sorry. Do give him my best wishes for a speedy recovery.'

'He asked me to apologize for not finishing your meeting, but he will write to you shortly when he has considered your request for help and will do what he can to help the project reach fruition although he is not particularly hopeful. We have to have our loans agreed by Head Office, you see, and we are expected to keep the loans at an acceptable level. I'll telephone you when I have some news and we'll make another appointment.' He held out his hand obviously expecting her to take the hint and leave.

Clare remained sitting down. 'The problem is I don't feel I can wait.' *I can't give up this easily. If losing my temper hasn't worked I shall try another line of attack.* 'Perhaps, in his absence, you could help me.' He looked taken aback and she said hurriedly, 'I do wish you would sit down for a moment and hear my proposition in a little more detail. I'm sure we could find a way round it.'

To her relief, after a moment's hesitation, he sat down in the manager's chair and opened the file Mr Woodrow had left on the desk. When he had finished reading it Clare launched into her requirements while Mr Griffiths made a few additional notes.

'I don't see any major problems,' he told her cheerfully. 'At least, nothing we can't deal with. We do have certain discretionary powers although, as I mentioned earlier, they do have to be approved by our superiors.' He smiled. 'Don't look so worried, Miss Wishart. It sounds like a very sensible, if unusual, idea and I hope we can find a way to accommodate your needs. What are banks for if not to lend money? That's how we make our profits.'

He promised to keep in touch and, encouraged by her unexpected success, Clare rose to take her leave. As she walked from the bank with her head held high she was aware of a glow of satisfaction that she had argued her case and won. She felt more like a businesswoman and less like a supplicant; the heady feeling was new to her.

Minutes later she was hailing a taxi to take her home and this reminded her that she still had no form of transport. Jonty was dead and so was Jimmie and she needed to replace both of them. Then, with a horse to pull the pony trap and the mower, she would set the new gardener to cut the neglected lawns and see to the flower beds and shrubbery. Merle Place must not be allowed to fall into neglect while she was still trying to sell it.

Fifteen

Clare was surprised, as time passed, to find that she missed Donald; not for his sparkling wit or experience but as another person in the house. She was thankful for Mrs Parks and Molly. Even when she was closeted in the study writing, she knew they were around and for the first time she wondered what she would do if she bought herself a much smaller house. If she didn't need servants, she would have nobody. Grimly, she reminded herself that she was only one of millions of single women who would live lonely lives without families.

So don't you dare to feel sorry for yourself, Clare Wishart! You have most of your life ahead of you and must make plans so as not to waste a moment of it.

Two days had passed since her trip to the bank manager. With a sigh, she stood up from her chair in the study and crossed to the window to stare out over the neglected garden. She had advertised for a gardener and a young man was coming later for an interview. Perhaps he knew something about horses. If not she would turn to the vet for advice, sure that he knew most of the animals in the area and would be able to judge their suitability or lack of it. Everything was changing and she found it unsettling. But not only for her.

Not for the first time, she thought about her cousin, trying to imagine him fitting in to the very different way of life he had now. His life was also undergoing serious changes, not least because he would now be working on the farm under Tom Jenner's eagle eye. Clare crossed her fingers, hoping that his marriage would last and be happy. At least she would be a godmother and she could look forward to seeing Donald's children grow up. But what was she going to do with the rest of her life apart from that? She would move from Merle Place but where to?

The assistant bank manager had written an encouraging letter about the possibility of a loan and she had spoken to him on the telephone, emphasizing the fact that she expected to be earning money as a full-time writer so should have a reasonable income.

'I'm surprised,' she had told him, 'that you think my application will be successful. Mr Woodrow seemed very doubtful that he could help me.'

'Apparently poor Mr Woodrow was in great pain during your interview and was later rushed to hospital,' he'd said. 'He might even have to have some surgery so possibly he was rather distracted when he spoke to you. I'll be dealing with your proposition and I'm very optimistic.'

They talked about her desire to retain some part of Merle Place and he suggested she talk to the family solicitor. A small but significant success, she thought, and made an appointment to see her solicitor later in the week. One step at a time – it was a daunting process but she was determined not to give in.

There was a knock at the door and Mrs Parks came in.

'That gardener chap's at the back door,' she told Clare. 'He's turned up early on the off chance, he says, because he's got to take his son to the doctor at three so if you can't see him now . . .'

'I'll see him,' she said.

The housekeeper hesitated in the doorway. 'He's a far cry from Jimmie,' she remarked. 'We'll never find anyone to replace Jimmie. This one's half his size and looks far too young to have a family. Just a bit of a lad really. Bit slow on the uptake, too, if you ask me.'

'Jimmie was young once, Mrs Parks.'

'Jimmie was devoted to Merle Place.' Mrs Parks shrugged. 'You'll see.'

The mention of Jimmie reminded Clare that she must find out about the headstone his sister had ordered. 'Show Mr Martin up, please, Mrs Parks.'

Minutes later Eddie Martin thundered up the stairs and

Clare smiled at his approach. At least he had plenty of energy, she thought. When he came into the room, however, she saw what the housekeeper had meant. He was small, thin and wiry with a thatch of untidy brown hair and eyes like boot buttons, but at least he had a ruddy complexion and looked hearty. He was obviously wearing his work clothes and launched into an explanation about why he had come so early. Clare stopped him in midstream and asked him to sit down.

'Give me some idea, please, Mr Martin, of your experience as a gardener,' she began.

He frowned.

'How long have you been a gardener, for instance?' she prompted.

'Years. Long as I can remember – since I left school.'

'How old were you at that time, Mr Martin?'

'Not quite sure.' He scratched his head.

'And may I ask how old you are now, Mr Martin?'

He gave it some thought then said cautiously, 'I reckon that'll be twenty-five.'

Clare was surprised. He looked about eighteen. 'And do you have any kind of reference with you? A letter from one of your employers, perhaps.'

He shook his head then changed his mind, plunged a hand into the pocket of his corduroy trousers and handed her a folded sheet of paper. 'Ma says to give you this.'

Clare opened the note that was written in pencil on lined paper.

> *Ed works for the vicker and old mrs Crewe and another chap, the brother of doctor Haddon.*

Her hopes were slightly dashed by this. It sounded as if he were already fully employed, but suddenly inspired she said, 'Shall we take a quick turn around the garden so you can see what you would have to be dealing with. I had hoped for someone full-time but part-time would be better than nothing.' She would also have to tell him that Merle Place was on the market, but she could promise to recommend him to the new owners.

Clutching his cap in both hands, Eddie Martin trailed silently behind her as she gave him information about the maintenance of the garden.

'Roses, obviously – they can be pruned quite severely in the autumn, but I expect you know that already. Over there – ' she pointed – 'that was once an orchard, but most of the trees are past their best now. I keep intending to plant a plum tree and maybe a pear and peach. Maybe the ones that grow against the wall. We do have a wall but it's part of the disused greenhouse. There's an old rustic summer house and beyond that a reasonable greenhouse. We grow grapes, mainly.' He made no comment but gave an occasional nod. 'You may have heard that I'm trying to sell the property, but if I do I could give you a very good reference so you would probably be able to stay on here.'

Suddenly Clare remembered the note he had brought. 'Do you still work for the vicar and Mrs Crewe and the other man?'

Eddie Martin closed his eyes; it seemed to help him focus on the question. 'I do the vicarage hedge once a month; Mrs Crewe's bit of grass Saturday morning; and I don't go to the doc's brother any more because he never had the right money and kept me waiting, like sometimes it was two or three weeks, and me ma said he was a dodgy payer and to give him a miss.' He opened his eyes, lapsed into a gloomy silence and stared fixedly at his boots.

Clare decided that perhaps he was distracted by the problem with his son and felt a little guilty for taking up so much of his time. 'I can show you the rest some other time, if you prefer,' she suggested. Why hadn't she enquired after the boy? She should have shown an interest, she thought, cross with herself. 'I hope there is nothing seriously wrong with your son,' she said.

He shrugged. 'It's his cough. Day and night. Cough, cough, cough!' His eyes gleamed suddenly and he pointed ahead. 'Stables? You got horses, have you?' He turned to her hopefully. 'I love horses, I do. Should've been a farrier like my uncle, but I wasn't old enough when he needed a new lad 'cos Buster, his nephew, had gone sudden like, died of his lungs just afore his wedding, and I missed my chance. If he'd hung on for a couple more years . . . Still, what's done's done.' He smiled. 'Me and horses, we're like that!' He held up a thumb and forefinger pressed closely together.

'We normally keep one horse,' Clare told him, 'but he died recently and we have to get another one. Perhaps you . . .'

'Could find you a horse? Of course, no problem!' Now his face was one large grin. 'You tell me what you want to pay and I'll find you one. I could take you to look at two this very day if you wanted. I'll see you proud, see if I don't!'

'We have a rather ancient trap and I drive myself most of the time, but you would be in charge of his food and general care – and he also pulls the mower. There is also the possibility of accommodation,' she said, remembering somewhat belatedly. 'If you wished to live in the small flat over the stables I would deduct something in lieu of rent but if not—'

His eyes widened. 'What just me in a flat?' He looked worried. 'I dunno what my wife would say.'

Clare pressed a hand to her mouth in exasperation. 'How silly of me! You're a married man. Forgive me. I quite forgot . . . Let me see now. You'd come in daily six days a week and would eat in the kitchen with Mrs Parks and with whoever is our maid. Your predecessor used to?'

'My what?'

'Our previous gardener was also willing to do a few odd jobs around the place when necessary – unblocking drains and that sort of thing.'

Eddie scratched his head and frowned. 'I could do that for you.'

He seemed willing enough, thought Clare. She came to an abrupt decision. A man who loved horses. He was young but he had a family and that was settling. His experience was limited but he looked fit enough and hopefully he could learn.

'Mr Martin, if we can agree your wages, you've got the job for six weeks and if you prove suitable it will hopefully become permanent.'

They shook hands on the deal.

Sixteen

Three days later, Margaret Hampden opened the door to the flat and looked none too pleased to see her son.

'It's gone ten at night,' she said crossly. 'What on earth brings you here at this late hour?' She led the way into the sitting room.

'I was on my way home from the opera and thought I'd call in and . . . just to see how you are.' He settled in a chair, stretched his legs and crossed his ankles. 'I was invited to go to *La Bohème* by Austin and his wife.'

'At Covent Garden?' She sat down opposite him and folded her hands neatly in her lap. She was not deceived by her son's attempt at nonchalance. A late visit usually meant that Steven had something on his mind and needed to talk about it. 'Did you enjoy it? It's one of your favourites, isn't it?'

'Very much so. Austin and I went to the crush bar for a whisky in the interval. His wife stayed in the box and we sent up an ice cream. She doesn't drink . . . A nice woman though.'

Ah! Now it was becoming clearer, she thought. 'Time you thought about getting a wife,' she said with a careless smile. 'Somewhere in England's capital city there must be a young woman with whom you could share your life.'

He sat forward eagerly. 'Before you ask how Miss Wishart is going to find her way to London for the dinner party, I'm motoring down earlier in the day to bring her back with me. Afterwards—'

'You are not going to put her up in your flat, I hope.'

'Certainly not! I have booked her into the Grosvenor Hotel for the night. On the Saturday I shall probably show her the offices where I work and then take her to the matinee at the Garrick. Miss Wishart is something of a country mouse – in the nicest possible way, of course, and I want her to get a taste of life in London. Then I shall take her back home to Kent.'

Margaret's mind began to work overtime. 'So I take it you are no longer seeing the other girl – what was her name? Laura? Letitia?'

'Lavinia Brooks. Yes, Mother, I am no longer seeing her. We stopped seeing each other a few months ago. It was never very serious – she was a friend of Harold's sister.'

'Harold at the office, you mean?'

He nodded. 'Lavinia was over with her parents visiting from Canada and she didn't know anyone. I was simply someone to escort her around the usual landmarks. Oh Lord! She was indefatigable! We saw the Tower of London and Trafalgar Square and trooping the colour – the whole caboodle!' He laughed.

'I hope you took her to the National Gallery. No visitor to London should miss that experience.'

'Oh, yes. I'd forgotten the NT. And the King personally gave us a guided tour of Buckingham Palace and—'

'Now you're being silly!' She tutted. 'You were rather a silly boy on occasions, but I hoped you'd have grown out of it by the time you reached forty-three! So you spent a lot of time together, but you didn't like her?'

'Or she didn't like me.' He grinned. 'Let's just say that we didn't *dis*like each other, but we didn't fall in love. That's what you are really asking.'

'Don't be awkward, Steven!' Exasperated, she sighed heavily. 'As if I would be so indelicate.'

Obliging her curiosity he said, 'Lavinia was pleasant enough but not my type. A little too brash for my taste. Miss Wishart is quite different. Rather quiet and solitary. I think the dinner party will be rather a test for her.'

'A test? Nonsense, Steven. None of my guests are allowed to find the evening a test. I shall be very nice to her – we all will. Where exactly does she live?'

'Near Maidstone – but don't imagine her as a country

bumpkin, nor as a delicate flower. During the war she worked in her own house, Merle Place, as a sort of ward maid. She's not afraid of hard work or of getting her hands dirty. She is currently selling the house, Merle Place, which has about a dozen bedrooms and acres of gardens. It was left to her by her grandfather.'

'A dozen bedrooms. Good heavens!' Margaret made a quick adjustment to her earlier impression of her son's new friend. Perhaps Miss Wishart could turn out to be a suitable wife for her son. 'I am looking forward to meeting her, Steven. And of course she writes in *The Ladies Own Journal*. Clarinda Hart. I like her style of writing. But now she's writing a novel for you.'

He nodded.

'How old is she?'

'I don't know, Mother.' He laughed. 'Perhaps nearing thirty. You know perfectly well a man can never ask a woman a question like that. I'm surprised at you!'

'Have a guess, dear, and stop being difficult.'

'Late twenties, then.'

'And not already married?' This was worrying, she thought.

'She was engaged but her fiancé was killed in the war. Six years ago. Apparently they were both killed by the same shell – not her, of course. I mean her cousin and his best friend, Simon, to whom she was engaged. She had tears in her eyes when she told me. I wished then that I hadn't asked about it.'

'Poor young woman! How positively ghastly.'

'It must have been horrific hearing how it happened. The letter from his commanding officer said that he had shown extraordinary courage under fire and had brought credit to the unit.'

'Maybe that is some comfort,' said Margaret, 'but how does one choose between a dead hero and a living coward?'

'Mother, what an odd thing to say!' He stared at her, shocked.

'You're not a mother, Steven. I am.'

'But he sounds like something of a hero. Something to live up to. She's obviously terribly proud of him.'

'I'm not intending to demean him in any way, but I suspect the officers always say that in their letters to the family. It gives the grieving relatives something to cling to; something to make the blow a little less severe.' She shook her head. 'I feel particularly for the poor wives of the men shot as cowards – especially the volunteers. You'd have to be a hero just to enlist if you weren't forced into it. They were probably just too frightened to carry on fighting. You are so lucky to miss all that, Steven. The day war was declared I thanked God you were too valuable to be conscripted. Working in intelligence was just as important.'

He looked at her in surprise. 'Would you have wanted me to return if I'd been branded a coward?'

'Most certainly I'd want you to return!' she repeated and he saw the stubborn look in her eyes. 'Ask Clare about the men who came home shell-shocked, their minds in tatters.'

'Clare said that when the letter came from his commanding officer she wanted to die, just to be with Simon.' He sighed. 'I don't know if she will ever want to wed. Left to her own devices she could earn a good enough living as a writer. She doesn't need to marry. She may stay loyal to him.' His expression changed. 'Some women can only ever love one man. Isn't that true?'

Margaret shrugged. 'For some women maybe. I married again and I certainly didn't intend any disrespect to your father, Steven. He would have wanted me to remarry.' She smiled. 'Let's not look on the black side, dear. You know what they say about time, the great healer. There's a lot of truth in that. Your young lady might *think* she doesn't want another man in her life but when she meets the right one . . . Who knows?'

'I hope so – if I am the right one.'

Margaret gave him a searching look. 'Does she mean that much to you?'

'Yes. I'm afraid she does. Compared to Clare the other women . . . just shadows.' He stood up. 'I must let you get to bed.'

As she saw him off at the door she patted his arm. 'I shall be very nice to her and I'll make sure she enjoys herself. I'll be at the head of the table, with you and Clare on my right and left. Would that help?'

'That would be perfect. Thank you, Mother.' He kissed her goodnight. 'I knew you'd understand.'

She watched him go down the stairs. So that was the purpose of his late-night visit, she thought cheerfully – and the young lady was in her late twenties. Clare Wishart sounded very suitable and was still young enough to give her some grandchildren.

Sunday lunch at the Jenners's farm was a haphazard affair. Tom and Annie had invited Clare to join them. Donald and Molly finally arrived, though were later than expected. Molly explained that Donald had been trying to scrub his hands which were covered with wood stain.

'He's been repainting the wainscoting,' she explained proudly. 'It looks a treat. You'd be surprised what you can do with a lick of paint.'

Annie said, 'Well, now you're here, you can set the table and then tell your pa to be back in half an hour – he's doing the rounds with the dog.' To Clare she said, 'Tom likes to walk the boundaries, as he calls it, once a week to satisfy himself all's in order. Once a week, as regular as clockwork.'

'Always takes his gun,' Molly offered. 'Dunno exactly what he's going to shoot – now that me and Don are wed!' She sent her husband a wicked grin and he rolled his eyes.

'I think I had a lucky escape.' He glanced at Clare.

Although it was Sunday, and though a visitor was present, no special effort was made, Clare noted. It was as if she were part of the family. Molly collected knives and forks from the dresser drawer and began to set the places on the large kitchen table. An assortment of dinner plates were arranged on the table.

'How's that?' Molly asked her mother.

'It'll do.'

As an afterthought Molly took a pot of rather limp geraniums from the window sill and put them in the centre of the table.

Clare said, 'Very nice!' and Molly smiled.

Clare found her quite beguiling in her Sunday best. Her dress, which strained at the waist, was white sprigged with pink roses and made her look about fourteen. Clare tried to imagine her with a baby and failed.

Annie spotted the geraniums and snorted with dis-approval. 'Get that off my table!'

Molly bridled. 'It's like they do at Merle Place.'

'Well, you're not at Merle Place so move it. Where do you think I'm going to put the vegetables with that stuck in the middle? And don't settle yourself! You can go and find your pa and say one o'clock on the dot.'

Donald said, 'Shall I go? Molly can rest.'

'She doesn't need a rest, Donald. She's not ill – she's just in the family way.' Annie pushed back a strand of hair. To Clare she said, 'I never give a thought to Mrs Parks. All on her own, is she?'

'No. She's been invited to a friend's house. Is there anything I can do to help?'

'No, thanks. You're a visitor so make the most of it.' She gave Clare a brief smile and bent to peer into the oven where a big hen, surrounded by potatoes, was slowly roasting.

'Smells good!' said Clare.

'It should be all right. I simmered it a bit first because it was an old bird. Gave up laying a month ago or more.'

'Not much fun being a chicken,' Clare said with a laugh.

'Better than being caught by a fox.' She gave Molly a look. 'You still here?'

Molly gave in and prepared to go in search of her father, pausing only to glance hopefully at Donald. 'Want to come with me?'

'No, he doesn't!' her mother snapped. 'Get along, Molly, for heavens' sake!'

When she had gone, Annie turned purposefully to Donald and Clare.

'About our Molly,' she began, keeping an eye on the window. 'When she's due – I don't want no fuss with doctors.' They regarded her blankly and she ploughed on. 'I don't want her to get any fancy ideas. Old Evie Staddon brought her into the world and plenty others like her. I've had a word with Evie and she's prepared to come. Never lost a mother or a child in all that time.'

Clare glanced at Donald who was looking nervous at the way the conversation was heading.

Clare asked, 'Is Evie a midwife? A qualified midwife?'

'Every bit as good as! She's delivered nigh on thirty babies in this village so I reckon that makes her one.'

Donald said quickly, 'Suits me, then.'

Annie looked at Clare. 'What about you?'

'I'm just a cousin to Donald. It's not up to me to decide such things. I'd rather not interfere.'

Annie put her hands on her hips. 'Just as we know where we are with this. I don't want anyone giving her fancy notions.'

Donald narrowed his eyes. 'What's the alternative to old Evie then? I'm not sure I'm quite clear about the problem.'

Annie tossed her head. 'It's a silly fad, if you ask me, but I know of a couple of girls who have chosen the new doctor instead of old Evie. They call it moving with the times! Huh! Why do they need a doctor when they're not ill? Having a baby is perfectly normal – no need for any fuss. A man's not cut out to be a midwife. He's never been through it, has he? At any rate, it's not suitable. Not in my opinion. A bit too personal, a man, at a time like that.' She snatched up a pile of chopped cabbage from the draining board, thrust it into one of the saucepans and poured boiling water over it from the kettle.

Feeling rather useless, Clare glanced at her cousin, hoping he had an opinion although, as Annie had said very forcibly, he hadn't been through it so what did he know?

Donald said slowly, 'Shouldn't Molly have a say in it? She may be happy with Evie. If not I think we must let her decide. She's the mother. It's her child.'

Clare gazed at him in astonishment. Donald Wishart, husband and father-to-be, was certainly changing – and for the better. She found herself envying Molly. Why had he been so difficult for most of his life? Was it her fault in any way? Was it really, as she had often wondered, that he was jealous of her when they were children? When her mother had died she had spent a lot of time with Donald's parents when she lived with them, and they had made a great fuss of her, trying to make up for the loss of her mother. Did all his resentment stem from that time?

'Her child *and* yours.' Annie reminded him. Faced with an unexpected challenge, she had softened her tone a little. 'Well, call me old-fashioned but it's not quite right to my way of thinking.'

Clare felt that Donald deserved some support. 'I think Donald's got a point.' She turned to him. 'Why not ask Molly some time when no one else is around? We may be worrying for nothing.'

Annie slammed a lid on to the cabbage pan.

Donald caught Clare's eye and winked. 'Clare's right. *I'll* have a word with Molly tonight and I'll report back to you in the morning.' He smiled at his mother-in-law who, disconcerted, found nothing to say.

'That's settled, then!' said Clare.

Donald muttered something about 'a bit of fresh air' and went out into the yard.

With her hands on her hips, Annie watched him go.

Clare said quickly, 'Has your daughter put a spell on him, Annie? He's so different. Much nicer now.'

Annie hesitated. 'Maybe no one loved him before.'

Clare nodded.

Abruptly Annie reached for the pot of geraniums. She gave them a little water from the tap over the sink, found an old saucer to stand the pot on and set the flowers in the middle of the table. 'Why not?' she said and the two women exchanged a smile.

Clare arrived promptly at the solicitor's offices the next day – a minute before twelve o'clock. Encouraged by her interview with young Mr Griffiths, Clare was hoping to use her charms to impress Mr Lawrence's son but she was disappointed. Old Mr Lawrence shook her hand and explained that his son had recently set up on his own in Dorset.

'It was time for him to break away,' he said, waving her

to a chair and settling himself behind his desk. He was small and pudgy with round-lensed spectacles and he always made Clare think of Humpty-Dumpty. 'My younger son is joining the firm and hopefully my nephew will also work here when he is old enough.' He smiled at her. 'Now, what can we do for you, Miss Wishart? Selling Merle Place, I hear. Well, that's a shame. It's been in your family for a long time.'

Clare said, 'That's how I feel about it. I have to sell the house because I can't possibly afford to maintain it and don't want to let it fall into disrepair.' She then explained the quandary and her own idea for resolving it.

Half an hour later, she had argued her case successfully and with the solicitor's help had found a way to ensure that she need not sever all connections with her home. As soon as she arrived home, she hurried to the telephone and made contact with Alan Latimer.

'This is how it could be done,' she told him, after the briefest of greetings. 'I would sell the property to your consortium at an agreed price but would retain an interest in the stable block so that I could use the accommodation above as a place in the country. A place of my own. What do you think?'

To her surprise he hesitated. 'Wouldn't we need it?' he asked. 'When you replace Jimmie . . .'

'But I've already found a replacement. A young married man who lives in the village with his family so he doesn't want to live there. You could continue to employ him and I could easily rent out the stable and the tack room to the consortium for a very small annual fee. Will you think about it, Alan? Then, wherever I move to, I could return to Merle Place from time to time. I could come here to write, maybe.'

After a moment Alan said, 'Is your solicitor willing to see it through for you and to deal with our solicitor?'

'Yes.' She was somewhat taken aback by what she felt was a lack of enthusiasm in his voice but continued. 'He suggests that it's all fully documented in the normal and appropriate way, but in addition there should be a condition of sale which is a leasehold interest for me of say ninety-nine years in the stable block. Obviously you will need to discuss it with the other members of the consortium, but if they agree and a price is agreed it should be straight sailing.' She stopped for breath, then went on eagerly. 'Since I would be retaining a small part of the property we could lower the price accordingly.'

Crossing her fingers, Clare waited. Then she heard what sounded like a deep sigh.

'Clare, I don't want to throw a spanner in the works, but there is a small problem. One of the members has backed out. He thought he could manage it but it involved a bank loan and they've refused to give him the whole amount. I was going to tell you but you didn't give me a chance.'

No, this can't be happening! Just when I thought we were there. Clare closed her eyes and only just managed to hold back a groan of frustration.

'I'm sorry, Clare. I know how much it means to you but I'll go on trying.'

'I'm not blaming you, Alan, because I know how keen you are. After all it was your idea. What reason did the bank give for turning him down?'

'They weren't very impressed with the idea. I admit it's a new concept, but I thought they might have been willing to take a few risks. You know banks, Clare, they're very cautious.'

Now it was Clare's turn to sigh. 'Well, let's think it over for a few days. Something might crop up. I can't say I think it will, but it's too early to despair.'

The conversation ended on a falsely cheerful note but Clare was not allowed to worry for too long. Mrs Parks hurried into the study to inform her that Eddie Martin was at the back door and wanted to see her.

'He asks us to call him Mr Martin,' she informed Clare with a sniff. 'First names not good enough for him, I suppose.'

Clare accompanied her downstairs. 'I suppose he is a married man and entitled to respect.'

Mrs Parks bridled. 'I told him, "Right then, it's Mrs Parks to you, young man." '

'But we all call you Mrs Parks.'

'We called Jimmie by his first name!'

'Only because he asked us to, remember. He liked to feel he was one of the family.'

And he might have been. He might have wed me and become one of your employers! Do please give in gracefully, Mrs Parks.

Mrs Parks said nothing but marched ahead to the kitchen where Eddie Martin waited at the back door.

Clare smiled at him. 'This is a surprise, Mr Martin. I thought we agreed you'd end the day at five thirty. It's nearly seven o'clock.'

'I've something to show you, ma'am. I've gone and come back, so to speak. It's a horse.'

Mrs Parks cried, 'A new horse? May I come down with you to see it?' She remembered her indignation too late and gave Clare a sheepish look.

'Miss Wishart may not like it,' he warned, 'and I've brought it on spec, like. Rode it here to see how tractable it is.' They walked towards the stables as he talked. 'Very decent animal, to my mind and it's used to pulling a trap so that should be no problem. Only problem is the mower but I reckon he could get used to it.' He laughed. 'It's not the mower that's the problem – it's getting the leather shoes on it! He's called Boxer. Don't ask me why.'

They rounded the corner and saw the horse tied to a ring in the stable wall. He was taller than Jonty and much darker with an uneven white flash between the eyes. He turned to watch them approach and Clare noticed that his ears pricked well forward. His eyes watched them inquisitively but without any sign of fear.

'Where did he come from?' Clare asked as Mrs Parks kept a respectful distance between herself and the animal.

'From a friend of my grandfather. Harry Field – lives about three miles from here on the Maidstone road. He's a carrier by trade or was. He bought it for the business, but when he was injured he gave up. Sold up but kept Boxer for a few months because his wife was fond of him.'

'And now?' Clare asked.

'He needs the money. He says if you want you can keep him for a week or two and see how he turns out. If he suits then he is yours. You can agree a price then.'

'And you think he's suitable for the work he'll do?'

He nodded.

Mrs Parks said, 'He's a nice looker, if that's anything to go by. Can I pat him? Is he friendly? I used to give Jonty a carrot. He loved carrots.'

'Oh, yes, he's a friendly chap, aren't you, Boxer?' He turned to Mrs Parks with a smile. 'Give him carrots, Mrs Parks, and he'll be your friend for life!'

Boxer's ears went forward again at the sound of his name. Mrs Parks patted the horse's neck and Clare stroked his nose while Eddie Martin watched with amusement.

'I know there's more I should ask,' Clare told him. 'How old he is and if he's in good health – things like that. Is he used to being alone or do we have to buy a goat to keep him company?'

'He's nearly five years old, in good health and he doesn't keep a companion.'

Clare laughed. 'Thank you, Mr Martin. Then let's give him a week's trial.' She glanced at Mrs Parks. 'He can't replace Jonty in our hearts but even Jonty was new here once upon a time. What do you think of him?'

Mrs Parks looked thoughtfully at the horse then nodded. She drew in a deep breath and said, 'I think Mr Martin has found us a very good horse.'

One problem appeared to have been solved but that left the business of the consortium and the sale of Merle Place. When Clare went to bed that night she lay awake for hours, tossing and turning anxiously until the early hours of the morning. She felt she was still no nearer to a solution.

The day of the dinner party arrived and Margaret spent half the morning in the kitchen with the cook, checking and rechecking the menu. The cook had been with her for more years than she cared to remember, but she still believed in keeping a sharp eye on things. One could never entirely trust a servant. That's what her mother had taught her. 'You have all the ingredients for the asparagus soup, Mrs Lamb? And the bread rolls are already made?'

'All ready to be warmed through at the last minute, ma'am.'

'Good – and there is plenty of smoked salmon? You know how well the men eat and they'll all profess to be starving!'

Mrs Lamb nodded. 'As usual, I have it all under control.'

'Of course. And the quails? They looked beautifully fresh and, of course, the vanilla trifle and the—'

'Fresh fruit salad and nuts and figs and the cheeseboard.' Exasperated, but trying not to show it, the cook straightened up and wiped her face with a handkerchief. 'I assure you everything will be perfect, ma'am.'

'I have every faith in you.'

With a smile, Margaret gave a slight nod and retired from the fray feeling that she had done her duty. Woe betide Mrs Lamb if anything was disappointing in any way.

The other half of the morning was spent supervising the maid who was setting the table with exquisite glassware and the treasured silver candlesticks, which had been passed down from Margaret's grandmother. Above the long table there was a chandelier that looked a little mundane presently but would glitter delightfully when the lights were turned on later. The newly washed dinnerware – white edged with gold – was stacked in readiness on the sideboard alongside cutlery, and Margaret's newly arranged roses stood proudly in a corner on a small round table.

Satisfied, she made her way to the drawing room where she stood for a moment in front of the piano on which her treasured photographs were arranged. For a long moment she allowed her gaze to wander over the record of her life. She smiled at herself aged ten on the sands at Bognor Regis, kneeling beside her favourite uncle as he fashioned an enormous sand castle. She stared without enthusiasm at a group of people posed in front of a car; another uncle had just bought it and he had transported

Margaret and her mother on a trip to Margate to enjoy the Whitsun Fair. Nanny Jessop was standing between her and her mother. Now Margaret poked her tongue out at her.

'Nanny Jessop! I hated you!' she murmured.

Margaret could still feel her cold dislike of Nanny Jessop through the mist of the intervening years. Nanny Jessop had been entirely two-faced, she thought.

You were sly, Nanny Jessop. You shut me in that cupboard and when I told Mama and cried you pretended it was all a joke and Mama laughed at me and called me Silly Billy!

Determined not to let the past spoil her day, Margaret turned her attention to her first wedding photo and smiled wistfully. *You should have lived, dearest man! You should never have left me.*

'And here you are again!' she told the youthful Margaret, seizing the photograph in its ornate silver frame, the likeness of her young self which she cherished, the image which she held most dear – a head and shoulders photograph of herself when she was twenty and had recently 'come out' at a lavish ball in Bloomsbury given by a friend of her aunt on her mother's side of the family. The photographer had brought out her best features in the shot – the soft shades of black and grey on white flattered the clearcut lines of her profile and softened the line of her throat while showing to advantage the gently waving hair. It also caught the gleam of her eye. In fact it showed her special kind of delicate beauty in the best possible light.

Don't look at me, she told the twenty-year-old Margaret. Don't see what the years will do to you. Don't discover what you will become – an old lady with fading looks and poor health. You stay the way you are!

She pressed the photograph to her heart and, closing her eyes, worked hard to hold back the sob that was rising in her throat.

When she was once more in control of her emotions she replaced the photograph without another glance then turned and made her way upstairs to her bedroom. Tonight it would be Clare Wishart's turn to sparkle, she told herself.

With characteristic generosity of spirit, Margaret would see to it that her son's visitor would be made to feel very special indeed.

As Clare and Steven sped through the Kent countryside she wondered aloud why they were travelling so early since the dinner party was to start at eight in the evening.

He gave her a quick glance. 'I've lots to show you, Clare,' he told her. 'I hope you don't mind but I wanted you to see our offices – where the business of publishing is carried on. There's so much you don't know about us and I'm so proud of what we stand for. And, of course, you will now be a part of it. And at Christmas we hold a party for all our authors so you can get to know one another.'

'It sounds interesting,' she said, 'but daunting.'

'Daunting? Nonsense. I can see you've been tucked away in the country for too long. I want you to relish your new role. Soon you'll have a chance to talk to Frank Leonards, who designs most of our book jackets . . . and to discuss publicity and whether to tour America.' He laughed as Clare turned to him in panic. 'Only teasing you!'

She let out a sigh. 'You wretch! That was so unkind.'

'I'm sorry, dar—' Shocked, he stopped mid-word.

Clare, equally shocked, looked straight at him but he was at once distracting her by requesting road directions. She applied herself to the map and the careless moment appeared to pass. But not for Clare and not, she suspected, for Steven. He had been about to call her 'darling' which surely meant that he often thought about her that way or imagined a time when he would do so. Clare's heart skipped a beat as she tried to appear composed while her imagination took flight. To herself she admitted that she had thought about Steven more than might be expected from their superficial relationship – a new author and her editor – but she now knew there was something more between them. Something deeper.

For the next few minutes they concentrated on the journey but at last Clare asked cautiously, 'What have you told your mother about me?'

'Nothing and everything,' he answered airily. 'All that I know, but then I don't know much, do I?'

Clare then launched into the latest disquieting news about Merle Place and they talked about ways and means without reaching any conclusions until Steven introduced another surprise which he had planned.

'I thought you'd like to see where I live – I have my own flat in Pimlico. It's nowhere near as attractive as my mother's apartment, but handy for the Underground and plenty of buses. Would you mind coming to see it – without a chaperone! I promise you'll be quite safe with me.'

'I'd love to,' she said, delighted. 'I-I often wonder about you and what you are doing. It's hard for me to imagine you in your world – we seem so far apart.'

A strange silence fell between them and Clare had the feeling that something more should be said but remained silent. Steven, however, seized his chance.

'We needn't be so far apart,' he said. 'I mean, our paths have crossed which must mean something. And we have so much in common – literature for example.' He faltered, apparently concentrating on his driving on a broad, straight stretch of road with no other vehicle in sight.

'Like literature and literature!' she agreed with a smile. 'You are a town boy and I'm a country girl. What else do we have in common?'

Without answering he abruptly steered into a small lay-by and stopped the car. 'I can't do two things at once,' he confessed. 'I can't drive and convince you. I can't be expected to steer and change gears when all I can think about is how to persuade you.' He swallowed, turning towards her.

'Persuade me to do what, Steven?' she asked breathlessly.

'To allow me to kiss you.'

Clare's smile was radiant. 'I wondered what it was I was waiting for – now I know.'

As they kissed an open-topped tourer materialized in the empty road and as it passed them the driver tooted the horn and cheered.

They drew apart, shyly, and Steven said hoarsely, 'He seemed to approve!'

'I did, too!' Clare laughed shakily. 'But he interrupted us. Do you think we should try that kiss again?'

'Oh, Clare!' He held her at arms length unable to believe his good fortune. 'Oh, yes! I think so.' He glanced up and down the now empty road and drew her close. 'I'm sure we can do better.'

On reaching London, Steven had installed her in a small but elegant hotel room and left her to unpack and shake the creases from her new clothes. Then he had returned to take her out to lunch and from there they had walked hand in hand through the crowded streets to visit his place of work.

'Of course it looks a bit empty today,' he had apologized, as he led her through the various rooms, 'but wait until you see it in full spate! It's a madhouse. So much activity – telephones ringing, typewriters clattering, visitors coming and going, as well as manuscripts being delivered and . . . But you'll see for yourself, Clare, and you'll become a part of it!'

Once it would have sounded terrifying, but today Clare thought about it with calm enthusiasm. She trusted Steven entirely. If he believed she would enjoy it, then she would.

He had then taken her to see his flat and she was finally able to see him in his home, where she was relieved to discover a new side of him. Gone was the hectic businessman, wheeling and dealing in a frantic office. As soon as they crossed the threshold she recognized it as his retreat from the world. The large shapeless sofa was full of mismatched cushions, a small table was covered with an untidy collection of china animals, the ormolu clock on the mantelpiece had stopped and there was a small pile of unopened mail on the sideboard.

She said, 'Very nice, Steven. Very cosy and welcoming.'

He grinned. 'I gave it a bit of tidy up when I knew you were coming. I'd show you the bedroom if you wouldn't mistrust my motives.'

'It's part of the flat. Part of your home.'

He threw open a door and she immediately laughed.

'A double bed! Does your mother know?'

'No, she doesn't and I don't expect you to tell her!'

The room was as casual as the previous room, but the window was wide open and fresh air and sunlight streamed in.

'And now the kitchen!' He led the way.

This small room was, to Clare's surprise, much neater than the rest of the flat with a row of copper pans on the wall, closed cupboards, a clean cooker and a gleaming white sink.

She hesitated, impressed. 'Do you cook?'

'Often. Nothing fancy but after a day in the office I toss a few things together for an informal dinner . . . it helps me to unwind. Friends often appear without warning and who wants to drag them out to a restaurant. We do enough of that with agents and authors during the day. Mother feels that in my position I should have a manservant like so many of my friends, but the truth is I value my privacy.'

Clare leaned against him, resting her head against his shoulder and his arm slid round her waist. 'Tell me what you cook.'

'Oh, let me see now. I do a mean Welsh rarebit, egg and bacon, ham omelette, mashed potato with cheese – that's one of my favourites. Need I go on?'

'No, I'm bowled over.'

Clare tried to imagine herself in the kitchen preparing something for the two of them. Having Mrs Parks had made her lazy, but surely she must be able to cook something appetizing. The thought made her panic.

Learn to cook, Clare. He obviously loves you and maybe you'll marry him one day. So learn to cook the kind of meals he likes. Not too much to ask, surely.

She made up her mind to buy herself a cookery book at the very first opportunity.

Later that evening, in the Grosvenor Hotel, Clare sat alone in the room that Steven had booked for her. She was watching the clock, waiting for him to arrive to take her to his mother's dinner party. The event which she had secretly dreaded now held few if any terrors as she sat in a glow of wonder, still breathless with excitement and dazed with joy – hardly able to believe the rapidity with which her life was changing.

Earlier they had parked in the lay-by for nearly half an hour, talking and trying to come to terms with the strength of their feelings for one another. For Steven, she understood it had been a long-held dream come true, but for Clare it had been a revelation. Surely she had known in her heart that she was falling in love with him – or had she deliberately ignored her emotions out of a mistaken kind of loyalty to Simon? Whatever the reasons for her reluctance to face the truth, she was now convinced. Simon would understand, she told herself. He would want her to be happy.

Sitting on the edge of the bed, watching the hands of the clock crawl round, she looked at herself in the long swing mirror and was amazed at how different she looked. Determined not to let Steven down she had bought a new outfit for the occasion – a jacket and long skirt in a soft blue grey, trimmed with coffee-coloured lace – and it suited her. She had taken extra care with her hair, which she had swept up, and she was wearing a double-stranded necklace of purple and grey beads; it had once belonged to her mother.

Her eyes shone and it had taken an application of pale face powder to subdue the bright colour in her cheeks.

The telephone rang and the reception desk informed her that Mr Flint had arrived. With a last quick glance in the mirror, Clare snatched up her purse and let herself out of her room.

Margaret's guests were all seated for dinner by quarter to nine. The maid was making her way round the table, carefully ladling the asparagus soup into each warmed bowl, carefully avoiding letting any drip on to the rim of the dish or, worse still, on to the spotless tablecloth.

Earlier Steven's mother had introduced Clare Wishart

to her guests by describing her as an extremely promising addition to her son's stable of new authors.

'We are all going to hear a lot about Clare Wishart,' she told them. 'Unless she retains her nom de plume of Clarinda Hart. I've read some of her work and she has a most inventive mind and a very original voice. Steven discovered her, so naturally he is delighted with his protégée.'

Clare had listened with mixed feelings to this praise, half wanting to believe it and half knowing that as yet she was untried as a novelist. Still she had drunk two glasses of champagne and was feeling more confident especially as Steven kept his promise and rarely strayed from her side. Together they had chatted to Colonel Dickson, listening sympathetically to details of his late wife's illness and to Alice Jefferys who had given them each an invitation to her latest exhibition.

'It's not being held in one of the better known galleries,' she told them earnestly. 'Instead I've secured a private exhibition at the home of Mrs Hetherington who is immensely well-connected in the art world and has guaranteed the attendance of at least two art critics. You must come, Clare. Insist that Steven brings you.'

Steven shook his head regretfully before Clare could answer. 'I'm afraid Clare is terribly tied up at the moment. She is selling her very large house to a consortium who—'

'Very large? How large are the rooms?' She gazed hopefully at Clare. 'You see a really large room might well prove ideal for a private viewing of my work . . .'

Recognizing the danger she was in, Clare said, 'Unfortunately the deal is almost done and the completion might take place any day soon. There is no way I would dare arrange anything.' She saw the disappointment in the young woman's eyes and felt sorry for her. 'The consortium might consider it, of course,' she suggested. 'If you care to give me one of your business cards I'll pass it on to them.'

Beaming with gratitude, Alice did just that. Margaret moved towards them and drew her son aside for a whispered conversation and Jack Lewis stepped in to take his place. Jack was short and comfortably plump with thinning hair and a slightly donnish look. Clare couldn't imagine him travelling alone in the wilder areas of rural Spain, but she soon found herself explaining yet again about the consortium's plan for Merle Place. 'They refer to it as a kind of retreat. Somewhere where creative people could spend a few weeks or even months to concentrate on a work in progress, whatever that happened to be. It must be rather difficult if you have a family to find enough time or space.'

Jack's eyes narrowed. 'It could be a life saver,' he agreed. 'I rather like the sound of it. I'm not finding it easy to work on my diaries. Did Margaret tell you I've been travelling a great deal and am expecting to publish my experiences. I live alone but am finding it difficult. Small distractions are my downfall – the cat needs to be fed, the laundry has to be done or the neighbour knocks at the door to use my telephone. I have a deadline – dreadful word – and my editor is nagging me!' He rolled his eyes. 'I expect you have the same problems.'

'I would do – except that Steven is my editor and is being very patient.'

A moment or two later, dinner was announced and the guests began to walk through.

'You were too soft with Alice,' Steven whispered, before they sat down on opposite sides of the table. 'She has no talent whatsoever.'

'She has to start somewhere,' Clare insisted. 'We women have to struggle in a man's world.' She smiled. 'We really do have to stick together.'

The asparagus soup was delicious and Clare suddenly realized that she was actually enjoying herself. Steven's mother was an expert hostess and the conversation was never allowed to flag. The fish course arrived and was duly appreciated and in the lull between the smoked salmon and the next course, Jack, seated next to Clare, returned to the subject of Merle Place.

'I've been thinking that my father might consider

joining the consortium,' he told Clare. 'He's got money to burn from wise investments and he also likes to write – mostly poetry, but he's never been published. Just finds satisfaction in it. I could have a word with him if you'd like me to.'

'I'd be delighted to pass on Alan's name and telephone number,' she told him. 'Please remind me after dinner.'

'But I must say a retreat sounds awfully dull. D'you know what I mean? Smacks of plain food, no talking and lights out at ten! It has a slightly religious ring to it.'

Clare rolled her eyes but she could understand his reasoning.

He went on. 'Something like a "centre for creative arts" might sound better. There's something rather monastic about a retreat, don't you agree? Rather spartan.'

'I'm inclined to agree with you. If your father does become involved I'm sure they'll be open to suggestions. It really is very early days.'

Before they could talk further Margaret tapped a fork gently against her glass and, intrigued, the guests turned to her.

'My son has something to say,' she told them briefly and all heads turned in Steven's direction.

He stood up and glanced round the table. 'I'm taking a terrible risk,' he said, 'but please bear with me for a moment or two. I have met a very sweet woman and I have an important question to put to her. She won't be expecting this – I haven't dared to raise the question until now . . .'

He turned to Clare who, shocked, felt the colour rise in her face. 'Dearest Clare, I'm afraid I'm not the most romantic man in the world – just a rather lonely bachelor, but could you possibly consider marrying me?'

Clare froze, staring at him. He was proposing! It came as a complete surprise and, despite her delight, for a moment or two her voice failed her. On all sides of the table the diners were silent, terrified that she was going to refuse him.

He said shakily, 'It's very sudden but I'm very sure. Please tell me you are willing to take the risk.'

'I . . . Yes, I am, Steven. Oh!' In a happy confusion she managed to stand and at once he left his seat and walked round to her side of the table and drew a small box from his pocket, opened it and offered it to her. A ring winked up at her in the light from the chandelier – a diamond and two dark emeralds in an intricate gold setting. He took it out of the box and slipped it on to her finger, and before anyone could see the tears of happiness in her eyes, he had drawn her close and was kissing her while around them the excited guests applauded wildly, showered them with good wishes and talked delightedly to each other.

Margaret reached up and tapped Steven on the elbow. 'Let the future mother-in-law kiss the future daughter-in-law,' she said.

Clare leaned down and felt warm frail arms close gently around her.

'Steven will take good care of you, my dear,' Margaret whispered.

'And I promise to make him happy.'

'I know you will, Clare. It may seem very sudden, but my son assures me you were made for each other. You can trust his judgement, my dear.'

Somehow the meal was resumed but for Clare it passed in a wave of deep contentment broken by occasional and brief moments of disbelief.

Afterwards, as she lay in the unfamiliar hotel bed, she tried to recall the rest of the dinner party but it had all merged into one joyous round of congratulations, questions about the future and plans, if any, for an early wedding.

What had surprised her most was the fact she had agreed so quickly and without the slightest hesitation. Did she feel any now, she wondered, waiting for possible doubts to creep in but none came. She stayed wide awake, not wanting to sleep, trying instead to imagine Steven in his double bed in his flat. Was he sleeping soundly or was he, like her, also too excited to want to waste a moment in sleep?

And what of Steven's mother? Was she content that at last her son was going to marry and hopefully raise a family?

'Better late than never,' she had joked with Clare when they finally parted at the door. The three of them had sat on together after the other guests had gone their various ways and Clare had found the conversation comfortable and reassuring as they sipped milky cocoa. There had been so much to talk about.

'Once we're married we can share our time between my flat and Merle Place,' Steven had suggested to Clare. 'We could keep it and go down together some weekends and you could spend time in London with me . . . until our children arrive!'

Clare looked at Margaret, who at five past midnight was still wide awake and missing nothing. 'You must come down and see Merle Place,' she told the old lady. 'It would be wonderful to be able to keep it, although the consortium will be disappointed. It's been part of my life for so long. It's very peaceful. I think you would like it, Mrs Hampden. You can wander in the garden or drift in the boat on the small lake – and also meet my cousin Donald and his young wife who live nearby. Mrs Parks is my housekeeper and we have a new horse and . . . Let me think. Oh, yes! A new gardener.' She laughed. 'Now I come to think about it, there have been so many changes recently.'

'Country life sounds interesting,' Margaret conceded doubtfully. 'I've rarely lived anywhere but London, though I'm sure I shall enjoy a visit.'

The time had passed quickly until Steven insisted that his mother must be very tired and they had left her to her rest.

Now, as a nearby church clock sounded three thirty, Clare turned over in bed, still far from sleep. *I'm going to be wed. I shall soon be Mrs Steven Flint. In a matter of months I hope I shall be expecting our first child. How astonishing. Unbelievable . . . And our children will have cousins who live on a farm* . . . She had secretly envied Donald and Molly but now she would be sharing their hopes and fears for the future. Family life – with all that that entailed – both good and bad!

The sound of the telephone made her jump and with a thumping heart she sat up and snatched it from the rest. An indignant night porter informed her that there was someone on the line for her.

'Darling Clare, I'm sorry if I've woken you.' It was Steven.

Clare smiled in the darkness. 'I was awake. I can't sleep. It's so good to hear your voice. Are you as happy as I am?'

He hesitated. 'I haven't steamrollered you into this, have I? I'm panicking slightly in case you change your mind. In the cold light of day it might all look different. I'm a few years older than you, Clare. Are you sure it—?'

'Am I sure it doesn't make a difference, Steven? Of course I'm sure. Age doesn't matter at all. It's loving each other that matters. And I love you so you can stop panicking! In the morning everything will be as wonderful as it is now.'

'Oh Lord! I can't believe how much I love you.'

'I can, Steven, because it's mutual. Go to sleep, dearest.'

'And I'll see you in the morning?'

'You most certainly will – and after the wedding it will be *every* morning.' She heard him catch his breath at the prospect.

'My dearest Clare,' he said softly. 'It can't be soon enough.'

P